SILENT GRAVE

A gripping mystery with a huge twist

PATTI BATTISON

(DETECTIVE MIA HARVEY THRILLERS BOOK 3)

JOFFE
BOOKS

First published as "The Dead Do Speak" in 2012

Revised edition 2019
Joffe Books, London
www.joffebooks.com

Please join our mailing list for free Kindle crime thriller, detective, mystery books and new releases.
www.joffebooks.com

For Norma and Ronnie with love

PROLOGUE

'…WE THEREFORE COMMIT Barbara's body to the ground; earth to earth; ashes to ashes; dust to dust; in the sure and certain hope of the Resurrection to eternal life….'

The words had seemed far too loud, boomed out like those of a thespian striving to reach a theatre's back row, crowding out all else. As there were only six followers around the grave – ten, should the professional pallbearers be included – there was little need for oral projection. The vicar was a show-off, intent on hogging the 'stage'.

Then came silence – a crushing silence.

Detective Sergeant Mia Harvey was unable to watch the coffin's descent into a grave which already contained her beloved father. She glanced around and found that everything was too bright: the purple of the vicar's robe; the reds and lemons of the flowers; the white of those now redundant service sheets still clutched tightly by all.

Muted whisperings surrounded her; eyes watched her slyly … pityingly. She wanted to get away, *longed* to be else-where, but knew that flight was impossible. She was there to deliver her mother's body to the grace of God.

And regret was her unsolicited companion.

Barbara Harvey – leading lady in this particular production – had spent the final years of her earthly existence in the confines of St Stephen's nursing home: unaware; uncommunicative, the victim of a cruel and vicious stroke.

She'd become an unwanted encumbrance in the life of her only child Mia, all of whose visits had been so grudgingly made. She would check her watch surreptitiously, repeatedly and leave as soon as was justifiably proper.

Why, then, did Mia now wish with such fervour to be in that tiny room, holding her mother's hand, telling her again and again that she'd always loved her – that she still did?

Oh God....

A hand on her arm. 'You all right, darling?'

'What?'

She looked down at the hand, realized it belonged to Detective Chief Inspector Paul Wells, her superior officer and constant support on that ghastly day. Wells squeezed Mia's arm gently, motioned towards the vicar who was offering her a wooden tray laden with soil. She grabbed a handful, tossed it into the grave, shuddering slightly as it clattered on to the coffin with such abysmal finality.

There wouldn't be a wake. Mia had been adamant about that. So one by one the meagre followers – just two carers from St Stephen's and a couple of Barbara's friends from way back – offered their condolences and made to leave, the pallbearers were already sidling away.

Mia was approaching the vicar, her words of thanks half-formed, when an almighty cry filled the air: a man's voice, terror-filled. She turned as one with Wells and scanned the large cemetery for signs of a disturbance.

The vicar huffed: muttered words emerged from his neatly-trimmed beard. No one, after all, likes to be heckled during a performance.

'My apologies … I'll soon put a stop to that,' he said. Then, gesturing towards the grave, 'Stay as long as you like. You won't be disturbed.'

But before he could take a step two dirt-smeared men came running towards them, arms flailing, faces deathly white.

'Oh Christ, help us,' the first man yelled. 'We've found a body.'

'And it ain't in no coffin neither,' screamed the other.

CHAPTER 1

'THIS IS INTERESTING,' said DCI Wells, staring down at the newly-exposed find.

'It can't be human,' said Mia. 'Look at the hand. It's a dummy, it's got to be.'

'No, darling, it's mummified.' Wells rubbed at his jowls. 'Nicely preserved, an' all.'

They were on a long stretch of land about thirty yards wide and effectively detached from the cemetery by a four-foot-tall picket fence; the impressive tower was all that could be seen of St Matthew's church from their point of view.

Wells' intense glance scanned the immediate area: he took in the lush carpet of meadow flowers and tall grasses, their heads buffeted in sequence by a brisk summer breeze that whipped across the exposed space. The River Stratton – a short distance from where they stood – flowed quietly by, its rippled surface catching the sun's rays beautifully.

It was a pretty spot, tranquil and unsullied, apart from a section of approximately twenty-square-yards which had been cleared and tilled quite recently. At the centre of the square was a rectangular hole about four feet deep, its edges piled with the resulting mounds of dark soil and heavy clay.

4

The right-hand wall of the hole had partially collapsed, exposing one quarter of the body. It lay on its back, the cloth-clad arm rigid and fixed at an angle; its head and the majority of its torso still covered. The hand was the only visible part of the corpse; its leathery skin pulled taut and blackened, giving it a strangely synthetic appearance.

The two gravediggers had retrieved their spades and were now standing in shocked silence beside the vicar, whose richly-coloured vestments lent a sense of the absurd to the grisly scene.

DCI Wells approached them. 'Why were you digging here?' he asked.

It was the vicar who answered. 'We've run out of space,' he said, gesturing beyond the fence towards the gravestones. 'This stretch is actually part of the cemetery, but it's been flooded a couple of times and the powers-that-be thought it wise to abandon it. No money for flood defences, you see.'

'So why use it now?'

The vicar gave a dramatic shrug, arms outstretched, heavy cassock billowing with the effort. 'When my congregation was told no more burials would be allowed at St Matthew's, all hell broke loose. They're sods at taking no for an answer. So we applied to have this bit reopened – the last flood was quite a few years ago now – and our application was granted.' He nodded towards the river. 'We're hoping to have some sort of barrier built between here and the bank, make the place a bit more secure. Not that the council are going to be throwing money at us. We'll be raising it ourselves … God willing.'

'How many years has this section been cordoned off?' asked Wells.

The vicar gave a discreet sigh. 'Look, I don't want to appear rude, but I really need to inform the police….'

'I should've said, vicar, we are the police.' Wells produced his warrant card. 'Detective Chief Inspector Paul Wells, Larchborough CID.'

'And I'm his detective sergeant,' said Mia, reaching for her card before remembering she'd left it at home.

The vicar gave her an astonished look. 'You're a police office? I'd no idea.'

Wells said, 'Would you answer the question, Mr...?'

'Fisher. Charles Fisher. Charlie, as a rule.' All signs of that confident actor from the graveside were now gone. The vicar was dithering, in serious need of a prompt. 'Sorry, what was the question again?'

'How long has this bit been cordoned off?'

Fisher thought for a moment, his Bible clutched close to his chest. He gave another shrug. 'Sorry, can't tell you offhand.'

'Find out,' said Wells. 'Quick as you can.'

One of the gravediggers edged forward, spade held aloft. 'Shall we finish the job?'

'No, mate, you can leave it to us.' Wells pulled a face at Reverend Fisher. 'There'll be no funeral taking place here, vicar. This is a crime scene now. You'd better make other arrangements.'

Fisher was almost as tall as the DCI's six-foot-five, and heavily muscled too; but he seemed to shrink before their eyes, his amiable features crumbling into a tortured grimace.

'I see … right … OK …' he mumbled, fingers beating out a tattoo on the Bible as his thoughts raced. He turned his apologetic stare towards Mia. 'Not quite what we had in mind for today, Miss Harvey.'

'Not quite, no,' she said, still scanning the hole, her professional curiosity fired up.

Reverend Fisher cast a withering glance at the corpse, as though reprimanding it for blasting a hole through his schedule. 'What should I do now, Chief Inspector?'

'Find me that information,' said Wells.

'No, I mean about the burial. Can it go ahead a bit further along?'

'Not until we've cleared the site.'

'How long will that take?'

'God knows, but the sooner you let us get on, the sooner we'll be out of your way.'

Fisher glared at the DCI, seemed about to parry the sharp words with a few of his own. 'I'll be in my office at the front of the church,' he said, turning on his heel. Then, hovering tentatively by the hole for a moment, he made a swift sign of the cross and marched away, the gravediggers following.

'You can bugger off an' all,' the DCI told Mia.

'What? Oh no, sir.'

'Oh yes, sir. You've been given compassionate leave and you're taking it.'

'But the body….'

'You've just buried your mother, darling. You need time to get over it.'

'I'll only get depressed at home, sir. This is just what I need … help take my mind off everything.'

Wells let out a long breath. 'One of these days you'll do as you're bloody told,' he muttered, ruffling his hair as he weighed up his options. 'OK, but the moment it all gets too much, you take yourself off home. Understood?'

'Absolutely.'

Mia could have kissed that corpse. Thanks to John or Jane Doe down there she could put off having to cope with her newly-acquired orphan status for a while. No doubt she'd be storing up all kinds of problems for the future – her mother's death had hit her harder than she could ever have imagined – but any excuse to delay the grieving process was to be grabbed with both hands.

'Shall I get the scene secured, sir?'

'I'll do it,' said Wells, already turning on his mobile phone. 'And hopefully we can get John Lloyd to retrieve the body.'

Mia frowned. 'I thought he'd retired.'

'Semi-retired – wants more time to study Sanskrit or some such crap. But if I know John, he'll be champing at the bit to get his hands on this one.'

Mia turned back to the corpse, surveyed the small section of desiccated flesh on view while the DCI scrolled through his numbers list for Silver Street Police Station.

'Why do you think the body didn't decay, sir?'

'Haven't the foggiest. That's why we need John.' Wells depressed the call button and grinned. 'Exciting, ain't it?'

'I wonder how the funeral's going,' pondered Detective Constable Jack Turnbull.

He was waiting with his colleague, Detective Inspector Nick Ford, in the corridor outside courtroom number one at Larchborough Crown Court. They were there to give evidence in a rape case involving a music teacher from the local comprehensive and one of his more nubile female pupils. The fifteen-year-old in question was beautifully formed – and highly knowledgeable in the art of seduction (as well as piano playing) according to the testimonies given that morning by a number of men whose lives and marriages had been terminally ruined by their association with the girl.

According to Nick, if she put half as much energy into her studies as she directed towards her flourishing sex life then a place at one of Britain's top universities would be hers for the taking. In fact, both detectives were of the opinion that the schoolteacher was the real victim in this case, but they were batting for the prosecution so would need to keep shtum on that particular point.

Nick tossed aside his crumpled newspaper – he'd finished the crossword, read everything on the sports pages, had even consulted the horoscopes – and offered Jack a jaded shrug.

'She'll be dancing on the grave by now.'

'Oh nice one,' Jack said, tutting.

'What?' said Nick, all wide-eyed innocence. 'Mia couldn't stand going to that nursing home every week. Can't say I blame her either. Talk about land of the zombies….'

Jack gave a pronounced wince. 'You missed your vocation, mate. You'd have gone all the way in the caring services.'

'Whatever.' Nick consulted his wristwatch. A mere three minutes had dragged by since the last time he'd looked. 'It must be our turn soon … *please*.'

They fell silent, took to watching the steady stream of humanity passing before them: sharp-suited solicitors; uniformed police officers; pompous court officials; tremulous witnesses; a fair selection of society's drop-outs, most of whom sported that season's must-have items: the over-sized hooded top and matching electronic tag. *Sit here long enough*, Nick thought, *and you'd catch a glimpse of Big Foot being chased by a yeti*.

'Shall I fetch another coffee?' Jack asked.

'Only if you fancy caffeine poisoning.'

Just then the imposing door of the courtroom creaked open and an usher appeared. 'Court's adjourned,' she said. 'All those for Regina versus Fairbrother reconvene here at two o'clock.'

'Fucking great,' Nick hissed. 'It'll take all day at this rate.'

'At least lunch'll be on expenses,' said Jack, who always looked for the silver lining.

The detectives chose a cosy curry house in a side street near the courts where the food was tasty but cheap and the watery lager cheaper still. Forty-five minutes later, duly fortified, they decided on a bit of retail therapy and were about to sidle into River Island when a scuffle started outside the HMV store opposite.

It would seem that a bungled theft was in progress. A couple of hefty youths clutching large holdalls were struggling with two store assistants, both of whom were determined to keep the thieves on the premises.

A furious battle raged in the doorway for several moments before spilling out on to the street, scattering passers-by with its violent undertones and the foul language issuing from the robbers' indignant mouths. Then one of the youths produced a knife, his crazed look proclaiming that he'd like nothing better than to use it.

As Jack followed Nick's haphazard path through the lunchtime traffic the youth with the knife broke free and hurtled past the shoppers, knocking a couple of them flying and dropping his bag in the process. Nick sprinted after him, keeping to the empty gutters, his determined glare never leaving his quarry's heaving back.

Jack was left to tackle the second youth still being held by the shop assistant. 'You're nicked,' he said, feeling in his pockets for warrant card and handcuffs.

The assistant – believing his heroics were no longer required now that the cavalry had arrived – let go of his catch. And his relieved sigh became a gasp as the thief threw his heavy bag at Jack's face, knocking the detective off his feet.

Jack was trying to straighten up when the youth's fist connected with the top of his head, plunging his senses into a quagmire of agony which deepened considerably after a second punch to his upturned chin.

The robber grabbed Jack's lapel and pulled him upright, continued to jab at his face, the frazzled detective powerless to stop him. Jack was aware of a strong alcoholic stench, could sense the youth's spiralling anger. He knew that he needed to block the punches but couldn't quite work out how to do it; that first hit had left him severely disorientated.

The fast-growing crowd kept to a safe distance, their faces showing shock and excitement in equal measure, not one of them tempted to intervene.

Jack tasted iron and, managing to twist slightly to the left, spat a load of bloody saliva at the pavement, noting with surprise a number of red patches already there. Was that *his* blood? He was frightened. He was going to get seriously hurt unless he upped his game. How though? The youth still had hold of his jacket, pulling him off balance, making it impossible for him to retaliate.

The attack was relentless, and the yob seemed invincible as Jack's half-hearted lunges kept missing their target. And that's when the detective got lucky. The youth suddenly let go of the lapel and grabbed Jack's shirt instead, but with way too much aggression. As a number of buttons were ripped from the material, Jack – who in any other situation would have cried real tears for the demise of his favourite designer shirt – found himself free to move for the first time since the beating began.

Taking advantage of the unexpected lull Jack kicked out, aiming for his opponent's genitals, but connecting with his thigh instead. It was enough to shock the yob for the vital second it took Jack's fist to find his leering features. The right hook was ineffectual, hardly finding any purchase, and Jack was trying to line up another when Nick appeared at his shoulder.

As Nick shoved his handcuffed captive inside the store, throwing the youth's retrieved holdall in there after him, Jack's assailant made a valiant move to escape. The DI was too nifty on his feet though. Before the yob could get away Nick was on him, grabbing his arms and holding them at an impossible angle behind his back.

'Jack, give us your cuffs,' he hollered, almost pulling the thief's arms out of their sockets as he attempted to break free.

The young detective merely stood there, his bloodied expression unreadable.

'Jack, throw us your fucking cuffs.'

This time the words registered and Jack managed to free them from his pocket before everything went black and nothing hurt any more.

By late afternoon scene-of-crime officers had erected a tent over the hole, keeping their discovery safe from prying camera lenses. DCI Wells knew that once the story broke, the local media would be out in force and the notion disturbed him; the positioning of the body and the openness of its surroundings would offer plenty of assistance to those intrepid reporters. Wells would be seeking publicity soon enough, but he wanted to be calling the shots when the time came. He needed complete control or the investigation could quickly become a farce.

It was essential that the body be removed to a more secure location as soon as was possible and, after calling for officers to secure the scene, Wells had set about tracking down John Lloyd, Larchborough's most revered pathologist.

'Fascinating,' Lloyd murmured, taking his first look into the partially-dug grave.

'Knew you'd like it,' said Wells. 'Otherwise I'd never have disturbed you.'

The pathologist had been searching for his golf ball in the rough (the second time that day) when Wells' call came through on his mobile, so he'd been more than willing to abandon the game even before the DCI had made him aware of the unusual condition of the body. He stood now in rapt wonder, like a small boy in Santa's workshop.

'Think you'll be able to get it out?' asked Wells.

'It's been years since I've done this sort of work,' said Lloyd, patting his thickening waistline. 'That body'll need careful handling. Not as robust as it looks. But, yes, I'll manage.'

'How long, do you reckon?'

'To dig it out?' Lloyd pursed his lips. 'Hard to say. There'll be all manner of evidence in that soil. Wouldn't want to ruin any of it.'

'I've every faith in you,' Wells assured him.

Mia was at a gate in the fence, chatting with the forensics team, all of whom had an eye on the tent, eager to start their duties. And the minute the men left the tent, they descended *en masse*.

The pathologist trudged across to Mia, his smile sympathetic. 'Paul's told me about your mother, dear. I'm terribly sorry for your loss.'

'Thanks.'

'She's dying to know why the body didn't decay,' said Wells. 'Any ideas, John?'

Lloyd gave a noncommittal shrug. 'Bacteria in a dead body need a certain set of conditions to be present before the decaying process can begin, Paul. Now, excessive heat prevents those conditions from occurring and that's why mummification is usually confined to hot dry countries.' He gave a sudden chuckle. 'When is our climate ever hot and dry for more than five minutes, eh?'

'We've had a couple of hot summers recently,' said Mia, 'but I'm thinking when you say hot you mean the scorching weather in places like … Egypt?'

'Exactly,' said Lloyd. 'Now, let's look at conditions here.' His gaze took in the pleasant surroundings. 'We've got the river not too far away. We've got the heavy clay soil that's characteristic of the area….'

'And clay holds water,' Mia cut in.

'Right again,' said Lloyd, chuckling.

Wells had to stifle a sigh. 'OK, what's the punch line?'

'Punch line?'

'How come we've got a mummy in dank and dreary Larchborough?'

The pathologist lifted a shoulder. 'It's a guess rather than a punch line, Paul, but I'd say it was frozen.'

'Frozen?'

'Yes, if the killer managed to get the body into a deep freeze soon enough after death then the decaying process couldn't begin. Freezing temperatures prevent the bacteria from doing their job in much the same way as excessive heat. And if the body was kept in that freezer for long enough then even after thawing out putrefaction wouldn't begin.'

'Even if it's buried in damp soil?'

The pathologist nodded sagely.

'Will the internal organs still be intact?' Mia asked.

'I'll let you know when I've got it open,' said Lloyd, with yet another of those chuckles that set the DCI's teeth on edge.

'When can you start?' Wells asked.

'Now, if you like, I've got everything I need in the car.' Lloyd patted his stomach again. 'Get a few hours in before dinner, eh?'

Wells was about to accompany the pathologist to the car park when his mobile phone buzzed. He broke away to take the call, his fierce expression telling Mia that the news wasn't good.

'Shit,' he muttered, hastily pocketing the phone. 'Mia, think you're up to a hospital visit?'

'Of course,' she said. 'What's happened, sir?'

'It's Jack … the poor sod's in a coma.'

CHAPTER 2

JACK WAS IN the Accident and Emergency department on the ground floor of Larchborough General Hospital. In order to reach him, Mia had to pass the same set of lifts she'd used to visit her mother in Intensive Care. As she approached the lifts, saw the familiar posters and notices, smelt the coffee at the WI's dinky little shop, she was overcome by a shattering melancholy.

Her mother's death had been slow and difficult to watch; the viewing of the corpse hours later so unlike those serene affairs featured in the majority of Hollywood tearjerkers. Barbara's ravaged face had shown all too clearly the effort involved in leaving this life. That image would haunt Mia forever.

DCI Wells was constantly teasing his DS about her burning quest to champion the underdogs of this world. He called it her 'Mother Teresa Complex'; said she ought to be in social work, so strong was her desire to help those in need. And it was true; she did empathize with the disadvantaged. Yet for years she'd blatantly disregarded her own mother, left her to the mercy of those paid to care. She'd been wrong to do that. And now it was too late to make it right.

Mia ducked into the nearest lavatory, horrified to feel tears welling in her eyes. A young mother was holding her daughter's hands under the dryer. When she offered a smile, Mia was unable to return it. She edged into a cubicle and sat there, waiting for them to leave, waiting for her emotions to settle. She couldn't let Nick see her in pieces. She had to keep on top of the job. It was all she had left.

Mia found him sitting in the A & E reception area, his face crumpled with concern. Nick Ford was one of her least favourite people. Their working relationship was stormy, always had been; it contained far too much animosity for even a hope of them ever gelling now. Nick was an enigma: stunningly gorgeous on the outside, but rancid as hell within. What you saw was most definitely not what you got with him. Even so, the moment she sensed his fear, the moment she saw his boyish relief at the sight of her, Mia felt Mother Teresa jostle for space in her heart.

'Any news?' she asked.

'Not yet.' He noticed the tell-tale redness around her eyes. 'You look like shit.'

'I'm fine,' she said, turning away. 'What happened to Jack?'

Wells had given her a sketchy outline. Nick proceeded to fill in the gaps.

'… and now they can't wake him up,' he finished, his voice cracking.

'Bastard,' she muttered through gritted teeth. 'You'd better have got him.'

'Oh yes,' he said, stretching the words out. 'And he'll get what he fucking deserves. They both will. Joey and Syed picked them up.'

Mia managed a vicious grin. Joey Champion and Syed Shah were huge officers with tempers to match; they made the Incredible Hulk look like Noddy.

Mia sat beside Nick while her gaze took in the large area. God, she hated hospitals: the relentless bustle; those horribly distinctive smells; that feeling of dread hovering over everyone….

'Been waiting all afternoon?' she asked.

'No, I had to get back to court. Only just got here myself.'

Mia gave him an incredulous look. 'Jack's been here alone? Why didn't you phone earlier?'

'How could I? You were planting your mother.' He gave her a swift repentant glance. 'Sorry ... Anyway, he's not on his own. Michelle's with him.'

'Good.'

Mia twisted around in the seat, her back towards Nick. For a short while there she'd felt almost at one with him, Jack's predicament cementing a bond between them. But now they were back to square one. Chalk and cheese. Cat and dog.

Her back still towards him, Mia said, 'Which room's he in?'

'Twelve,' said Nick.

Wishing she had her warrant card Mia hurried towards the reception desk, pushing aside the long queue as she uttered tepid apologies. The receptionist was on the verge of objecting when Mia offered her name and rank.

'Any news on DC Jack Turnbull, please, room twelve?'

The girl tapped a few computer keys; a model of frigid efficiency. 'Not yet, but you can go in if you like. Through that door there,' she said, pointing.

'Thanks.'

The door led them into another large area with a number of small rooms on either side. A long nurses' station filled the centre space. Room twelve was to their left, its door ajar. The detectives hovered outside while a young Indian doctor busily checked Jack's vital signs.

Michelle – Jack's wife – was hunched in a moulded plastic chair beside the bed, her features haggard as she scrutinized the doctor's every move. When she caught sight of the detectives Michelle rushed to greet them.

'How was the funeral?' she asked Mia. 'I thought about you.'

'Bless you, sweetie, it was OK,' said Mia, squeezing the girl's hand. 'How is he?'

'Better than we thought, actually.' The words were aimed at Nick. 'He's still unconscious, but it's not a coma.' She nodded towards the doctor. 'That chap's been brilliant. He says there's no permanent damage, just bad concussion. It'll take a while, but Jack should be fine.'

'Thank God for that,' said Mia. 'Can I get you anything?'

Michelle shook her head. 'I'll have to be going soon. Mum's got Jamie.' Jamie was their three-year-old son. 'Doctor Patel said it's best to come back tomorrow. They'll be keeping Jack asleep till then, anyway.' She motioned towards the room. 'Want to see him?'

'No, I'll wait till he's awake,' Mia said hurriedly. After a day spent with her mother's coffin and then Tutankhamun, Mia didn't think she could stomach even a moment with the injured Jack. She'd had enough grief for a while.

'Do you need a lift?' she asked Michelle.

'No, got the car, thanks.' She nodded again towards Jack. 'Mind if I go back in?'

'You carry on. And, don't worry, Michelle, one of us'll be here first thing tomorrow to get Jack's statement. The bastard won't get away with this.'

As they trudged towards the car park Nick said, 'The funeral went all right then?' to cover the awkward silence between them.

Mia nodded and went on to tell him of their surprising find.

Nick gave a brittle laugh. 'Brilliant … lose one mummy and straight away you find another.'

Mia stopped in her tracks, unable to believe her ears. Surely even Nick wouldn't stoop to such a tasteless low. She spun around, eager to release all of her pent-up tension on the callous prat. But when she glimpsed the genuine sorrow in his deep brown eyes, Mia's mouth opened on to nothing but silence.

'Come here,' he whispered, spreading his arms wide.

And as Mia felt tears looming once more she was only too happy to oblige.

It was seven p.m. and John Lloyd had decided to call it a day. Cocooned in thick grey overalls, latex gloves and black wellington boots, he'd spent the better part of four hours scraping at the soil around the corpse with a trowel and almost two-thirds of it was now exposed.

The procedure was mind-numbingly slow and required great attention to detail; each newly-revealed portion had to be photographed and reported upon for the benefit of Lloyd's handheld recorder. All soil removed from the hole was deposited on to a tarpaulin sheet for later inspection by the forensic team.

Conditions inside the tent were far from ideal: heat from the day's mild weather and Lloyd's excited breath were causing a chemical reaction to occur within the exposed flesh and a terrible stench fast permeated the steamy air; a stench which kept even the hardened DCI Wells at a safe distance.

Sweat glistened on Lloyd's forehead as he scrambled from the hole. 'Knew it was too good to be true,' he said to Wells.

'What's that?'

'A great chunk of the torso's decayed.'

'Thought so, it stinks.'

'We'll need it guarded overnight,' said Lloyd, peeling off his gloves. 'That might be a stink to you, Paul, but foxes and the like will think it's yummy.'

'Good point,' said Wells, nodding. He took out his notebook, cast Lloyd a hopeful glance. 'Any first impressions, John?'

'It's definitely female,' he said, looking back towards the tent. 'Can't guess at an age yet, but I'll have a decent stab when she's back at the lab. She's fully clothed, and bits of the clothing are in near perfect condition, you'll be pleased to hear. There's even some hair still attached to the scalp.' Lloyd grinned suddenly. 'Can't wait to get her cleaned up for a proper look.'

'When will that be, do you think?'

'With an early start in the morning, she could be in the lab by lunchtime at the latest.'

'Better tell my boss the good news,' said Wells, delving for his mobile phone.

Lloyd raised a hand. 'See you back at the car park.'

The DCI held his breath as he selected the number for Superintendent Shakespeare. He wasn't looking forward to the call. Costs for the various aspects of the operation – an overnight guard; the huge forensic involvement; John Lloyd's bill for retrieving the body, to name but a few – would run high. And Shakespeare was allergic to spending money.

Wells deliberately kept the conversation short, his answers to the super's nervous questioning succinct. And he was cutting the call as Nick approached, the morose DI beating his legs like a crazed Morris dancer as the trousers to his immaculate suit became a magnet for clinging seed heads.

Wells had had no contact with his team all afternoon and still believed Jack to be in a coma. He hurried towards Nick, struggling to read his implacable expression.

'How is he?'

'The coma was a misdiagnosis, sir, but he's badly concussed. We'll know more in the morning.'

'OK. Where's Mia?'

'I had to follow her home, make sure she was all right. She got a bit emotional at the hospital.'

Wells let out a harsh breath. 'I bloody knew she wasn't up to it.'

At any other time Nick would have agreed, would have made more of Mia's fragile state than was the truth in order to dent the DCI's abiding faith in her. But this time, for some obscure reason, he felt compelled to defend her.

'Mia's adamant she'll be in tomorrow, sir, and perhaps it's for the best. She'll be better with something to do.'

Wells made no comment, merely ushered Nick towards the tent. 'Come and see the body,' he said, stopping short of the actual scene. 'Better hold your nose, mate. It stinks in there.'

Nick lingered inside the tent just long enough to get a quick glimpse. 'Jesus,' was all he said.

The corpse's babysitter arrived; introduced himself as Police Constable Steve Gardner; told them he was always getting the short straw. Wells offered him a sympathetic smile. It wouldn't be a pleasant assignment: stuck in the dark between one open grave and a cemetery filled with closed ones. Did the dead walk at night? He'd ask PC Gardner in the morning.

Most of the SOCOs had already left for the day, but a few were still busy. They needed to get that huge mound of earth safely back to the forensics laboratory and were transferring it into smaller, more manageable containers because it was a fair trek to the car park and their waiting van.

As the unlucky constable settled himself in his foldaway seat – lunch box and thermos at the ready, paperback novel, battery torch, and iPod beside them – Wells and Nick started the walk to their cars. But they'd hardly taken a few steps when a member of the forensics team called to the DCI, urging him to stop. The man hurried towards them, holding up a digital camera as though it were a trophy.

'Have a look at this,' he said to Wells, thrusting the camera towards him.

The DCI found himself staring at a picture of the corpse's decaying abdomen: a grisly mix of dirt-ingrained greens, yellows, and cloudy white – Mother Nature was clearly from the Abstract stable of artists.

'What am I supposed to be looking for?' Wells asked.

The scientist drew his index finger along a specific point on the small screen. 'See those bones?'

Wells wasn't sure that he could. Forensic detail, as far as he was concerned, should be meted out on a 'need to know' basis. His job was to track the murderer, not acquaint himself with the intricacies of putrefaction; he left that to the experts. Therefore he was woefully poor at deciphering the various components of a forensic snapshot.

He offered the camera to Nick. 'See anything?'

'No, sir.'

Wells turned to the scientist. 'OK, we give up.'

'It's hard to see, I'll admit,' he said, taking the camera, his finger once again outlining the portion of interest. 'See those tiny bones? They shouldn't be there. I reckon they're part of a foetus. I reckon there're two dead bodies in that hole, Chief Inspector.'

'That car park's full again. Even the police are using it now. For church use only, the sign says. Can't they read? I'm sick of it. Rehearsals start in less than an hour. Well, they'll just have to move. Shall I go and tell them, darling?'

That verbal barrage came from Kate Fisher – vicar's wife, stage director of St Matthew's theatre group, and the driving force (to her mind) on all of the church committees – as she burst into her husband's office like a whirlwind, flicking on lights as she flew around, filling the intimate space with more shadow than illumination.

When no answer was forthcoming Kate glanced at the vicar and found him slumped at his desk, forlorn face cupped in left hand, eyes focusing on nothing.

'Darling, what's the matter?'

Tugged out of his deep meditation by the sudden intrusion, Reverend Fisher sat back heavily and turned dull eyes on his wife. He said nothing. Dread swept over Kate as she sank into the visitor's chair before his desk.

'Charlie, has something happened?'

'We've found a body.'

Kate gave an incredulous laugh. 'You've what?'

'We've found a body,' said Fisher, his voice rising. 'We've found a dead body.'

'Don't be ridiculous.'

'All right, go and tell them to shift their cars. And while you're at it ask how the murder investigation's coming along.'

Eyes wide, a hand over her mouth, Kate said, 'They think it's murder?'

The vicar gave a cynical huff. 'She's hardly likely to have dug a hole and thrown herself in.'

'It's a woman?'

Fisher ran a hand across his beard. 'How the hell should I know?'

'Where is she?'

'In Noah Bailey's plot. I've told the family the funeral's cancelled. Didn't say why. Said we'd be making other arrangements to suit them. They're not happy.'

'Let Frank deal with them, darling. It's about time he earned his keep.'

She was referring to Frank Lessing, their verger. Lessing, a devotee of St Matthew's for over thirty years, was an indispensable fountain of local knowledge and the possessor of such a joyous disposition that even the most obstreperous of parishioners could be instantly browbeaten into submission by his beatific smile.

Charlie Fisher saw him as a Godsend and Kate hated the fact. *She* was the powerhouse behind her husband's ecclesiastical career, not some pompous and overbearing old bachelor with too much time on his hands and thoughts well above his station.

'Frank's busy,' said Fisher. 'I've sent him to help at the crime scene.'

'But that's your job,' Kate said with a sharp tut-tut of displeasure. 'You shouldn't let him steal your thunder all the time, darling. I do keep telling you.'

'And I keep telling *you* to mind your own business.'

Kate held up her hands in a placating gesture and sat back. There followed a moment of quiet contemplation and then she suddenly brightened. 'I think somebody needs a drink,' she said in a sing-song voice.

Humming softly, Kate retrieved a brandy bottle and glass from the walnut cabinet behind her husband's desk and poured a large measure. 'There, darling, that'll do you good,' she said, placing the glass before him.

Fisher glared at her. 'Don't pretend you actually care about me … *darling*.'

Biting back a bitter response, fixing a conciliatory smile to her lips, Kate returned to her seat. 'Please, Charlie … not here.'

Fisher gave her another withering glance. 'What are we going to do?'

'Well, you can say a prayer for that poor woman,' Kate said, reaching for the telephone receiver, 'while I tell everybody rehearsals are cancelled.'

CHAPTER 3

'ARE YOU ALL right?'

'I'm fine, sir.'

'You don't look fine.'

'I am, honestly.'

'Why don't you go home?'

'I don't want to, sir.'

Paul Wells tutted loudly; it was easier to get his hyperactive grandchildren into an early bed than it was to coax the stubborn Mia Harvey into believing that her way wasn't necessarily the best. While she settled at her desk he poured her a coffee, scrutinized her face carefully as he handed her the mug.

'You look bloody awful,' he said.

And he was right. Mia had had a lousy night. She'd slept fitfully, her fractured dreams bringing images of both parents in happier times. And although those images had offered a welcome – if fleeting – relief, they'd also compounded her grief a hundredfold as she struggled towards wakefulness, clutching at the duvet, her cheeks awash with tears.

Crying into her pillow would solve nothing, however. She needed to get a grip. And she would. Work would be her refuge from now on: their team her only family.

'Has Nick gone to see Jack?' Mia asked. It was 9.30 a.m. He should have been in by now.

Wells nodded. 'We phoned first. He's awake … and moaning nonstop, apparently.'

Mia found a smile. 'You know Jack, sir. He can't be without his hair gel.'

'And those hospital gowns are hardly designer standard,' said Wells, with the beginnings of a grin.

'Did they mention his injuries?'

The DCI's grin morphed into a growl as he reached for his notebook. 'Concussion. A few loose teeth. Badly blurred vision. Cuts and bruises on his upper body….'

'God…. Why did it happen, sir?'

'The nasty bleeder was pissed. High as a bloody kite, an' all. Him and his mate had been celebrating the birth of his son and heir – first in a new line of law-breaking scum,' said Wells, scowling. 'Anyway, daddy wanted to buy the kid a present, only he'd spent all his dole on the booze and drugs. What could they do? Oh yes … pinch a few DVDs and sell them on. Top marks for initiative, Mr …' Wells consulted his notes. '… Jason Perry.' He shrugged. 'So, of course, when Jack dared to stop him, our Mr Perry took offence.'

'Where are they?'

'Still in the cells till we get Jack's statement.'

'They'll not get bail, surely?'

'*He* won't,' Wells said heavily. 'Not if I can help it.'

The threat of physical violence was a constant in their job. That was one of the reasons why they went around in pairs, but life was fluid, circumstances variable; you only had to be in the wrong place at the wrong time and … Mia sighed inwardly. She'd try to call in on Jack later. Take him something nice.

Picking up her pen and reaching for a wad of papers from her Intray Mia attempted to rouse a little enthusiasm.

'I thought you'd be at the cemetery, sir.'

'I'm going when Nick gets back. You can come, if you like.'

Thank God for that, Mia silently breathed. She'd been certain the DCI would keep her chained to a desk for the rest of that week at least – and brain-numbing paperwork was the last thing she needed. She smiled her thanks at him.

'Fancy another coffee?' he asked, about to get to his feet.

'Let me,' she said, quickly leaving her desk. Mia was forever complaining to the others about her thankless role as the DCI's unelected tea-lady. But she'd rather pander to him; it wasn't in her nature to accept being mollycoddled.

She was handing across his mug when Nick burst in, red in the face and breathing heavily. 'The lift's broke again,' he muttered.

While Mia filled a mug and took it to his desk, Nick opened his briefcase and gave Wells a copy of Jack's statement. 'He couldn't remember everything, sir, but it should be OK.'

The statement covered two pages. Wells scanned Jack's neat handwriting in silence. Then he went over it a second time, occasionally making notes on a scruffy piece of foolscap.

He looked up at Nick. 'Have you given your account?'

'Yes, uniformed have a copy.' He pulled a Xeroxed sheet from his briefcase. 'Here's one for you, sir.'

'How is Jack?' asked Mia.

'Knackered,' said Nick, between swigs of his coffee. 'When I got there he was writing a formal statement for the prosecution in the rape case.'

Mia tutted. 'Couldn't they let him wake up properly first?'

'They're summing up this afternoon so …' Nick shrugged.

'Poor old Jack,' she said, laughing. 'He's already done a day's work and it's not even eleven o'clock yet. No wonder he's moaning.'

'What're downstairs doing Perry for?' Wells asked Nick.

'Apart from the shoplifting? – assault occasioning actual bodily harm.'

'Good. He'll likely get a custodial with his list of previous.'

'Jack might be going home tomorrow,' Nick went on.

The DCI frowned. 'Bit soon, isn't it?'

'Michelle's mum's a retired nurse. She's offered to move in with them till he's better.'

Mia snorted. 'He'll be back here by the end of the week, checking his pretty-boy face in the mirror every few minutes and stinking the place out with TCP.'

'Doubt that,' said Nick, perching on the edge of her desk. 'His vision's still not right. They're fast-tracking an appointment with an eye specialist.'

There followed a fearful silence; when Mia's horrified gaze settled on Wells, his spirits sank. He'd seen that look a thousand times on his daughters' faces – when they were small and life had cruelly disturbed their safe and seemingly uncomplicated world. *Do something,* it said; *make it better.* But there was nothing he *could* do. He was powerless.

'Won't be a minute,' said Mia, on the verge of tears as she grabbed her shoulder bag. 'I need the loo.'

She was making for the door when it opened on to Jim Levers, their usually mellow duty sergeant.

'You won't bloody well believe this,' he said, coming to a stop before the DCI's desk.

Wells smiled, thankful for the timely interruption. 'Tell us anyway.'

'That bastard, Jason Perry … he's only made a complaint against Jack for assault.'

'That's ridiculous,' said Mia, her laugh hollow.

Wells frowned. 'He's already lodged the complaint? Who interviewed him?'

'Greg Taylor.'

'What's the dozy bleeder playing at? He knows the state Jack's in.'

'He'd no choice,' said Levers. 'A witness came forward, said it was Jack who started the fight. She's willing to testify in court. Said we're all a load of animals and we've got to be stopped.'

Wells's hangdog features lengthened considerably, but after a moment's contemplation he let out a short staccato laugh.

'Why are we worrying?' he said. 'It'll never get to court.'

He sounded certain enough. He just hoped to Christ he was right.

So they were fast-tracking an appointment with an eye specialist. Mia gave a tiny shudder in the passenger seat of Nick's car. They didn't do that for nothing. When her mother's glaucoma had become especially problematic a couple of years ago, they'd waited almost six months before Mia finally ran out of patience and paid for a private appointment.

Poor Jack. Poor *stupid* Jack. Why hadn't he hung on for Nick before charging in, all guns blazing? He could have even let the bastard go, rather than risk an injury that might ... She stifled a gasp. What if his sight never returns to normal? What if he goes blind?

It wasn't fair. Jack had never hurt anyone. And his life had been going so well. His marriage to Michelle – although rocky to begin with – was strong and an absolute joy to witness. Their little boy was gorgeous and well above average intelligence; the nursery teachers said so. Jack was studying hard for promotion, with Wells backing him all the way.

And now this.

What if Jack couldn't watch his son grow into a man?

As the sunlit countryside zipped past her passenger window Mia mentally chastised herself, trying to banish all such morbid thoughts from her mind; she couldn't carry on like this. She'd have to snap out of it. In their job they faced death and near fatal injuries regularly; they were trained to distance themselves, almost to stand outside their bodies whilst witnessing the atrocities human beings inflict upon each other with such shattering regularity.

Why then was she allowing such ghoulish thoughts to take a hold? Was her subconscious mind forcing her to wallow in the macabre as a punishment for abandoning her mother at the very time the poor woman had needed her most? Was death merely a distant concept … until it crept stealthily into your personal zone, showing you that life wasn't everlasting, that one day it would be your turn?

Mia's breath caught in her throat.

What's Mum got to do with Jack? What's death got to do with *anything*? Jack wasn't dying – at least they could all be thankful for that.

A tight band of anxiety wound itself around Mia's chest, taking her completely by surprise. She couldn't breathe; couldn't even let Nick know she was in difficulty. She was battling with the seat belt, trying to wrench it from its latch, when a wad of tissues appeared on her lap and dragged her back to the present.

She gave Nick a puzzled frown. 'What're these for?'

He was guiding the car into a lay-by, his handsome face hugely troubled. 'Take a look,' he said, pulling down the sun visor in front of her.

Mia glanced up into the small mirror attached to the visor. And a stranger looked back at her. A stranger with rivulets of black mascara running down her sallow cheeks.

'You look like Coco the fucking Clown,' said Nick, in that terribly alluring way of his.

She didn't know what to say. She hadn't even been aware that she was crying.

Thankful for the tissues, Mia set about repairing the damage. She risked a glance at Nick. 'You won't say anything to Wells,' she said, cringing at her pleading tone. 'I don't know what's the matter with me.'

'I do,' said Nick, pulling on the handbrake. 'I thought you'd be better off coming into work today, Mia, but now I'm not so sure.'

'Oh don't you start,' she said, sighing. 'I have enough of that from the boss.'

Nick released his seatbelt and sat back, arms folded. 'You've just lost your mum. It is OK to grieve, you know.'

'Yes, I do know,' she said, turning towards the side window.

'So give yourself a break. Take that compassionate leave they've offered.'

'You'd like that, wouldn't you? Let Wells see me crumble when things get tough. That'd suit your purposes just fine, wouldn't it, Nick?'

He gave a couldn't-care-less shrug, reached for his cigarettes on the dashboard and opened the driver's door wide before lighting up.

Mia left the car and flounced towards a sickly hedge bordering the lay-by, seemingly intent on studying its sparse dust-covered leaves. Nick watched her closely. He knew what she was going through because a number of years ago he'd lost his pregnant wife in a car crash.

His whole future taken away by a patch of black ice.

And instead of facing the trauma head-on, he'd done exactly what Mia was trying to do now. He'd carried on as though everything was fine. But it hadn't been fine. Unable to cope with the endless sympathetic glances from his colleagues, with the way in which they were forced to pussyfoot around the subject of his loss, Nick had put in for a transfer to Larchborough, and once there he'd kept his past a secret, had hidden his grief behind a tough-guy image which served only to alienate him from almost the entire workforce.

He'd been vile to Mia on many occasions; indeed, he'd almost come to enjoy their open rivalry in front of DCI Wells. They were like two toddlers, vying for Daddy's attention. Nick laughed inwardly as he pulled on the cigarette, his gaze still on Mia's back. Life was such a fucking joke when all was said and done.

He'd been racked with guilt after his wife's accident. He was supposed to have seen to the car's loose brakes and he hadn't. Now Mia was experiencing that same guilt over her mother, and it would destroy her if she wasn't careful.

Nick didn't want that to happen. He wanted to save her from herself. Why? Because even when he was at his most vicious, compromising her professional integrity and stabbing her in the back, Mia always rose above it, always found strength within herself to put the job first. She wasn't one to bear a grudge. And the times she'd covered for him….

Nick took a final drag on his cigarette, tossed the butt on to the road, and meandered towards her, hands in his trouser pockets. Mia heard him approach and, her back still towards him, started rifling the depths of her shoulder bag with all the eagerness of Robert Langdon in search of the Holy Grail.

He stopped beside her, moved to rest a hand on her shoulder, but thought better of it. 'Can I say something?'

'Depends on what it is,' she said, her attention still on the bag.

'If you ever need to talk – about your mother … Jack … anything – then I'm always here to listen.'

She turned to him and snorted, her eyes searching for that tell-tale piss-taking light in his. 'You what?'

'I'm just saying….'

Mia was still searching his eyes, still looking for the hate she normally found there. But all she could see in those fathomless brown depths was compassion.

Highly flustered, she fastened the bag and hitched it on her shoulder. 'We'd better get off,' she said, heading back to the car. 'The boss'll be wanting an update.' Wells was at the hospital, informing Jack of Jason Perry's audacious claim.

They'd travelled probably half a mile when Nick said, 'The crime scene … is it anywhere near your mother's…?'

'Grave? Is that the word you're searching for?' Mia sighed heavily. 'No, it's not. And look, Nick, I'm fine.'

'Oh yeah? I wasn't the one nearly flooding the car back there.'

'If you ever mention that again … I'm fine. It was—'

'It was a panic attack, Mia. You're not fine.'

'I know what you're up to,' she said, letting out a savage laugh. 'You're trying to undermine me. This is the first mummified corpse we've found and you want it for yourself.

Well, tough, Nick. I've beaten you before, and I'll do it on this one. You see if I don't.'

'I wouldn't bet on it. And as your superior officer, I'll be taking the lead with the Reverend.'

'Thank God for that,' Mia said to the side window. 'He's back to his normal juvenile self.' She gave him a sideways glance. 'Don't try to be nice, Nick. It doesn't suit you.'

CHAPTER 4

FRANK LESSING WAS in the chancel, chuckling to himself as he retrieved hymn sheets left there by careless choirboys after last night's practice session. Well, it wasn't often he got the better of Charlie Fisher on matters of film and television.

Each morning Frank presented the vicar with a question on entertainment through the decades. What was the significance of the colour red in *Sixth Sense?* Who played James Stewart's other half in *It's A Wonderful Life?* Where was television's *The Office* based?

As a rule Charlie was on the ball, got the answer straight off. But today's question had him flummoxed. Who played Alexander in Oliver Stone's 2004 film of the same name? Frank had asked. And the vicar hadn't a clue. Couldn't even hazard a guess. Oh sweet victory.

Of course, Charlie wasn't functioning at his best today. Frank had picked up on that the minute he'd lurched into the vestry – collar askew and hair a mess – at ten minutes past eight. He was supposed to have been in at 7.30, and it wasn't like him to be late. The poor bloke looked as though he hadn't slept a wink all night. It must be the flu. There was a lot of it about; even at that time of year. He'd have to see that Charlie didn't overdo things, didn't stretch his limited resources. A difficult task at the best of times; the vicar's days were usually chock-a-block.

Frank descended the steps into the nave and stood before the rows of pews. The church was empty apart from Edna Templeton seated at the back, head lowered, wrinkled features blissful in prayer. Edna was there most days, knew the Books of the Old Testament better than Charlie, and wasn't shy in demonstrating that knowledge to anyone with a spare minute. Most of the flock thought the old lady was a few sandwiches short of a picnic – they could be an uncharitable bunch at times – but Frank knew differently. She was simply beguiled by the old church. As he was.

Frank loved St Matthews: every stone, every carved feature, all of its historic significance. Over the years thousands upon thousands of worshippers must have stood where he was now. It was a sobering thought.

But he couldn't spend all day in rapturous repose. He needed to get on. Charlie Fisher wasn't the only one with a busy day. He'd get those hymn sheets back to the office and start on his list of things-to-do. The council men were due at any time to start work on those old graves that had settled; he'd have to make himself available for them.

Thoughts of graves brought Frank's mind back to yesterday. Terrible business that. Who'd have thought a body could have been buried all that time and nobody knew a darn thing about it. Charlie had been in a right state ever since its discovery. On top of the flu as well.

Frank was shaking his head and making his slow pigeon-toed way towards the office when the main doors of the church burst open, causing Edna to flinch. Mia entered first and Nick followed, all the while aiming whispered threats at her back.

Ignoring him, she marched along the aisle towards Frank, her warrant card held high. 'Detective Sergeant Mia Harvey,' she said, her words bouncing off the stone walls. 'We're here to see Reverend Fisher.'

Frank did a comical double-take as she approached. 'Either you were with us yesterday, Miss, or you've got a doppelganger right here in Larchborough.'

Mia was pulled up short. If she was to be reminded of her mother's burial at every turn then this case might well prove to be too much. But Nick had already said she wasn't up to it and if she gave in now he'd be right. She couldn't have that. She'd just have to plough on.

'I *was* here,' she said, recovering well. 'My mother's funeral …'

Frank gave a gracious nod. 'My condolences.'

Nick edged forward. 'DI Ford,' he said, holding up his card. 'Where can we find Reverend Fisher?'

'At the hospital,' Frank told him with a cheery smile. 'Tuesdays he visits the wards, offers succour to the sick and dying.'

'When will he be back?'

Frank sucked in a breath. 'Might be a while yet. He does home visits on Tuesdays as well.'

Mia said, 'Could we have your name, sir?'

'Frank Lessing. Verger.' He held out a hand. 'You've come about the body?'

'Yes,' said Mia, wincing at his hearty grip. 'Our boss wants to know when that section of the cemetery was cordoned off. Reverend Fisher said he'd find out.'

The verger touched a finger to the side of his nose. 'Then you don't need Charlie. Fifty-odd years I've been paying homage to this beauty. Never married, I haven't. And why should I? This place is mistress enough for anybody.' He turned sharply, motioned for them to follow. 'Let's find you them files.'

The office was a small dark cluttered room to the right of the main doors. Flicking on the overhead light Frank tossed the hymn sheets on to a solid wooden desk and pulled up two straight-backed chairs, pronouncing that the detectives should sit as he made his way towards a grey metal filing cabinet.

'Over four hundred years old she is, and still looks like a goddess,' Frank said, as he tackled the second drawer down. 'Of course, she's had a few facelifts, a few nips and tucks …' He fell silent, searched with more urgency through the drawer. 'Charlie must have already taken it out.'

He threw up his hands and sank into the olive green captain's chair behind the desk. 'Not to worry. Should be able to work it out if I set my mind back.'

Mia shared an anxious look with Nick. DCI Wells wouldn't accept a date pulled out of thin air by the aging verger. He'd expect substantiated evidence to back up the man's claim.

'Perhaps we should wait for Reverend Fisher,' she pondered.

'No need,' said Frank. 'Let's see, the last flood was around 1999, and the church council battled for a good two years after that to get proper flood defences. No money available, though, was there? Them graves are full of dead people – that's their view – and dead people won't bother about a bit of water. Never mind the relatives. They don't count.'

The man's argument was gathering momentum, his aggressive hand gestures moving to auto-pilot.

'Mr Lessing … the date?' Nick prompted.

Frank focussed on the detective, a grin slowly forming. 'Sorry, best not to get me started. Anyway, when we realized we'd have to raise the money ourselves we put on a number of events….' He continued in silence, his gaze drifting skyward as he scanned the historical sequence. 'Three years,' he said, at last. 'Three years we've had that fence. Couldn't afford anything stronger. Times were hard. Still are. People need to watch the pennies. We thought a fence'd do for the time being.'

'And was that bit normally maintained to the same standard as the rest of the cemetery?'

'It should've been, but no's the answer to that.' Frank gave them a knowing look. 'Money again, you see.'

'So basically it's been left to grow wild.'

Frank nodded. 'And very pretty it is, too. Don't you think?'

'Very,' said Mia. 'Does anybody keep an eye on it?'

'No.'

'So anybody can gain access without the church's knowledge.'

'That's right.'

Nick said, 'According to our boss, Reverend Fisher wasn't happy about using that land. He only agreed after pressure from the congregation. Is that right?'

'Yes, Charlie was mindful of the complications we'd be left with if it flooded again. A decent headstone can cost thousands. One ends up under two or three feet of filthy water and the church is liable.'

'How long has Reverend Fisher been here?' asked Mia.

'About four years. The faithful love him. Especially the ladies. He's been in a right state since that body turned up. He *does* care, you see. He feels for people's suffering.'

'OK,' said Nick, getting to his feet. 'You've been very helpful, Mr Lessing. Thank you.'

'Any time you have a question about St Matthew's, you come to me,' said Frank as he headed for a small rear door, its key already in the lock. 'I'll let you out this way. Just turn left and you're in the car park.'

The detectives made to go, but Nick stopped in the doorway. 'Who has access to this room?'

'Everybody who helps out,' said Frank, shrugging. 'It's Charlie's office, of course, but he's not the mean type. Me and the missus are always squabbling about who's going to use the desk. I win, as a rule, though. Charlie always backs me up.'

Mia lifted a suspicious brow. 'I thought you said you weren't married.'

'Not *my* missus … Charlie's.' He chuckled. 'Can't wait to see the back of me, can our Kate. Then again, can't say I'm a big fan of hers.'

The detectives moved out into sunshine that was awfully bright after the gloom of the tiny office. And they reached the deserted car park, *en route* to the crime scene, to find Edna Templeton hovering nearby.

'Christ, what now?' Nick muttered.

Mia approached the woman, gave her a smile. 'Can we help?'

'I heard you say you're the police.'

'Yes, we are.'

Edna viewed them hopefully. *'The eyes of the Lord are in every place, beholding the evil and the good.* Proverbs, chapter 15, verse 3.' She grabbed Mia's arm, turned her pointed gaze on Nick. 'Please … warn Charlie. Warn him. He won't listen to me.'

'Bloody hell, Jack, the nurses should have warned me,' said DCI Wells, standing like the Spectre of Death at the foot of the young detective's hospital bed.

Jack's fingers went to his cheekbones and prodded gently. 'Looks bad, doesn't it, sir.'

'Your face is OK, mate. I've just never seen you without the quiff before.'

Jack's bruised face instantly crumpled and as he toyed with his red hair, battled with gravity in a bid to get back that beloved quiff, Wells mentally kicked himself. He'd been trying to inject a little lightness into his arrival, but had clearly aimed the needle at a sore spot.

Quickly changing the subject, he said, 'I brought you these,' and handed Jack a number of magazines, their subjects ranging from computer programming to grooming and fashion, with a little soft porn thrown in for good measure.

'Thanks,' said Jack, flicking through the top one. 'That's really good of you, sir.'

Wells was making himself comfortable on the side of the bed when Jack's quick inhalation of breath alerted him to a problem. 'What's wrong, mate? Shall I get somebody?'

'You can't sit there,' Jack whispered. 'They go mad if you sit on the beds.'

Wells stifled a curse; he couldn't do right for doing wrong. Feeling like a newcomer in a foreign land he went in search of a chair.

After his initial barrage of tests and examinations Jack had been transferred to Bartlett-Trent, a general ward for men. Three of the eight beds were occupied by women, however; very ancient women whose wits had left them; women who had moaned and yelled drug-induced profanities throughout the night. Sleep had been impossible.

Add to that deprivation a stuffy atmosphere tinged with the scents of vomit and loose bowels, the Nazi-inspired temperaments of the staff, the stone-like feel of his mattress, and Bartlett-Trent Ward was an almost perfect match for Jack's imagined version of hell.

Wells' thoughts were travelling along similar lines as he attempted to cram his gangly frame into a thoroughly inadequate plastic chair to the right of Jack's bed.

'You slept OK?' he asked. Jack rolled his eyes and made a slight scoffing sound. 'Never mind, mate, you'll be out tomorrow, so I hear.'

'I hope so. This place is doing my head in.'

Wells allowed his gaze to settle on the next bed. Its occupant – a man of Wells' generation – was connected to a number of drips, had an oxygen mask covering his pasty features. A see-through plastic bag hung at the side of the bed – only inches from the DCI – into which bright orange urine dripped sluggishly.

Wells had to force back sour bile as he turned back, silently promising God that he'd never again take his robust health for granted. And he found Jack blinking hard and squinting at one of the magazines, trying without much joy to read the headlines on its cover.

'Your eyes any better?' Wells asked, knowing full well that they weren't.

'A bit, sir.'

'When's your appointment with the specialist?'

'In the morning.'

'That's good.'

Wells shifted his weight in the chair. How could he tell the poor sod he'll soon be facing an assault charge? He risked another glimpse of Jack's face. The bruises seemed bigger, even angrier than when he'd first walked in. Jason Perry must have had a field day.

Shit, he'd just have to tell him. He couldn't sit there all day.

Wells took in a juddering breath and held it for several seconds. Then he said, 'How's the little 'un?'

Jack tried to smile, a hand going to his aching mouth. 'He's OK, sir. Missing me though. He sent me this.' He pointed to a sheet of white paper blu-tacked to the side of his locker.

Wells found himself staring at a few blobs of yellow and red. 'Is that supposed to be you?' he asked, smiling.

'No, it's Superman. Jamie's mad on him. He's got Superman wallpaper, a Superman blanket …' The bed suddenly shook as Jack let out a sob. 'God, I'm sorry, sir.'

'What for?'

'For getting myself into this mess. *I'm* hardly bloody Superman, am I?'

Wells rested a hand on Jack's sheet-covered shin. 'Settle down, mate. Upsetting yourself ain't gonna help.'

'I couldn't stop him. He was all over me. I tried to hit him back, but I kept missing. Nick must think I'm a right twat.'

Wells tutted. 'You're a twat for thinking it. We're all behind you, Jack. You should know that.'

'What's his name, sir?'

'Jason Perry,' said Wells, the words sticking in his throat.

'What's he being done for?'

'Shoplifting, and assault occasioning actual bodily harm. He'll be going down, don't you worry.'

'Good.'

There followed a few moments silence; ample time in which Wells could have acquainted Jack with the charge being brought against him. The words were in his mind – lined up like obedient little soldiers – but his thin lips refused to let them march.

'I'll be back before you know it,' Jack was saying. 'I'm well on track with my sergeant studies, sir. I'm determined to pass, for Jamie's sake.'

Wells pulled himself to his full height in the uncomfortable chair, those last few words breaking down the wall of his crippling inertia. 'Jack, we've got a problem. Perry's put in a complaint against you for assault.'

Jack wanted to frown, wanted to laugh out loud, but his injuries made those small reactions impossible. Instead, he simply stared at the DCI, his fingers working on that quiff while he struggled to take it in. 'But I hardly touched him, sir.'

'A witness came forward, said you'd started the fight.'

'No way,' said Jack, getting seriously het up. 'I'm not saying I didn't want to hurt him – I'd have bloody killed him, given the chance – but he'd got me off balance. I couldn't get a fair shot.'

Wells' gaunt features were indignant. 'I don't want any of that talk. Do you hear me? You were trying to apprehend him, that's all. You didn't want to fight.'

'I did, sir.'

'You did not,' said Wells, in a snarled whisper. 'You start banging on about wanting to kill him and the prosecution'll be quids in.'

Jack gave Wells a dismal look. 'Oh yeah.'

As the young DC sank back into his mound of pillows Wells' heart went out to him. He looked broken, dejected. He looked as though he'd given up already. And his next statement only served to underline the fact.

'That's it then. Might as well clear my desk now.'

'For Christ's sake,' Wells muttered. 'You're right, mate, you ain't bloody Superman.'

'What can I do, sir?'

Once again the DCI was subjected to a 'Make It Go Away' glance. And this time he was better equipped to deal with it.

'You maintain a dignified silence at all times,' he said, trying to infuse a modicum of confidence into his tone. 'Say nothing to anybody outside your immediate circle. This is bound to make the local papers and journalists are a sneaky breed. Perry hasn't got a hope in hell of getting this to court, but we don't want to play into his hands.'

'Who's the witness?'

'Not sure yet.'

'What happens next?'

Wells sat back, folded his arms. 'You get better, mate. You get your eyes seen to. You get your pretty face back. I need you in the office. I can log on to the bastard computer, but after that I'm lost.' He was getting to his feet when a series of loud high-pitched bleeps cut through the surrounding chaos. 'What's that?' he said, as a posse of grim-faced nurses emerged from nowhere and power-walked towards an adjoining bay.

'Somebody's stopped breathing,' said Jack, as casually as only a fellow patient could.

'No,' said Wells, horrified.

Jack nodded. 'Second time today.'

'Christ.'

Sounds of curtains swishing closed, the urgent murmurs of the staff, and still the shrill beeping continued. As everyone in Jack's part of the ward fell silent, all of them listening to the heroic battle being waged beyond the thin partition, Wells watched as two women – smartly dressed and sobbing quietly – were led to the comparative safety of the nurses' station by a tall, well-built, dark-suited male.

The man had his back to the DCI and was comforting the women in hushed tones, when he turned briefly to gesture towards a drinks machine – the women shaking their heads – Wells found himself staring at the ravaged features of Reverend Fisher.

Wells felt the hairs on his arms do a little jig. Never before had he seen such a marked change in a man. Yesterday the vicar had appeared strong and self-assured; a little disconcerted when the body was discovered, certainly, but still in control nonetheless. Now, though, he resembled a man whose shoulders held a thousand worries, whose eyes had witnessed untold horrors.

Why? Had something terrible happened since yesterday afternoon? Or was the sight of yet another dying person taking its toll? He must have to sit at many deathbeds in his line of work. Indeed, the DCI had to gaze upon many abused and mutilated dead bodies in *his* job. Just because it happened often, didn't mean you ever got used to it.

That bleeping stopped as suddenly as it had started, the resulting quiet almost deafening. Then, after a beat of about three seconds, normal service resumed: muted gossiping, chairs scraping, coughs and groans….

Wells needed to get out of there. Grabbing his chair he said a brisk, 'Don't worry', and a hearty farewell to Jack and headed towards the exit. He was adding his chair to the precarious stack near the doors when he spied Reverend Fisher lurching towards him, shoulders still hunched, Bible clutched tightly to his chest.

'Nasty moment, vicar,' he said, intercepting Fisher before he could leave the ward.

The man gave him a dismissive glance. 'Sorry?'

'Back there … A goner, is he?'

Fisher studied the detective's face for a long moment. 'Do I know you?'

'DCI Paul Wells,' he said, holding out a hand. 'We met yesterday at the crime scene.'

'Of course … forgive me.' He grabbed Wells' hand, pumped it with enthusiasm. 'Yes, I'm afraid *he* has passed on.'

'Shame.'

'It's a blessing, really.'

Wells followed Fisher into the corridor where people chattered softly on the single row of fixed seating and the pings of arriving lifts provided constant background music of sorts. The vicar moved with an almost sluggish gait, yet his gaze darted all ways. He seemed desperate to be away.

'Are you OK?' asked Wells. 'You don't look too well, if you don't mind me saying.'

Fisher gave a dry snort. 'I'm being sorely tested, Chief Inspector. The Great Man – He never makes things easy. The deceased was another of my congregation, so his poor family will of course be expecting a burial at St Matthew's. But where to put him? – that's the big question.'

'If it's any help I can try and speed up the forensic examination of the plot, see if it'll ease your burden.'

'That's very kind of you, especially as you've troubles of your own.' Fisher nodded towards the doors of Bartlett-Trent. 'A family member?'

'A member of my team. He's just been sorely tested an' all. Like they say, vicar, "these things are sent to try us".'

'Indeed. Anyway, must get on,' said Fisher, already heading for the lifts. 'I need to check that the chapel's free. His daughters want to pray.'

'You carry on,' said Wells, walking alongside him. 'And say one for me while you're there.'

Fisher offered his hand. 'It was good to talk to you again.'

'We'll be talking many times, I dare say.'

The vicar gave a lukewarm smile as he pressed the lift button, darting in almost before those inside had alighted. And as Wells stood there, jingling the loose change in his trouser pockets, he could only wonder why the man had taken the lift to the fifth floor when he knew damn well that the chapel was on the first.

A cool oasis in a sweltering desert. A soothing shoulder to cry on. A helping hand. Those blessings and many more like them were sent by God to ease our often troublesome paths through life.

And Reverend Charles Fisher gave thanks in abundance as he approached the door to his own personal oasis in the Psychology Department at Larchborough General Hospital.

A sign on the door read: ALISON PARKER Clin.Psy.D.

And it was Mrs Parker's cheerful 'Come In' which rang out in answer to Fisher's strained knock. She was seated at her desk; a vision – or mirage? – in beige linen and Angel perfume.

'Charlie, I've been trying to call you all morning. Where have you been?'

'Don't ask,' he muttered, pulling up a chair.

'I was worried. When Kate called to say rehearsals were cancelled I thought—'

'The police are crawling all over the church grounds.'

'I know,' she said, slowly removing her spectacles and placing them on the desk. 'It was on the radio.'

Fisher's eyes took on a haunted look. 'I thought things couldn't get any worse, Ali, but now….'

'Charlie, stop it. What can the police do?'

'They'll ask questions, and they'll keep on asking until the whole ugly truth's been exposed.'

Alison's grin was sardonic. 'Who's going to tell them? We won't, and *she's* hardly likely to talk.' She left her seat and stood behind him, massaged his shoulders, felt the knots of tension there.

Fisher grasped her hands. 'I'm finished, Ali. I knew she'd destroy me in the end.'

'No, she won't,' Alison murmured softly. 'I'll see to that.'

CHAPTER 5

THE TENT WAS still in place and SOCOs still swarmed about its edges like scarabs around a dung ball – very much as it was yesterday. Only now the stench was gone, replaced once more by the heady scents of wild flowers and meadow weeds.

Mia was thankful for the change. It was bad enough having to endure Nick's constant complaining, without having to hold one's breath at the same time.

They were at the fence, watching the action from a distance. Not that there was much to watch. Actually, their entire visit had been a waste of time. They'd learned nothing of any use, had found no leads with which to further the investigation, and wouldn't either until the post mortem results became available. That was the trouble with this stage in the game. They were all walking blind.

'What was that old lady's problem?' Mia pondered aloud.

'Dementia, I should think,' said Nick.

She nodded agreement. 'What now then?'

'Fancy a chat with your mum?'

'No, I'll wait till the headstone's ready. Have a bit of a ceremony then.'

Nick stared into the distance, at the snaking river and a large copse of beech and ash trees towering beyond it. 'She's better off, you know.'

'Of course she is,' said Mia, her tone dripping with derision.

'And so are you.'

'You think?'

'You are, Mia. You can get on with your life now.'

'I haven't got a life.'

'That's your fault,' he said, shrugging. 'Decide what you want to do and get on with it.'

'Like you, you mean?' Nick failed to respond; simply lowered his gaze. 'See, that's shut you up.' She hitched her bag on to her shoulder, took one last glance at the SOCOs and headed for the gate in the fence. 'Let's get back to the office. I'm gagging for a coffee.'

The graveyard was huge, with burial plots dating back to the early seventeenth century. Many of the very ancient ones had fallen into disrepair and – nearer to the church – council workers were toiling hard to save as many as they could. Mia regarded them with a wry smile because the verger was amongst them, pointing and gesticulating and offering his pearls of wisdom, no doubt.

The cemetery was a beautiful spot, with huge oak and hawthorn trees offering shade and shelter at various points, well-worn paths meandering, and birdsong filling the perfumed air. It was lovely; so utterly peaceful. Mia felt her cares falling away as they negotiated the path towards the headstones. Even Nick had lowered his shoulders, looking less like a boxer psyching himself up for a fight.

The graves started about a metre from the fence and Mia moved slowly, studied the crumbling inscriptions as they edged further away from the crime scene.

'Oh, my God … look,' she suddenly cried out.

Nick turned to find her pointing towards a modern headstone in shiny black marble. He trudged back, read the gold lettering with a heavy heart.

ANNA CHAMBERLAIN
Born and Died – 15 July 2006
Beloved Daughter of THOMAS and GRACE
Rest Well, Darling
Our Love Will Be With You Always

There was a large oval cut into the marble to the left of the inscription which showed the red and wrinkled face of a new-born child, her eyes shut tight, her mouth open in a mewl of undisguised fury. Fresh rosebuds in pink, yellow and white filled four bulbous containers at each corner of the gravelled plot. And a number of bedraggled soft toys – two teddy bears, a pink elephant, and a small penguin – were shackled to the base of the headstone by thin unobtrusive wires.

'Born and died on the same day,' Mia murmured. 'How awful.'

Nick said nothing. He didn't dare open his mouth for fear of divulging the secret of his own daughter. And the truth of it was he felt jealous of Thomas and Grace because they'd at least glimpsed their child. They'd held her and kissed her and told her how much she was loved. He hadn't been fortunate enough to experience even that small blessing. His daughter hadn't even managed to be born.

'Let's go,' he said, turning sharply on his heel. 'I thought you wanted a coffee.'

Mia watched him tramp away, his head down, shoulders hunched again. 'Heartless git,' she muttered.

'Thought I'd find you here. Checking up on me, are you?'

'Now, Frank, what have I told you about that attitude of yours?'

'You're the only one who thinks I've got an attitude.'

Kate Fisher let out an exaggerated huff as she slammed shut the file she'd been studying and fixed the verger with a superior look. 'If you must know I've come to help Charlie. He's not had a good night.'

They were in the office, the overhead light bulb casting ominous shadows upon Kate's features, showing up dark lines beneath her eyes and a pinched appearance to her mouth. As a rule she scrubbed up well for fifty-two; could pass for ten years younger. Not today though.

'I hope it's not catching,' said Frank as he leant against the filing cabinet, keeping a fair distance between them.

'Catching?'

'What Charlie's got. You look a bit under the weather yourself.'

'He hasn't got anything, Frank. He's perfectly well.'

'You've just said he had a bad night.'

Kate glared at him. 'Charlie's fine. OK?'

Frank held up his hands. 'Don't want the congregation coming down with flu, that's all.'

'They won't.'

'That's all right then.' He turned away from her, started rummaging in the filing cabinet. 'Can't praise your hubby enough, Kate. One in a million, he is.'

Isn't he just? she thought, staring at the verger's broad back. To everyone else. Not to her though. Never to her.

Charlie couldn't do enough for acquaintances, for strangers. Charlie would put himself out, go that extra mile, with hardly a thought. Why then couldn't he see that she was suffering so badly? Why couldn't he help her?

Kate's thoughts went back to the previous night. She saw again the loathing and recrimination in his eyes; heard again the door slamming as he stormed out in the early hours.

What had she done to deserve such rancour?

Still, they'd made up after he'd eventually returned. They'd managed a few hours' sleep. Things could be worse.

'The police are still busy at the crime scene,' said Frank, his words pulling her back to the present.

Kate opened up the file again. 'Are they?'

'They'll be—'

'I don't want to know.'

Frank shrugged. 'Rehearsing tonight?'

'Hopefully. If everyone's available.'

'Let me know if you want me to set up.' He turned to face her, a number of papers in his hand. 'If you can bear my presence, that is.'

After he'd gone Kate stared at the closed door for a long time. Frank Lessing was a thoroughly decent soul, solid and reliable to a fault. Every one of their congregation saw him as an extension of her husband, used him as a dumping ground for their troubles. And the old man seemed to thrive on it.

Trouble was he'd sided with Charlie from the outset. They'd never get along now. She was the enemy, the one to avoid. Kate sighed. If only she could tell Frank *her* troubles. If only *she* could confide in him.

'Bruises? How the hell can he be covered in bruises?'

Nick baulked at the DCI's vicious tone. 'That's what Jim Levers said, sir.'

'The doctor was called,' Mia added gingerly. 'Perry was complaining about the pain.'

They'd arrived back at CID to find Paul Wells in a quarrelsome mood. He'd been genuinely shocked by the sight of Jack's injuries and was ready to lash out. Jason Perry was the one he really wanted to batter, but as such a move was out of the question Nick and Mia were getting the backlash.

Wells hurled them a scurrilous glance and snatched up his telephone receiver, punched out the numbers with heavy disgust. 'Jim, it's Paul. What's all this about Perry?'

'He collapsed in the cell, Paul. We had to call the quack.'

'Bollocks,' Wells barked. 'He's putting it on.'

'That was my first thought, but the doc says he's got heavy bruising to the stomach and kidneys.'

'How? Jack reckons he never landed a punch.'

'Dunno, but Perry's solicitor's doing a photo shoot as we speak. On his second role of film apparently.'

Wells's furious breath drenched the telephone receiver while his long jowls trembled with suppressed fury. Jason Perry was a no-good waste of space with cardboard for brains, but put him in a custodial situation and he could win *Mastermind* with his knowledge of beating the system. Wells had met his type before: clued-up toe rags who knew every loophole, every crack through which to wriggle free. Not this time though. Not if he could help it. Jack had sworn that he hadn't landed so much as a slap on the arsehole and Wells believed him.

'Jim, let me know when the solicitor's buggered off. I want a look at Perry's so-called injuries.'

Wells slammed down the receiver without so much as a goodbye. He sat back, stared at the steaming mug of coffee that Mia had wordlessly positioned before him.

'Thanks,' he grunted, nodding towards the drink. 'Nick, did you get any impression that Perry was hurt?'

'None, sir. There was blood everywhere, Jack could hardly stand, but Perry hadn't got a mark on him.'

Wells narrowed his eyes. 'Were *you* a bit rough with him?'

'No way, sir. I'll admit I could've been gentler with the cuffs, but I've got more sense than to beat up a collar in front of a crowd.'

'All right, mate, I had to ask.'

Mia was sipping her coffee, only half-listening to their dialogue. Her thoughts were following an altogether different route.

'Nick,' she said, carefully replacing the mug, 'didn't you say Joey and Syed answered the call?' He nodded. 'Then I'll bet you anything they had a bit of fun in the car.'

Nick let out a derisive snort. 'They'd maybe give him a hard time, but they wouldn't go that far.'

'They've done it before. That bloke who raped and set fire to little Phoebe Wilcox. Remember?'

'Shit,' said Wells. 'OK, I'll take a look at the damage and then I'll have a word with them.' He sat back, let out a heavy breath. 'Christ, this is looking bloody bad for Jack.'

'They couldn't know Perry would press charges,' said Mia. 'I'm sure they wouldn't have done it otherwise.'

'But he has and they did,' Wells fired back. 'And this could cost Jack his job.'

Nick jumped in. 'Why cite Jack though? Why not them? Anyway, we don't know they did anything yet. Innocent till proven guilty – isn't that the way it's supposed to go?'

'Somebody did something,' Wells snarled. 'His solicitor's used up a roll of film already.'

It was then that his phone buzzed. Wells snatched it up, heard John Lloyd's ponderous tone. 'You'd better have something I can use, mate.'

And it would seem that he had quite a bit. They watched Wells scribble away for many moments, the ensuing silence punctuated by the occasional grunt and murmur, even a raucous laugh now and again.

'OK, kiddies, listen up, John's given us some good stuff,' he said, replacing the phone. 'First off, he reckons Mommy Dearest's been dead for about two years. She was white, approximately five-foot-six. He's put her age around late twenties. She wasn't hard up. She was wearing expensive designer gear and she's got a mouthful of veneers. Expensive veneers, according to John.'

'They can cost thousands,' Mia interjected.

'These were top of the range, apparently. That'll make it easier to track the dentist.'

'What killed her?' asked Nick.

'Intracranial bleeding caused by blunt force head trauma,' said Wells, reading the words verbatim. He glanced up. 'A crack on the skull to you and me.'

'Could he tell what was used?'

'You know what it's like, mate, they can make a guess but that's all. John says the wound – at the back of the head – was quite small. It was bleeding in the brain that finished her off. Could have been caused by a heavy ornament or such like. He found traces of resin and gilt, said he'll get back to us when they've been tested further.' He gave them an intense look. 'Also, the woman had a healed fracture in her left shin bone – something else to help identify her. And her hair was dyed. Brown to dark blonde, John reckons. She was right-handed, and would have had a slim build before the pregnancy.'

'What about the foetus?' asked Mia.

Wells consulted his jottings. 'It was a girl. In the third trimester, so the woman was over six months gone, although John reckons she was nearer to eight.'

Mia glanced over her own notes. 'Sir, there's the grave of a new-born girl very near the crime scene.'

'So?' said Wells, shrugging.

'It's really immaculate … fresh flowers … toys … the grass around it well-trodden. And the baby died nearly three years ago. If the family keep such a keen eye on it they might have seen something fishy around the time of our murder.' She made a face. 'Worth a thought, don't you think?'

Wells raised a dubious eyebrow, but nodded nonetheless. 'Track down the parents. Let's see what they've got to say.'

'Will do, sir.'

Wells took another call. It was Jim Levers. Jason Perry's solicitor had just left the building, grinning like a hyena on crack. The DCI left Levers in no doubt as to his feelings about the over-confident brief before cutting the connection. After which Wells took a moment to slow his breathing and focus his thoughts.

'OK, let's get organized,' he said, scratching his head. 'We'll need a list of all females reported missing between … let's say June 2006 and June 2007. If that brings nothing, we'll go further back.'

'I've got that,' said Nick.

'And we'll need a list of cosmetic dentists. John's promised his report by tomorrow lunch at the latest, so we'll have photos and X-rays by then. I'll leave that with you as well, Nick.' He suddenly hissed out a snarl. 'Christ, we could really do with Jack here. There's gonna be a load of bloody computer work.'

'I'm planning on seeing him tonight,' said Mia.

'Don't mention Perry's bruises.'

'Of course not, sir.'

Wells glanced at his watch. 'Listen, let's call it a day and start early tomorrow. Eight o'clock sharp.' He shot Mia a probing look. 'Bearing up, are we?'

She nodded. 'Thanks for letting me come in, sir. I'd be climbing the walls at home.'

He gave her a hasty smile and rustled together his notes. 'Right, I'll transfer all this to the whiteboard. Then I'm off downstairs to give poorly Perry a dollop of my particular blend of TLC.'

Mia didn't stay long at the hospital. She'd arrived to find Michelle and Jack's mother huddled around his bed, fussing and tearing his nerves to shreds – if his waspish expression was anything to go by. As each patient was allowed only two visitors at a time – and she'd have felt guilty should either of the women have had to drag their heels outside – Mia dumped a bag of Jack's favourite sweeties and the latest Snow Patrol CD on his bed, gave him a swift peck between the bruises, and hotfooted it out of there.

Back at the car park, pulling in a lungful of clean air, Mia swallowed a curse. Merely stepping through the hospital doors had her hurtling back to the moment of her mother's death, leaving her trembling and hating herself for such weakness. Mia liked to be in control. What she didn't like – what she couldn't stand – was that sense of emptiness that kept hitting her in waves, unexpected and unremitting.

What to do now. She was loath to go home. Her mother's belongings were there, waiting to be sorted.

Just two small boxes and a bag of clothes.

Not much to show for a life.

She'd put everything in the spare bedroom. Out of sight, but not out of mind. They goaded her constantly; she felt accused and vilified each time she passed the door.

No, she couldn't go home.

She'd head back to St Matthew's, see if anyone was around. She could ask about the parents of Anna Chamberlain. Save herself a job in the morning.

Yes, it was a plan.

'God,' she muttered, approaching her car. 'Maybe Nick's right. Maybe I *should* get a life.'

'Mr Perry, we meet at last,' said Wells as the custody sergeant pulled open the cell door.

Jason Perry, hunched on the low bed, lifted his shaved head. 'Who the fuck're you?'

'DCI Wells, sir.' He nodded to the sergeant, left his briefcase in the doorway. 'I'm the boss of that copper you thrashed to a pulp.'

'He done the thrashin', bruv.'

Wells leant against the wall, hands in his trouser pockets, a contemptuous look on his jowls. 'Let's have a shufti then.'

Perry left the bed, lifted his grubby T-shirt, wincing dramatically as he did so.

Wells's stomach fell as he stared at the stretch of bruised flesh around Perry's middle; made his pocketed hands into fists as the boy turned to show a matching patch at the small of his back.

Trying valiantly to keep the shock from his face, Wells said, 'Who did that to you, son?'

'Your g'rilla, bruv.'

Wells forced a laugh. 'Come on, we both know that's not true.'

'You callin' me a liar?' said Perry, easing himself back on to the bed. 'S'licitor says I'll get money outta this … *compensation*.'

Wells lifted his brows. 'That's a big word, son. If nothing else your vocabulary's improved.'

'Fuck off.'

'Language,' Wells scolded. He took his hands from his pockets, folded his arms. 'So you're the victim here, Mr Perry. Is that right?'

'Yeah.'

Wells nodded towards the boy's grazed knuckles. 'Looks to me like you got a few in yourself.'

Perry shrugged. 'Protectin' meself, wern I?'

He was sweating heavily. Large stains showed at the neck of his T-shirt, across his scrawny chest, beneath both armpits. His left leg jigged constantly. A full plate of food sat beside him on the bed.

'You haven't touched your dinner, mate.'

'Ain't hungry,' he said, his gaze fixed to the floor.

Wells's grin was vicious. 'Missing the drugs?'

'Ain't into that shit,' said Perry, flinching momentarily.

'Glad to hear it. You've a new baby, I'm told. Got to be a role model now – teach him right from wrong.'

'I will,' he said, eyes still on the floor.

'Shame really. You stuck in here. Not being able to see him. Must be hard.'

Perry looked up then, gave the DCI a cocky grin. 'Got the magistrates in the mornin'. S'licitor says I'll get bail.'

'Really?'

'Yeah, no problem. 'Specially with me injuries.'

Wells' expression was hugely sceptical, but he let it go. 'What did the doctor say?'

'Wants me to have a blood test,' said Perry, a hand going to his stomach. 'Says things ain't right inside.'

'Oh dear.'

Perry's eyes narrowed. 'Your slave's gonna fuckin' pay for this. S'licitor says so.'

'He's paying already. In a hospital bed.'

Perry lifted a shoulder. 'Had to retaliate, bruv.'

'Your solicitor teach you that word an' all, did he?' Wells pushed himself away from the wall, shook his head. 'What's the world coming to, eh? Can't even shoplift in peace now.'

Perry adopted an indignant pose. 'I was buyin' them DVDs for me partner. A present, like, for havin' the kid.'

'Fifty-odd?' said Wells, smirking. 'She must really enjoy her films.'

'Fuck off.'

'OK.' Wells reached for his briefcase, took his time. Straightening up, he said, 'By the way, Mr Perry, who's your witness?'

The boy grinned. 'One o' God's angels, I'd say.'

'You haven't got a name?'

Perry shook his head. 'She saw everythin' though. She must've gone to Specsavers – you reckon?'

'You know it was a woman then?'

Wariness showed momentarily in the boy's sunken eyes. 'S'licitor told me ... yeah ... yeah, that's it.'

'Strange,' said Wells. 'He tells you her gender – sorry, her sex – but doesn't give a name.'

The jittery Perry started rubbing his thighs, gave the DCI an angry frown. 'I forget, all right? S'licitor says she's legit. S'all that matters.'

Wells made for the door. 'Good night, then, son. Sleep tight.'

'Wait. I ain't gonna get no sleep. I'm in agony. Can you get me some tablets, bruv? Somethin' to knock me out?'

Wells smiled. 'As a slippery arsehole once said ... fuck off.'

The small church car park was almost packed when Mia eased her Fiat through the gates. She grabbed her bag, activated her locking device, and was heading for the main doors when Frank Lessing came into view, an empty lunchbox and crumpled newspaper in his chubby hands.

A smile of recognition lifted his leathery features when he spied her. 'Hello again,' he said.

'I was worried the place might be empty,' she told him, motioning towards the cars. 'Seems like I was wrong.'

'Play rehearsal,' said Frank, a caustic look in his eyes. 'The place'll be a tip come morning.'

'Who's in charge?'

'Charlie's missus ... the dreaded Kate.'

Mia glanced towards the church. 'Is the vicar in there?'

'Didn't see him. Then again, I just set everything up and get out quick. I keep out of her way as much as I can.'

'OK, thank you,' said Mia, already approaching the doors.

'Before you go …' She turned back, and Frank gave her a thrilled type of look. 'Clint Eastwood's *Dirty Harry* film was the first to be inspired by the Zodiac serial killer. Yes?'

'If you say so,' said Mia, itching to get away.

The old man was almost hugging himself. He loved his daily quiz. 'But what was the title of the latest one in 2007, and who starred in it?'

Mia, swallowing a sigh, thought for a moment. 'OK … it was called *Zodiac* … funnily enough. And it starred …' She was hooked now, desperate to remember. She snapped her fingers. 'Jake Gyllenhaal and Robert Downey Junior. Am I right or am I right?'

'Oh, you're good,' he said, pointing a finger, a slow grin stretching his features. He backed away, the finger still pointing. 'You've set me a challenge, you have. I'll have to put my thinking cap on for you.'

'Do your worst,' she responded with a laugh.

Feeling ridiculously buoyed by that small triumph Mia pushed through the heavy doors to find the foyer-type entrance area transformed into a small stage. A row of three hard-backed chairs were positioned at an angle. And more chairs and boxes were scattered at various points. To signify pieces of furniture? Or doorways?

She was turning her attention to the pews – their backs to the stage – where a number of people sat in groups, a few of them poring over battered scripts, when a woman rushed up to Mia, her gaze accusatory.

'Can I help you?'

'Kate Fisher?'

'Yes. Who are you?'

Mia brandished her warrant card. 'DS Harvey. Larchborough CID.'

As Kate studied the card Mia studied her. And she had to admit that Mrs Fisher was something of a surprise. After listening to Frank Lessing's hardly complimentary assessment of the woman Mia had expected to find a gargantuan-schoolmarm-dragon type; an assumption which couldn't have been further from the truth.

Kate Fisher was tiny, trim-figured, and her flowing ankle-length skirt accentuated her youthful femininity beautifully. Her skin was almost flawless; the few lines that did show around the eyes only added interest to her attractive features. Standing there, towering over the woman, Mia felt ever so slightly jealous. And fat.

'Have you come about … about the body?' Kate stuttered.

'In a way,' said Mia, pocketing her warrant card. 'I was hoping for a word with your husband.'

'He's not here. Not yet. He's …'

Kate appeared to be flustered. And Mia wondered why.

'Is it OK if I wait for a bit?'

'Shall I get him to call you? Wouldn't that be better?' said Kate, attempting to herd Mia towards the doors. 'I'm sure you've got better things to do with your evening.'

She hadn't. Unfortunately.

'Absolutely. But you know how it is – no peace for the wicked.' Mia moved towards the pews, turned to face the stage. 'Which play are you doing?'

'The Ghost Train,' said Kate, stifling a sigh. 'Can I get you a cup of tea as you're staying?'

'If it's no trouble.'

'We can't start yet anyway. Still a few stragglers to come.'

A large tea urn stood on a table to the side of the stage, stacks of polystyrene cups beside it. Kate filled one of the cups – added the milk to which Mia had nodded acceptance – and then led the detective to a quiet pew well away from the murmuring group.

'Sorry if I seemed a bit, well, eager to get rid of you just then,' said Kate. 'But we're so behind with rehearsals. We're on in four weeks and haven't finished blocking the moves yet. Personally, I don't think we'll be ready, but Charlie says I should trust in God, so I am.'

Mia took a tentative sip of the tea. It was rather good. 'I used to do amateur dramatics,' she told the woman.

'Really? Then you should join us. We're always in need of experienced helpers.'

'I don't think so,' Mia said, hurriedly. 'I don't have much spare time.'

'Oh well.' Kate started to fidget, was clearly desperate to keep their flagging conversation alive. 'My husband was a professional actor years ago. He played Steve Webber in *Temple's Crest*. Did you ever watch it?'

'Oh, thank you,' said Mia, resting a hand on Kate's shoulder. 'I *thought* he was familiar. It's been driving me mad. *Temple's Crest* … of course. I watched it all the time when I was growing up.'

'You've met Charlie?'

Mia gave a sombre nod. 'We buried my mother yesterday.'

'Ah, you were here when the body was found. He mentioned you.'

A gloomy silence followed. Eventually Kate said, 'You're lucky to have found a plot.'

'Mum went in with Dad. He's been here since the mid-nineties.'

Kate flushed. 'Gosh, I'm sorry. Talk about making things worse.'

'It's fine, honestly,' said Mia, with a smile. 'Your husband did a brilliant job.'

Just then the doors opened and a taller, more delicate version of Kate Fisher burst in. She was conducting a hushed conversation with a very handsome young man, their hands linked, eyes oblivious to anything but each other.

'Oh good, here's Grace,' smiled Kate. 'Only Charlie and Alison to come now.' She rose from the pew. 'DS Harvey, come and meet my daughter.'

Kate introduced the two women. 'And this is my son-in-law, Tom. Isn't he a dish, Detective Sergeant?'

Isn't he just. She shook his strong warm hand. 'It's Mia, by the way. I'm not actually on duty at the moment.'

'Mia … what a lovely name,' said Tom, staring straight into her eyes. 'Can I get you a cup of tea?'

'I've already got one, thanks.' Then, realizing that her hand was still in his, Mia sprang away. 'I'm waiting for Reverend Fisher.'

'Let's wait together,' he said, his smile teasing. 'I want a word with him myself.'

'Darling,' said Kate, taking her daughter's arm, 'come and see the gorgeous costume I've found for you.'

Grace allowed herself to be led away, but kept her eyes firmly on her husband. 'Hands off, Tom. I'll be watching, don't forget.'

Mia was puzzled. The girl had said the words lightly, had giggled almost uncontrollably as they left her mouth; and yet Mia had the distinct impression that the sentiment behind them was heartfelt. God, how awful … If a handsome husband can make you *that* paranoid, maybe she should look for somebody a bit more frayed around the edges.

She went back to the pew, retrieved her drink. Tom followed; a little too closely for Mia's liking. Sidling along the bench, leaving a gap between them, she said, 'What business are you in, Tom?'

'I'm an actor,' he said, the words spoken with much conceit. Then he laughed. 'Well, I will be when somebody gives me a job. Haven't had one in ages.'

Mia sipped her tea. 'Difficult, is it?'

'Virtually impossible. We should be living in London, right in the thick of it, but Grace will insist on staying here.'

Tom was lounging on the pew. He was wearing dark blue denim jeans, a blue-and-white-striped polo shirt and brown brogues. The outfit looked carefully casual, shabby even, but Mia knew designer gear when she saw it; she'd worked with Jack for long enough. Here was one out-of-work actor not short of a bob or two.

'What do you do while you're waiting for work?'

'Nothing,' he said, with actual pride in his voice. 'The theatre's my life, Mia. Well, TV and movies, hopefully. I haven't got time for anything else.'

She frowned. 'But you've just said you can't get any jobs.'

'True, but it won't last for ever.' He pointed to his face. 'Wouldn't I make a brilliant Bond? Come on, be honest.'

'It must be a struggle financially,' she said, deliberately ignoring his question.

'Not at all. My wife's a doctor. A GP, actually. She earns enough.'

So, you're a kept man. I'm going off you, sweetie.

Mia drained her tea, put down the cup. 'Your father-in-law used to be an actor, I'm told.'

Tom shot forward, suddenly impassioned. 'That's why I'm here. Charlie said he'd get on to some of his mates, put in a good word. He was meant to call me, but the old sod's making me sweat.'

'Are you in this play?'

Tom laughed. 'Be serious, Mia. I've got better things to do with my time.'

No, you haven't.

'It's for a good cause though, isn't it – the flood barrier?'
'I wouldn't know.'

He turned to look at the assembled cast. Mia followed his gaze and found that a number of the women were staring back and blushing pink – even the grannies – as he threw kisses and generally played to his audience. If arrogance and self-love were equal to acting talent then this man was a future Oscar-winner.

Mia glanced at her watch. It was 7.30 p.m. Kate and her daughter had returned to the set. Kate was organizing everyone – they might as well block the bits they could do – her tone efficient yet nicely ingratiating. The whole group seemed to love her. Grace was making herself comfortable on the set, all the while flicking quick glances at her husband. Mia was beginning to feel very uncomfortable under the woman's scrutinizing glare.

'Any idea when Reverend Fisher's due back?' she asked Tom.

'He should be here by now. He's bringing their … leading lady.' He said the last two words with a sarcastic smirk.

Mia narrowed her eyes. *Patronizing prick.* 'Think she's any good … as you're the expert?'

'Alison?' He let out a howl of undisguised pleasure; then fell back, pretended to mop tears from his eyes. 'She's a clinical psychologist at the hospital and about as creative as this piece of wood,' he said, rapping his knuckles on the arm of the pew. 'She's Kate's little sister, and as nobody else wanted the part she got roped into doing it, poor cow.'

'At least she's having a go.' *That's more than you're doing.*

Mia rummaged in her bag for notebook and pen. She'd leave the vicar her mobile number and a message to call her in the morning. No point in wasting more time listening to God's Gift twittering on. Even sorting out her mother's stuff was preferable to that. She was flicking through the notebook, searching for the next clean page, when there it was.

ANNA'S PARENTS = THOMAS & GRACE CHAMBERLAIN. FIND THEM.

Tom and Grace.

God, she was slipping; she should have made the connection immediately.

She stole a look at Tom. He was buffing up his fingernails on his jeans, grinning as his wife mouthed 'I love you'.

'You're Anna's father,' Mia blurted.

His head jerked around, all signs of cockiness now gone. 'What?'

'Sorry,' she said, a hand to her mouth. 'It's just … I'm trying to find the parents of a baby named Anna Chamberlain and … Are you her father, Tom?'

'Yes.' He sat up straight, brushed back his glossy fringe. 'What of it?'

Mia explained her reasons for being there. '… and it would help a lot if you could remember seeing anything suspicious.'

Tom's effervescent charm was suddenly a thing of the past. He had half-turned on the pew, was fixing her with a virulent lour. Mia recoiled slightly. He probably would make a good James Bond – for all she knew he might be brilliant – but at that moment Tom bore more than a passing resemblance to one of the repulsive baddies.

'Leave it … OK?' he said, annoyance darkening the blue of his eyes. 'I don't visit the grave, so … just leave it.'

He was on his feet and racing towards the main doors before Mia could draw breath. She rushed after him, noting Grace's puzzlement. She just hoped the woman didn't think she was planning to ravage him in the car park.

Mia left the church to find him heading for a nifty red hard-topped sports car, the keys already in his hand.

'Tom, please stop. I'm sorry if I've upset you.'

He came to a halt, his back still towards her. The only sounds were from a helicopter circling overhead and the tinny tune of an ice cream van in an adjacent street.

Mia mentally chastised herself. How could she have been so thoughtless? Wasn't *she* hurting now? Her mother's death was tearing her apart. But at least her mother had had a life, a good one too until the final years.

How much worse it must be to lose a baby, to nurture and look forward with such tingling anticipation for nine whole months – only for the precious gift to be snatched away at the final hurdle. She couldn't even begin to imagine the pain, the mental torture involved. There could be nothing more horrific, surely.

Tom's arrogance – his terribly narcissistic attitude – must be a cover; a means of hiding his crippling anguish. Mia could see that now. And what of his wife's chronic possessiveness? After already losing her child, she must be terrified of losing him too. Poor Grace – effortless beauty and a good career were just meaningless trappings in the greater scheme of things. Not for the first time Mia gave silent thanks for her single status. Better to have nothing to begin with. Saves a lot of heartache in the long run.

Mia approached Tom carefully, rested a hand on his arm. 'I'm so sorry. It must be awful.'

'I'll tell you what's awful,' he said, spinning round to face her. 'Having to live in this dump because your wife won't leave the fucking grave.'

Mia's mouth dropped. 'What?'

'I wanted to have Anna cremated, take her to London with us. But, no, Grace wouldn't hear of it. And Kate's just as bad.' He straightened his back, showed his teeth. 'If they'd given half as much thought to my career as they do to those fucking bones, I'd be a major star by now.'

While Mia stood in shocked silence Tom got into the car, wound down the window. 'That woman you've found … I hope she's rotting in hell. And you know what? – I hope my daughter's with her.'

Frank Lessing was planning a bonfire. The evening was perfect for the task, with a nice south-easterly breeze to send any smoke scuttling towards the fields and well away from the houses. He wouldn't want to get Mrs Marshall's back up, again.

Frank's old stone cottage stood at the end of a short terrace in Barrack Street off Simpson's Landing – so-called because the fifteen-acre site had been used as an important landing point for surveillance aircraft during the last war, and was owned at the time by a farmer called Harry Simpson. Or so the story went.

The area, now council-owned, had become a favoured venue for fly-tippers. And Frank took it upon himself to clear away the smaller items regularly, so he had plenty to burn. His little shed was chock-full with heavy-duty sacks. It was time to make some space.

His narrow garden was over a hundred feet long, and Frank had constructed a large concrete square towards the end of it especially for fires.

When the rubbish was piled high and the flames had taken hold Frank hurried back to the cottage. And should Mrs Marshall have been spying from behind her immaculate net curtains, she would have noticed that Frank's expression – so genial, as a rule – was now tight and apprehensive.

Inside his kitchen Frank made for the table, on which lay his crumpled newspaper. He unfurled it slowly – his breathing ragged – and took from its pages the three sheets of paper he'd stolen from the filing cabinet in Charlie Fisher's office. Frank's heart beat rapidly as he tore the sheets into tiny pieces. Then he returned to the bonfire and threw them into the licking flames.

Feeling the weighty wrath of God on his sagging shoulders, Frank turned his face to the Heavens, tears clouding his eyes. 'Needs must, dear Lord … when the devil drives.'

CHAPTER 6

'MORNING, JIM, LOVELY day,' said DCI Wells, as he breezed into reception.

Levers held up a scrap of paper. 'No, it isn't.'

Frowning at the duty sergeant's disgruntled expression, Wells approached the desk and took the note. It told him that Jack was to attend an interview at the Discipline & Complaints office. The powers-that-be were taking Jason Perry's allegations seriously.

Wells crumpled the paper and tossed it on to the desk. 'Where can I find Joey Champion and Syed Shah?'

'Canteen,' said Levers.

The station canteen was heaving: all officers on nightshift had finished; those on dayshift about to begin. Champion and Shah were finishing their fried breakfasts when Wells came to a halt at the table, deposited his briefcase on the floor with a smile.

'Mind if I join you?' he asked, his tone deceptively mild.

'Gotta be off in a minute, sir,' said Champion.

'This'll only take a minute,' said Wells, pulling up a chair. 'Jason Perry – remember him?'

Shah scowled. 'Nasty prick.'

'Yes,' said Wells, 'he's a piece of work, that one.'

'How's Jack?' asked Champion.

Wells made a face. 'Not good. His injuries'll heal, of course, but how he'll manage when he's thrown off the job, with a little 'un to feed….' He shrugged.

'It won't come to that,' said Shah. 'They won't take that scum's word.'

'Looks like they have, mate. Jack's got to see Discipline and Complaints.'

'Christ,' said Champion.

Wells picked up the brown sauce bottle, started fiddling with it. 'How did Perry seem when you put him in the car?'

Champion lifted a shoulder, shot a glance at his partner. 'OK, I'd say. He was bladdered, but….'

'Did he look like he was injured?'

'No, sir.'

'What about you, Syed? Did you notice any injuries?'

'No, he hardly looked like he'd been in a fight.'

Wells paused for a moment, stared at the sauce bottle still in his hand. 'Nick reckons Jack was in a hell of a mess. Glad I didn't see him. I'd have wanted to tear Perry apart.'

PC Champion sat back, blew out his cheeks. 'He looked bad, sir. Good job he was out of it.'

Wells eyed them conspiratorially. 'I hope you two stuck to station policy. I mean, nobody would have blamed you if you'd wanted to get a few punches in, but we've got to play it by the book.'

'Yeah,' said Shah. 'His shins might have stung a bit, though, after we dragged him into the car.'

Wells grinned and nodded. 'So you kept your fists to yourselves?'

Champion was mopping up egg yolk with a piece of bread. He gave the DCI an arduous glance. 'Yeah, had a job though.'

'I'll bet,' said Wells. 'We've all done it, given the bastards a bit of what they deserve. You did good with that paedo a while back.'

'Thanks, sir.' He pushed his plate aside. 'You know, that little kid was alive when he set her alight. She was still screaming when we got there. You never forget something like that.'

Wells knew that to be true, but even so … 'Villains have rights as well, unfortunately.'

'Too many, if you ask me,' said Shah, folding his arms with a flourish. 'Law's too lenient nowadays.'

'Makes me sick,' said Champion.

'And me,' said Wells. He skimmed them a surreptitious look. 'So Perry was still intact when you brought him in.'

'Honest to God,' said Champion.

And that was when Wells's convivial mood took off at a rate of knots – along with the sauce bottle. It hit an adjacent wall, the plastic splitting on impact. Brown sauce showered the hair and uniform of a female officer who sat chatting with three others at a nearby table.

'So why is Perry covered in bruises?' Wells bawled. 'His torso's black and blue.'

Champion and Shah just stared at the DCI, speechless. In fact, everyone in the canteen fell silent, everyone except the female officer. She was protesting loudly, yelling for Wells to look at the mess. He ignored her, carried on eyeballing the two men, waiting for an answer.

'Well?' he said, jowls quivering. 'Hurry up, I haven't got all fucking day.'

Shah's breathing became rapid; DCI Wells was a formidable sight when angry. 'We didn't touch Perry,' he said. 'We've already told you, sir.'

'And I've already told _you_,' said Wells, lunging forward, 'that he's sustained extensive injuries, and I want to know how. He didn't get them from Jack.'

'Nor from us,' said Champion, pouting with indignation. 'Ask the custody sergeant – he might have done it. Or maybe the prick was already hurt when he laid into Jack.'

'Nice try,' said Wells through gritted teeth. 'But the bruising's too recent. So, how about confessing … get it over with.'

Champion rose to his feet, Shah following suit. 'I know you're upset, sir – we all are – but you're not gonna stitch us up.'

'I'm not stitching anybody up,' said Wells, replacing his chair. 'But I will find out the truth.'

The officers made to go, and then Champion turned back. 'Let us know when you do … *sir*.'

Nick and Mia were already working when Wells bounded into CID, red-faced and belligerent. He took one look at his fragile DS and hurled his briefcase at his desk.

'I thought I'd told you to stay at home if you weren't up to working.'

Mia's face *was* very pale. But she was coping, had even looked forward to coming in. It was good to be busy.

'I'm OK,' she said, shocked by his fierce entrance.

She shared a glance with Nick as Wells struggled out of his jacket and settled into his chair.

Nick said, 'Something happened, sir?'

Wells pushed out a breath and regarded them with a guilty expression. 'Perry's complaint's going ahead. Jack's got an interview with D and C.'

'You're joking,' said Mia.

Nick pointed to Wells' in-tray. 'There's a note just come in, sir, about the witness.'

Wells grabbed the wad of papers, found the relevant one. 'A Mrs Valerie Clarke,' he said, rubbing his jowls. 'Works at the cheap stationery store in Argyle Street. Out shopping in her lunch hour when she saw the fight.' He took to riffling once more through his tray. 'Where's her statement?'

Nick shrugged. 'That's all that came in.'

Wells tutted. 'I'll just have to pinch a copy from downstairs.' He glanced at Nick. 'Do me a favour, mate. Put her name in the system, see if you get anything.'

'Yes, sir.'

'I use that shop,' said Mia. 'Why don't I—'

But before she could utter another word the door was flung open by Superintendent Shakespeare. He marched up to Wells' desk, his pompous features pink with displeasure. He was wringing his hands and sweating. The superintendent hated confrontation.

'I've had a complaint from Inspector Blakeley,' he told Wells. 'He says you attacked one of his female officers with a sauce bottle. Care to explain yourself, Chief Inspector?'

Wells sat back, his cold stare causing the superintendent obvious discomfort. 'I didn't attack her, sir. The bottle shot from my hand. There's a difference.'

'The officer in question alleges that you threw it at her.'

'It shot from my hand. Is clumsiness a crime now, sir?'

'Inspector Blakeley is backing his officer. He has every right—'

'Was Blakeley there?' Wells interrupted.

Shakespeare gave a resigned sigh. 'No.'

'Then it's the officer's word against mine.'

Shakespeare jutted out his chin. 'It has also been brought to my notice that you were involved in a heated altercation with PCs Champion and Shah. What's going on, Chief Inspector?'

Wells folded his arms. 'Jack's facing disciplinary action for a crime he didn't commit. I was merely asking the officers if they knew how Jason Perry got his injuries. They took offence at my choice of words, that's all.'

'DC Turnbull is in a tricky position, I'll admit, but you can't go throwing accusations around.'

'I was backing up my officer,' said Wells. 'I have every right.'

Shakespeare was edging towards the door. 'I'll tell those involved that I've spoken to you. I'll give them your apologies and your sincere word that it won't happen again.'

'Give 'em what you like,' Wells muttered, reaching again for his intray.

'By the way,' said Shakespeare, his hand on the door handle. 'DC Turnbull will, of course, be transferred to another station while the complaint is being heard.'

'Oh no, he won't,' said Wells, his smile holding little humour. 'We need him here.'

'It's procedure, Chief Inspector.'

'Bollocks to procedure. The lad's innocent. He's coming back here.'

Shakespeare opened the door for a quick exit. 'I'll let you know when a suitable position has been found for him.' And then he was gone.

Over at the hospital Jack was blissfully unaware of the developments taking shape; developments that had the potential to totally wreck any stability he'd achieved in his working life. Indeed, his whole future hung in the balance.

At that particular moment, though, Jack's only concern was how to fit his few belongings into the miniscule overnight bag provided by Michelle.

Soon, everything was packed except for the magazines that Wells had brought in. Jack – still dodgy on his feet – shuffled towards an adjacent bed where a teenaged boy lay with both legs in traction.

'Mike, do you want these?' Jack asked, handing him the soft porn titles. He couldn't take them home; Michelle would be well upset.

'Ain't gonna do me much good at the minute,' Mike said, 'but, yeah, thanks, Jack, they're cool.'

'Mr Turnbull, can I have a word?'

Jack swivelled round to find a stunning brunette by the side of his bed, her slender leather briefcase on the blankets. She was laughing.

'Wow, your face *is* a mess … but there's not much wrong with your eyesight.' She pointed towards Jack's abdomen.

He looked down to find the start of an erection nudging his pyjama bottoms.

'I've … I've not been well,' he said, blushing.

Her laughter increased as she held out a hand. 'I'm Alison Parker, the hospital's psychologist. You're going home today, I hear.'

'That's right. After I've seen the eye specialist.'

Her own eyes held devilment, and Jack could guess what she was thinking as her gaze made another excursion to his lower parts.

'Anyway,' said Alison, moving on, 'your doctor asked me to talk to you. You've had a nasty experience. Do you *want* to talk about it?'

'No, thanks. I just want to get home to my family.'

'Have you heard of post-traumatic stress?'

'Sure, but I haven't got it. I'm fine, thanks.'

'How have you been sleeping?'

'I haven't. Nights in this place are like the football ground after a home win.'

That laugh came again. Alison Parker had really great teeth. Her face and figure weren't bad either.

Alison took from her briefcase a small white card and handed it across. 'If you do ever need to talk just give me a ring and we'll arrange an appointment. OK?'

No bloody way. 'OK.'

'Good luck, then.'

Alison was careful to keep her steps light and relaxed as she approached the nurses' station for the real purpose of her visit to the ward.

'Kirsty,' she said, tapping the staff nurse's shoulder, 'have you got any Paracetamol? I've had a headache for hours.'

Kirsty looked up from the patient notes she was studying and gave Alison a chiding look. 'I shouldn't … Oh, go on then, you know where they are.'

'I'll buy you a drink next time we're out,' said Alison, making her way to a room behind the desk.

'You'll buy me two,' said Kirsty, her attention already back on the notes. 'And don't forget to sign for them.'

The room was little more than a large cupboard. Floor to ceiling shelving covered opposite walls, on which resided all the essentials of a busy ward. Directly ahead, beneath a small reinforced-glass window stood a desk housing a large metal cabinet and an open ledger.

The cabinet was locked, but its key lay on the desk beside the ledger. Alison tutted through a nervous grin. Weren't the newspapers always saying that NHS standards had slipped?

'Bring back matron,' she whispered. 'But not yet.'

She unlocked the cabinet and quickly palmed two Paracetamol caplets. Then she took out one large box of a morphine-based painkilling drug and stood pondering as her fingers fluttered over a bottle of Valium tablets.

No, better not be greedy.

Quickly locking the cabinet and replacing the key, Alison dropped the drugs into her briefcase and signed for the Paracetamol.

Out on the ward, Kirsty was plumping up pillows for an elderly patient. Alison gave her a wave, mouthed 'thanks', and regretted bitterly that the girl would soon be in the mire.

'Rebecca Crawford,' said Wells. 'She's our most likely candidate.'

'The name doesn't ring a bell,' said Mia.

'Probably because she disappeared from Nuneaton.'

Fifty-six women had been reported missing in the period between June 2006 and June 2007. Fourteen of those had been found dead, and a further thirty-three had long since been reunited with their families. Of the remaining nine, only one woman came anywhere near to matching the colour, age, and financial status of the team's mummified corpse.

Rebecca Crawford.

'We'll follow this line of inquiry for the time being,' said Wells. 'No point in wasting resources till we know for definite she's not the one.'

Wells took the report over to the whiteboard, wrote her name and last known address. 'She was twenty-eight,' he said, still writing. 'Single, although she was seeing a bloke called Bryan Baxter. According to this Baxter was in Switzerland when Rebecca went missing. He worked for a pharmaceutical company – moved to Switzerland permanently about a year later.'

'Was Rebecca in the same business?' asked Mia.

'No, she was a personal trainer, from London originally, had a few of the rich and famous as clients. She was on the verge of opening her own fitness centre – a super gym, apparently.'

'In Nuneaton?' said Mia. 'A bit out of the way.'

Wells shrugged. 'Doesn't say where.'

'Anyway, she wouldn't be doing much training with an eight-month bump.'

'That's the thing,' said Wells, scratching his chin. 'There's no mention of a pregnancy in this report. Nick, can you find out the boyfriend's address, ask his local force to contact him?'

'Will do, sir.'

'And we'll need her dental records. Did you get that list of cosmetic dentists, mate?'

Nick grabbed his computer mouse, clicked a number of times. 'It's only partial,' he said, hurrying across to the printer where three sheets of A4 paper were dropping into its tray. 'I'll let you have the full list later this afternoon, sir.'

Wells winced when Nick handed him the sheets. 'This is only partial? Christ, I thought there'd only be half a dozen or so. It'll take for ever to work through this lot. Right, we're definitely having Jack – even if I've got to hide him and his computer in the bloody stationery cupboard. Sod Shakespeare.'

'What about Rebecca's family?' asked Mia.

'There's no mention.' Wells held up the report. 'This is only partial an' all.'

Nick made a note on his pad. 'I'll get on to Nuneaton and ask for the original case files, sir.'

'Thanks, mate. Oh, and while I remember … did you check on Jason Perry's witness?'

'I did.' Silence for a moment while Nick thumbed through the clutter on his desk. 'Here it is. Not that it tells us much. Valerie Clarke appeared in court last year as the plaintiff. She'd accused a neighbour of trying to poison her Yorkshire terriers – she breeds them – but the case was thrown out on insufficient evidence.'

'That's it?' said Wells, clearly hoping for more.

'Afraid so, sir.'

Wells' sigh was heartfelt. 'Worth a try, I suppose.' He returned to his desk. 'OK, where are we? Nick, you're on top of Rebecca Crawford, so to speak.'

'I am, sir.'

'And I'll track down the post-mortem report. John promised we'd have it by now.'

'What about me?' asked Mia. She felt like the little girl nobody wanted to play with.

'You could always make us some coffee,' said Nick, smirking.

Mia gave him a ferocious look, then said to Wells, 'Would you like one, sir?'

'Yes, please.'

'OK, I will then.'

She was handing out the mugs – a bit too heavily in Nick's case so that coffee split all over his paperwork – when she said, 'I found that baby's parents, by the way … the baby in the cemetery.'

'Oh yes?' said Wells, only half listening. He was dialling John Lloyd's mobile number.

'They're Reverend Fisher's daughter and son-in-law.'

'Really?' said Wells, the receiver to his ear. 'Could they tell you anything?'

'I only got to chat with the son-in-law but, no, he couldn't.'

'Pity.'

Lloyd picked up at that moment and Mia lost Wells' attention, so she targeted Nick. She filled him in on the previous evening's events, gave him her views on Tom and Grace and the state of their marriage.

'It's only been a few years since they lost their baby,' he said. 'They're bound to be fragile still.'

Mia hadn't really expected Nick to be interested in her observations. He very rarely was. And when he too lifted his telephone receiver, signalling that their conversation was over, she felt her sense of isolation increase.

Then *her* phone buzzed. 'DS Harvey….'

It was Jim Levers with an update on Jason Perry's appearance before the magistrates. Mia replaced her receiver in time with Wells.

'I told John we'd fetch the post-mortem report,' he said. 'It'll be quicker than …' He stopped; Mia's face was showing real horror. 'Oh Christ, what's up now?'

'Jason Perry got bail.'

Wells threw down his pen. 'Stupid bloody magistrates … The bastard'll be in the pub by now, celebrating all that compensation they'll be throwing at him.'

Mia slowly shook her head. 'He's at the hospital, actually, sir. He collapsed in the dock.'

'Why are we here?' asked Nick.

'You know why.' Mia gave him a sideways glance. 'You turning into a goldfish?'

'No, I mean, why are we *here*, in this life? What's it all for?'

They were in Nick's car *en route* to the hospital. Wells wanted them to pick up the post-mortem report and query Jason Perry's condition at the same time. Nick was silent for most of the journey – nothing new there – and Mia's thoughts were wandering yet again towards her mother when he suddenly spouted that age-old conundrum.

'You all right?' she asked with a laugh.

'There, you see? – we never talk.' He swiped the steering wheel. 'Nobody *ever* talks.'

Mia snorted. 'Listen to Mr Chatty. If I get a couple of sentences out of you in a day I feel lucky.'

'Oh forget it….'

But Mia didn't want to forget it. A trip into the dark recesses of Nick's psyche might be interesting. Better than dwelling on dead parents, anyway.

'No, tell me, what's brought all this on?'

Nick shrugged. 'I just wonder whether it's worth all the aggro, that's all. You get born, do your best not to screw up, and then what? – misery and high taxes.'

Mia turned towards the side window. 'I think I prefer you when you're quiet.'

He swung the car into a side street. No way was he going to pay for hospital parking again. 'I'm right, though,' he said, pulling on the handbrake and sitting back. 'That dead baby's parents – you said yourself they're in a mess. Rebecca Crawford's family … her boyfriend … Christ knows how they're managing without proper closure. And what's Jason Perry's story? He probably wouldn't be using if he wasn't so fucked up.' He turned to Mia, his expression an open dare. 'Name me one happy person. Go on.'

'Jack,' she said without a pause. 'Jack and Michelle couldn't be happier.'

'For now. But when he loses his job and that nice lifestyle they've worked so hard for, they'll be just as desperate as the rest of us.'

Mia was appalled. 'Give it a rest. God….'

Nick reached for his cigarettes, opened the car door and lit up. 'Take you and me,' he said, smoke escaping with the words. 'We're like a couple of mice stuck in a fucking wheel. Work and sleep, work and sleep … Where are the fun bits? Where are the rewards?'

'What exactly do you want?'

'I want more. I deserve more. We both do.'

Mia stared at him, marvelled at the way his dour expression only enhanced his good looks. 'Nick, are you asking me out?'

'What?' Now it was his turn to be appalled. 'Fuck off, I was just—'

'Well, thanks a lot, Nick. You could have *tried* to look a little less *repulsed*.'

Mia got out of the car, slammed the door so hard that the dashboard shook, and Nick could only watch her stomp away without a backward glance.

'Bollocks,' he muttered, tossing his cigarette into the road and following.

They were approaching the hospital's main entrance – their usual animosity now tinged with embarrassment – when Mia spotted Reverend Fisher looking furtive by a bed of tall shrubs. And she was pointing him out to Nick when he was joined by Alison Parker.

'Hello, what's going on there?' Mia said, as they watched the vicar lean in for a hug.

The couple's faces showed smiles and pleasure in the encounter, but their body language – Fisher's especially – told a different story. He frequently shot guarded looks around the car park, seemed to flinch whenever the hospital doors swished open.

'That woman looks familiar,' said Mia, stepping aside for a man in a motorized wheelchair.

'One of the doctors?'

'Not one of Mum's. Oh, hold on, she's Kate Fisher's sister. Tom told me she works at the hospital. She's got the lead part in their play.'

Nick laughed. 'He's keeping it in the family then.'

'Oh, trust you,' Mia said, skimming him a look. 'He's a vicar, for goodness sake.'

'Vicars can have it as often as they like. Only priests are celibate. And me … unfortunately.'

Mia managed a crooked grin. 'I'd have no problem getting into a nunnery, if you want the truth.'

Nick spread his arms. 'Like I said, work and sleep.'

Mia focused again on Reverend Fisher. He'd shifted position, was now around the side of the shrubs, pulling Alison with him. He was talking urgently, his face close to hers.

'They don't look very happy,' said Mia, frowning.

'Which just goes to prove my point,' said Nick. He started towards the main doors. 'Anyway, good luck to them.'

Jason Perry was still in the Accident and Emergency department, undergoing tests. He was awake, apparently, but not very coherent due to the large amount of narcotics even now entering his body through an intravenous drip.

'You do know he's a user,' Nick said to the helpful doctor who'd given up part of his lunch hour to fill them in.

'No, you're wrong. He said he's been clean for years.'

Mia gave a humourless laugh. 'For all of forty-eight hours, actually.'

'Pity the accompanying officer didn't mention it.'

'Mr Perry beat up one of our colleagues, doctor. We're not exactly in a rush to help him.'

'But if we'd known about his drug use we'd have tailored his treatment accordingly. As it is, we've probably made a bad situation a whole lot worse.' The doctor pulled on the stethoscope around his neck, clearly annoyed. '*And* we've wasted time and money into the bargain.'

Nick said with a lethargic shrug, 'When will you know what's wrong with him?'

The doctor gave a listless sigh. 'Give us a call on Saturday. We should know what's what by then.'

'So he's not going anywhere before the weekend?' asked Mia.

'Wouldn't think so. He's pretty sick.'

The detectives shared a worried glance. 'OK,' said Nick.

Kate Fisher couldn't keep still. She was pacing her living room, checking her watch. Charlie had promised to be back for lunch. Where was he?

His mobile was on voicemail. Should she call him? They'd parted that morning with angry words. Would a call antagonize him further?

If only he'd talk. How could she help if he didn't make the slightest attempt to communicate? Charlie used to be so considerate, would put her first all the time. She used to joke about him placing her on too high a pedestal, said it was hell for her vertigo.

Not any more. Not for a long while. They hadn't made love in ages. Charlie could barely look at her most of the time. He made her feel as though she was in the wrong when all she wanted to do was love him.

Now things were worse than ever. And that bloody corpse was to blame. Charlie's antagonism had worsened from the moment it was found and Kate could only wonder why. She knew that losing the space for more burial plots added to his worries. But it was only temporary; the police would release the land as soon as they possibly could. And, anyway, it wasn't her fault. Why should she be the one to suffer?

Getting to her feet once more, glancing again at her watch, Kate went back to counting the minutes.

Where are you, Charlie? Please, darling, *hurry up*.

CHAPTER 7

BRYAN BAXTER WAS waiting by the baggage carousel at Heathrow airport when the call came through. He peered at the display on his mobile and tutted. It was Gerhard Ryman, his immediate boss.

What now? Couldn't they manage without him for five minutes?

This was Baxter's first trip home since his relocation to Switzerland. Not that it would be much of a break. He'd had a garbled late night phone call from his twin sister, Claire: something about solicitors and bankruptcy courts. She needed him to fly over. And if he didn't come *right now* then Nigel could be hauled into jail and the kids taken into care, and *then* what would she do?

Claire had always possessed an overactive imagination, sensing trouble where there wasn't any. But he'd looked after her ever since that motorway pile-up had taken their parents back in 2000. He couldn't let her down now.

Grabbing his suitcase from the carousel, and musing that a spell in prison might do his hapless brother-in-law some good, Baxter took the call.

'Gerhard … hi …'

'Not disturbing anything, I hope,' said Ryman, with a bawdy laugh.

Baxter grinned as he headed towards the taxi rank. 'Give us a bloody chance. I've just got off the plane.'

'But English girls are always ready, always waiting. Isn't that what you said?'

'Sure, but I prefer a little privacy when I fuck. I'm old-fashioned.'

'Or repressed?'

'No, that's you,' Baxter said, laughing. 'Anyway, what's the problem? Have sales taken a nosedive without me?'

Silence followed, a very long silence, and Baxter was presuming that the call had failed when Ryman said, 'The police have been asking for you, my friend.'

Baxter stopped dead, almost tripping up a woman behind him. Apologizing profusely as he backed away, the hand with the phone held out towards her, Baxter hurried to a quiet corner where a tall potted palm stood beside a row of seating. He took the end seat, placed his suitcase alongside, and pulled in a steadying breath as he put the phone to his ear.

'Say again, Gerhard. The line's patchy.'

'The police called to speak with you.'

'When?'

'This morning.'

'Did they say what they wanted?'

'No, just that it was imperative that you speak with them.'

A young family chose that moment to procure the seats beside Baxter; the harassed parents speaking in rapid French to three bawling children who refused to be placated.

Baxter lowered his voice. 'What did you tell them?'

'That you had taken a plane to England. That you would not be back for two weeks. I gave them your sister's details, Bryan, said they could speak with you there. Did I do right?'

Baxter was staring at the crowds milling around the terminal, seeing nothing. What did the police want with him? He'd been so careful. They couldn't know.

'Bryan?'

'Sorry, Gerhard, this connection's really shit. No, no, that's fine. You did the right thing.'

'I hope your sister is all right. You let me know. OK?'

Christ, could something have happened to Claire? What if she hadn't been over-reacting? What if that pillock she'd married had done something crazy?

'Listen, I need to ring her right now. I'll be in touch.'

He cut the call and was scrolling for Claire's number as he lunged towards the automatic doors.

'Monsieur. *Monsieur* …'

It was the French bloke, calling him back.

Baxter failed to keep the irritation from his face as he turned. 'What?'

The man's smile was apologetic as he pointed to the suitcase still positioned by the potted palm.

'Oh … merci,' said Baxter, bowing to the man for some reason as he retrieved the case.

Baxter called his sister as he headed for the taxis. And as he listened to the ringing tone he really hoped that something *had* happened to Claire.

Because the alternative didn't bear thinking about.

'What're you doing here? You should be resting,' said Wells, as Jack hobbled into CID.

The young detective perched on the corner of Nick's desk and gave them all a look of doom. 'D'you want the good news or the bad?'

'The good,' Mia said, as she hurried to pour him a coffee.

'The consultant thought I might have a detached retina. Turns out it's only a corneal abrasion.'

'Oh sweetie, I love it when you talk dirty,' she said, trying to lighten the mood as she handed him the mug.

'What does it mean?' asked Nick.

'Not sure, but a course of antibiotics should clear it up.' Jack took a sip of coffee then placed the mug well away from Nick's computer. He was one of those dedicated techies who'd rather stick pins into those battered eyes of his than risk getting liquid into the works.

'Brilliant, mate,' said Wells, trying hard not to stare at his face. The swelling was drastically reduced and his bruises were turning a dirty yellow, but Jack still looked like he'd been in a war.

Wells quietly fumed as he squeezed the arms of his swivel chair, imagining they were Jason Perry's neck. 'OK, what's the bad news?' he said.

Jack looked as though he was fighting tears. 'I've got to see Inspector May at Discipline and Complaints in the morning.'

'Christ.' Wells waggled a finger at his DC. 'You're not to worry, mate. This won't go all the way. I'll see to that.'

Jack threw up his hands in hopeless misery. 'I didn't do it, sir. I swear….'

Wells stared at Jack as though his words had caused a mortal wound. 'We *know* that, you stupid bugger. And I'll tell you something else … the day a worthless bloody lying toe rag like Perry gets one over on us is the day I pack it all in. They can keep my pension, and I hope they bloody *choke* on it.'

Jack gave Wells the type of look a small boy might give his father after he'd diverted a disaster on his behalf. 'Why I came in …' he said. 'Well, I was wondering whether you'd got anywhere with the witness. Only Michelle's in a bit of a state. Actually, she's …' He fell silent, tried to swallow, but the lump in his throat wouldn't allow it.

Mia was at her desk, biting her knuckle hard, hoping the pain might halt the tears that were threatening. 'I could go and see her, if you like. If you think it might help.'

Jack's smile was half-hearted. 'It's OK. Her mum's with us. She's helping … a bit,' he said, pulling a face.

Mia gave him a nod. 'How's Jamie?'

'Confused. He keeps on about my "poorly" face, keeps wanting to touch it.'

Wells was making notes on a pad. 'There's not much we can do about the witness, but there's plenty more grief I can give the lying bastards who did it.'

Nick caught the questioning look in Jack's eyes, and said, 'Joey and Syed.'

'No,' said Jack, aghast.

'They picked the pair of 'em up,' said Wells. 'George Slater was custody sergeant on the day and he's hardly Rocky bleedin' Balboa. Champion and Shah have a history so unless Perry beat himself up I'm putting my money on them.'

'Did Perry get bail?' asked Jack.

All three looked away briefly, reluctant to heap more bad news on to the despairing DC. It was Wells who spoke.

'He's in the hospital. He collapsed in court.'

'Shit,' said Jack. 'Wish I hadn't asked.'

'Just remember, mate, you won't be done for it. I won't let it happen.'

Jack was fiddling with his mug, making overlapping coffee rings on a stationery application form. He looked completely crushed and Wells couldn't bear to see it.

'When will you be fit for work?' he said, unable to take the silence a moment longer. 'We need you.'

Jack glanced up, his expression unbelieving. 'But, I can't …'

'Says who?' Wells motioned towards the corner desk. 'It's all there for when you're ready. You just pick a time.'

'But the super called me. He said—'

'He changed his mind,' Wells cut in. 'He's behind you all the way.'

At the sound of those last words Jack's whole demeanour altered. He straightened his back, squared his shoulders, was totally oblivious to the quizzical glances his mates were aiming at their boss.

'Thank God for that,' he said. 'I was starting to feel like a leper.'

Wells gave him a grin. 'You've got a few bruises, mate, but your arms ain't dropping off. Could be a whole lot worse.'

'Yeah,' said Jack, grinning back. He glanced at his watch, got to his feet. 'Better be going. I've made an emergency appointment at the dentist. One tooth gone …' He pulled down his lower lip to show them. '… and two more loose.'

'Bring the bill to me,' said Wells. 'I'll get the force to pay.'

'Really, sir?'

Wells wasn't sure he could square it, but he'd pay himself if he had to. The bill would probably be astronomical. Why should Jack have to fork out on top of everything else?

'Really. Now, bugger off, your face is putting me off my coffee.'

'Right,' said Jack, edging towards the door. 'I'll phone you then, sir … when I'm ready to come back.'

'One more thing,' said Wells.

Jack turned, raised his brows.

Wells smiled. 'Good to see you've got your quiff back, mate.'

'Rebecca Crawford's gym would've been brilliant,' said Mia.

She was reading a sample copy of the brochure that was tucked into the case notes from Nuneaton. There was also a black and white photograph of Rebecca; a 10 x 8 portrait shot taken by a professional. Mia gazed at the girl's lustrous blonde hair with real longing. It grew past her shoulders, had a slight wave, a high gloss that almost shimmered, and was exceptionally thick. Mia wondered vaguely whether hair extensions had been in vogue a few years back. The girl's attractive face was expertly made up. And her teeth – those expensive veneers? – were extremely white; too white, if that were possible.

'She's very pretty,' Mia told the others. 'Very self-assured.'

'What I can't understand,' said Wells, 'is why there's no mention of the pregnancy. She was a professional woman, not some skanky lowlife living off the streets. Her friends, her family, they all must have known.'

'She might not be our mummy,' said Mia.

'True, but she's ticking all the boxes so far.'

'What does the report say, sir?'

Wells had the post-mortem report open in front of him. He went back a page and read for a moment. 'John says the foetus was definitely coming towards the end of gestation. The skeleton was fully formed. He's still claiming she was about eight months gone.'

Mia frowned. 'OK, the notes say she wasn't in constant contact with her family, so it's possible she hadn't told them about the baby, but the boyfriend should have known. Why didn't he say anything?'

'We'll be able to ask him soon?' said Wells.

'You've found him already?' Mia was surprised.

'I got the Swiss police on to it,' said Nick. 'Turns out he's staying at his sister's in Milton Keynes. He's coming in sometime tomorrow morning.'

'Very obliging of him.'

'His sister's got some trouble, apparently – that's why he's in the country – and he doesn't want to heap more grief on her, so he's coming to us.'

Mia fixed him with a fierce look. 'You're keeping a lot of stuff to yourself, Nick. Why didn't I know about this?'

Wells, sensing another heated exchange that he could well do without, said, 'The boyfriend called earlier, while you were in the toilet. Things had moved on when you got back.'

Mia closed her indignant mouth, seemed to visibly deflate in the chair. She'd rushed to the loo after Jack had made his exit; too emotional, too pissed off with his situation to stay at her desk. She'd bawled in a cubicle for a good ten minutes and then returned to their sympathetic stares, knowing full well that the water she'd splashed on her eyes had done nothing to eradicate the tell-tale puffiness.

'Who's going to speak to him, sir?'

'We can work that out tomorrow. Did you say her dental records are in the case notes?' Mia nodded and took the file to his desk. 'I'm seeing John Lloyd tonight. He can compare them to his X-rays.'

'Has he said any more about the resin and stuff he found in the wound?' asked Nick.

'Not yet. I'll ask him about that an' all.' Wells glanced at his watch. It was 5.26 p.m. 'Right, there's not much we can do till the body's been identified so we'll finish now. See what tomorrow brings.'

Mia dragged herself back to her desk, overcome by a sudden inertia. She didn't want to go home; dark thoughts plagued her there, accentuated her feelings of loneliness, made it impossible for her to find peace. She'd stay in the office if she could. Work through the night.

A vague idea had followed her around all day. It was in her mind again now. She said to Wells, 'Sir, there's a little theatre group at St Matthew's. They're doing *The Ghost Train*. Kate Fisher said I could help out if I felt like it. Is there any reason why I shouldn't?'

Wells was packing his briefcase. He stopped, surprise on his face. 'Is that what you want?'

Mia lifted a shoulder. 'It'd be something to do.'

'Can't see why not. It won't compromise the case.'

'OK, I think I'll go along.'

Nick was switching off the printer behind Wells. He was grinning, offering Mia a thumbs-up. She gave him her usual response: the pursed lips, the skimming eyes. But inside she was smiling.

'How many more to do?' asked Reverend Fisher.

'Just those few by the lych-gate,' replied Frank, pointing.

They were in the churchyard, inspecting the old graves that had been saved by the council workers.

'They're doing a good job,' said Fisher.

'Not bad. Have to stand over them though.'

While the vicar stooped to pick up a fallen tree branch Frank watched him closely, tried to gauge the man's mood from his weary movements and the frown lines on his forehead. And as Fisher deposited the branch into a lidded skip kept at a discreet distance from the graves, the words, 'my brother's keeper' suddenly appeared in Frank's mind, causing him to smile wanly. Frank definitely saw himself as Charlie's keeper: he would slay all manner of enemies in a bid to keep him safe.

Dragons. Warriors.

The police.

'Hasn't that missus of yours got you in with a doctor yet?' asked Frank, his sharp tone a clear rebuke.

Fisher was staring in the general direction of the crime scene, his mind elsewhere. 'I don't need a doctor,' he said.

I need a miracle.

'No? You could've fooled me.'

'You're as bad as my mother,' said Fisher, forcing a laugh. 'Stop fussing.'

Frank laid a hand on the vicar's shoulder. 'I'm here if you ever need me, Charlie.'

'I know.'

They stood for a few seconds, staring into each other's eyes, into each other's *souls*. Frank held his breath, hopeful that the man might at last begin to confide, but a squirrel – the same one that'd broken the branch, probably – chose that moment to scuttle noisily up the tree and the spell was broken. Fisher scratched his beard, gave a sigh, and turned towards the church.

'Better get on, Frank. I'm touching up scenery tonight.' He made a face. 'Or so I've been told by Kate.'

They were almost at the main entrance to the church when hurried footsteps came from behind.

'Hello. Has it started?'

They turned to find Mia rushing towards them, shoulder bag clutched to her chest. Frank took a step forward in a subconscious bid to protect his charge.

'Look who it is,' he said genially, horror twisting his stomach. 'What brings you here?'

Mia came to a stop and favoured them with a warm smile. 'Mrs Fisher said she could use me in the theatre group. I've had a bit of experience.'

Panic showed on the vicar's face for the briefest of moments, and then his acting skills kicked in.

'That's wonderful,' he said, smiling. 'The more the merrier.'

'You go in, Charlie,' said Frank, taking Mia's arm. 'I want this lady to myself for a minute.'

Mia was grinning like a loon. Steve Webber from *Temple's Crest* was standing right beside her. Amazing! She'd always been a bit star struck; she couldn't help it. Her mother had been a fan too, before the stroke. She would've been thrilled to know he'd buried her.

'I'd like a chat later, vicar,' she said. 'If that's all right.'

'I'm sure it is,' said Frank, leading her to an old stone bench across from the church.

Mia sat down, bag on her lap. It was ridiculous really, but she was almost quaking with anticipation of the next instalment of their quiz.

'OK, I'm ready, Mr Lessing? Have you been thinking hard?'

No, he hadn't. Entertainment trivia was the last thing on his mind. He hadn't even thought up a question for Charlie. First day he'd missed in years.

'If you're joining us, Miss Harvey, you'd better start calling me Frank,' he said, playing for time.

'Only if you call me Mia,' she laughed.

'Mia. Right.' What to ask. Oh yes. '*The Green Mile* …'

'Tom Hanks,' said Mia, anticipating.

'Yes, he starred in it,' said Frank, eyes narrowed. 'But who wrote the original short story?'

Mia sat back, knotted her brows. 'God, I ought to know this. I love that film.'

'Take your time,' said Frank, looking towards the church doors. *The longer I keep you away from Charlie the better*, he thought.

'Stephen King?' she said at last. 'Was it Stephen King?'

Frank slowly shook his head, eyes filled with admiration. 'Right again. How do you do it?'

'What can I say? – I've just got the type of brain that attracts useless information. If it'll never do me any good, never make me any money, then I remember it.'

The pause that followed was as pregnant as their corpse had been until Frank broke it with, 'How're you managing?'

'Sorry?'

'Are you coping with your loss?'

'Oh,' said Mia, her smile slipping. 'I'm OK, as long as I keep busy. You know how it is.'

There was nothing else for it. They'd have to go inside. 'Talking of keeping busy,' said Frank. 'I'm sure Kate's got plenty for you to do.'

'Good,' said Mia, getting to her feet. 'Just what I need.'

They entered the church to find a scene of organized chaos. Everyone seemed to be talking at once. And straight away Mia could sense that some tempers were seriously fraying.

The chairs had been positioned on the 'stage', but inaccurately according to a particularly blousy woman who was haranguing a stressed-out young man. Costumes had been strewn over the backs of pews, and these too were the focus of a heated debate.

Mia felt like the new girl starting school in the middle of a term. Frank had hold of her wrist, was scanning the crowd for Kate.

'Let's try the office,' he said.

The office door was ajar, and Mia caught sight of the vicar arguing with his wife in the brief moment before Frank – recoiling abruptly, as though he'd been stung – yanked her back to the scrum.

Mia was astonished. She turned to peer again at the thin sliver of office on view, hoping to catch another glimpse. Their argument had seemed very one-sided: the vicar towering over his tiny wife, gestures intimidating, vicious teeth showing white against his dark beard; while Kate – the so-called harridan – cowered before him.

Frank left Mia with a thin nervy woman called Ann Frost, after explaining that she'd come to help. Ann was the stage manager and too busy, apparently, to do anything other than sit Mia on a chair at the side of the 'stage' and leave her there to fester.

Not the friendliest of welcomes. Mia might have felt quite aggrieved had her investigative instincts not become aroused. While she sat there, overlooked and abandoned, Mia's thoughts were busily centred on Reverend Fisher. She'd always found him to be very meek, very considerate – the archetypal vicar – and was shocked to discover another side to him. No one was ever black and white, of course; we all have our grey areas, but, even so, he was a man of the cloth; he should be better than the rest of us.

'You're the police officer. DS Mia Harvey, isn't it?'

Mia was dragged from her musings to find Grace Chamberlain standing over her, a fur-collared black coat in her arms. Mia got to her feet. 'Not tonight. I'm just here to help out,' she said, smiling.

Grace was beautiful, yet strangely indifferent. There was no warmth in her eyes, no responding smile on those cupid lips. She resembled a shop window dummy; was lacking that vital spark of humanity. Mia was on the verge of harbouring a mild dislike for the woman when Nick's words came back to her. *It's only been a few years since they lost their baby. They're bound to be fragile still.*

'That's a lovely coat,' said Mia, striving to make an effort. 'Is it part of your costume?'

It was as though Mia had found the magic password. Grace underwent a startling transformation before her eyes, was grinning broadly as she held up the coat, her manicured fingers stroking the fur on its collar.

'Not very PC, of course, but isn't it gorgeous,' she said. 'Mum found it in a charity shop. It's the right period too.'

'Slip it on,' said Mia. 'Black should look brilliant on you.'

The coat was a perfect fit. And as Grace preened and paced, exaggerating her model poses outrageously, the two women bonded.

'Come and see the rest of the stuff,' said Grace, pulling Mia along. 'Mum's brilliant at searching out little gems.'

She was too. Each item fitted perfectly with the era of the play and the various circumstances of the characters.

'She found all this in charity shops?' said Mia, amazed at the quality and condition of the clothes.

'Dad helped her with a few things. He's got pals in the acting business.'

Mention of the vicar doused Mia's enthusiasm momentarily. But she shrugged it off. 'Did he help your husband?' she asked, her attention still on the costumes.

Grace recoiled slightly, gave her such a quizzical glance that Mia felt obliged to explain.

'He was telling me … your husband … that Reverend Fisher was asking around … you know … trying to get him an acting job.'

'No, he hasn't. Not yet, at least. Dad's still on it though.'

'Is Tom here?'

Grace's laugh was harsh. 'He wouldn't be seen dead anywhere near an amateur production. He's a professional. And he *will* make it. He deserves it so much.'

After their little encounter the other night Mia reckoned that all Tom Chamberlain deserved was a good kicking.

'Grace …' she said, hesitating briefly. 'I know about your baby. I'm so sorry.'

The girl looked away, swallowed hard. 'It's been really tough. You've no idea….'

She sank on to the nearest pew, gazed skywards, sighing. Mia sat beside her, and was surprised when the girl held her arm.

'Do you want to talk?' Mia dared to ask. 'I'm a good listener.'

'It seems I've done nothing *but* talk since it happened,' Grace said. 'Dad believes everything happens for a reason, every hardship teaches us something. And I have to admit I've more empathy towards my patients who're in the same situation, so it was worth it in that respect. It's just …' She shrugged, unable to go on.

'Will you try for another baby?'

'I can't. There's an 85 percent chance it'll happen again.' She shook her head. 'I decided not to take the risk.'

'Oh Grace, that's awful.'

'It's worse for Tom in a way. He's completely blanked it out. He won't visit her grave, won't discuss her … If I even mention her name he goes mad. The poor boy's hurting so badly …'

Yes, and I'm Cheryl Cole. God, talk about being blinkered. What was it with couples? Marriage should bring lovers closer together. And yet she'd encountered this very scenario time and again over the years – virtual strangers living under the same roof, keeping up a pretence to others … to themselves.

'Anyway, let's change the subject,' said Grace, getting to her feet. 'What's Mum got you doing?'

'Nothing, yet. I haven't spoken to her.'

Grace scanned the crowded space, caught sight of Kate enduring a lengthy lecture from Ann Frost.

'Mum,' she called, arms waving. 'Over here a minute.'

Kate Fisher, clearly relieved to be abandoning the fraught stage manager, made a beeline for her daughter.

'Mia's come to help,' Grace told her.

'Your father told me.' Kate turned to Mia. 'I'm so glad you decided to join us.'

But was she? Mia sensed a desperation behind the words. And her smile was fixed, a poor imitation of the real thing. Perhaps she shouldn't have come after all. Perhaps Kate's invitation had just been empty words, something to say.

Or maybe she was still smarting from that encounter with her husband in the office. Now that was more likely. Kate's cheeks were flushed, her movements jerky. She kept biting down on her lower lip, nervously clearing her throat. She was a different woman altogether from the one Mia had met two days ago.

'I've decided Mia's in charge of the costumes, Mum. She's got a flair for it.'

'I don't know,' Mia got in before Kate could respond. 'I might not be able to come again. My job's pretty hectic.'

'So is mine,' said Grace. 'But we all need time off. Tell her, Mum.'

And then the old Kate was back. 'Grace is right, darling. You must come again.' She gripped Mia's hands. 'I'll introduce you to everybody in the break, but we must start now while we've still time.'

The actors were instructed to take their positions; all others told to clear the 'stage' and keep quiet. Mia was to sit with Kate throughout the rehearsal, so she could see who was doing what.

'Help me get two chairs from the office, will you, darling?' said Kate.

Mia duly obliged, and was surprised to find the office empty. 'I thought Reverend Fisher was in here.'

'Charlie … helping with the play?' Kate said, with a withering snort.

'But he gave the impression he was staying. I told him I wanted a chat later on.'

Kate stiffened. 'Oh? What about?'

Mia gave an embarrassed laugh. 'I'm a big fan of *Temple's Crest*. I just wanted his autograph.'

'Then you shall have it,' Kate said, spreading her arms with a flourish. 'But not tonight.'

Kate was wearing a loose-fitting cardigan over her ankle-length summer dress. Mia thought she looked stunning. She was admiring the outfit now but as Kate opened her arms, causing the sleeves of the cardigan to ride up, Mia was shocked to see a number of large bruises around her wrists and further up the arms. They were a livid purple, looked freshly done.

The breath caught in Mia's throat. Could the vicar have done that? Threats and intimidation were but a breath away from violence for some people, and his body language had certainly looked threatening. Was he capable of such an act? Mia hoped not. The woman wasn't even half his size.

'How did you get those?' asked Mia, playing it down.

Kate was hugging herself tightly. 'Oh I'm always bruising myself,' she said, her tone matter-of-fact. 'Grace keeps telling me I should get a blood test or something. It's nothing to worry about.'

But try as she might, for the rest of that evening, Mia couldn't stop worrying.

CHAPTER 8

'NICK, I THINK Reverend Fisher's beating his wife.'

He said nothing, simply laughed in Mia's face.

'What's so funny?'

'You are,' he said. 'You think he's too much of a saint to be shagging the sister-in-law, and then you tell me he's knocking his wife about.'

They were going down the stairs to police reception (the lift was still broken) where Bryan Baxter was waiting. DCI Wells had decided to accompany Jack to his interview at the Discipline and Complaints department, so they were to question Mr Baxter without him.

'But I've seen the evidence, Nick – bloody great bruises all over her arms. We can't pin this one on Joey and Syed.'

'Is she willing to testify?'

'What do you think?'

'Then there's nothing we can do.'

'I know, but … Oh, it doesn't matter.'

They found Bryan Baxter sitting on the wooden bench opposite the desk. He was chatting easily with the duty sergeant, but his body language was tight and cautious. Not that that meant anything; most people were apprehensive in a police station.

'Mr Baxter,' said Nick, holding out a hand. 'Good of you to come.'

'What's this about? The chap on the phone wouldn't tell me.'

Neither of the detectives responded; they wanted him sitting down first before divulging any details.

'Would you come this way, sir?' said Mia.

They were using interview room number one because it had a window that actually opened. The air was very close that morning. Baxter settled into a chair opposite them, his wary gaze taking in the sleaziness of the cramped space.

'Will you be recording me?' he asked with a nervous grin.

'No need,' said Mia. 'We just want some information.'

'About what?'

The man was formally dressed in a suit and tie. While Nick found a fresh page in his note pad Baxter loosened the tie, undid the top button of his shirt. He was sweating. Quite a lot, Mia noticed.

Nick sat back heavily. 'How long have you been in England, sir?'

'I got in yesterday morning. Why?'

'So you won't know we've found a body in a local cemetery….'

'Whatever next?' said Baxter, grinning.

Nick shifted his weight in the chair. 'There's no easy way to say this, sir… We identified the body last night. It's your missing girlfriend, Rebecca Crawford.'

That disclosure had an unusual effect on the man. For a count of about five seconds he remained still, looked totally relaxed. Then he bent forward as though he'd been winded, was staring at the table top with wide eyes.

'We're really sorry you had to find out like this,' said Mia.

Baxter's eyes flooded and tears coursed down his cheeks. He fished a linen handkerchief from his jacket pocket and dabbed at the tears. 'I suppose a part of me always knew she couldn't still be alive,' he said. 'When did you find her?'

'Last Monday, sir. The church was having a plot prepared for a burial. Rebecca was discovered as it was being dug.'

'But she didn't know anybody in Larchborough. What was she doing here?'

'We were hoping you'd throw some light on that,' said Nick. 'That's why we asked you to come in. We've got the case notes from when Rebecca went missing, but they're not telling us much.'

'There's not much to tell. I know it's a cliché but Becky simply disappeared into thin air.' Baxter sat back, shrugged helplessly and blew his nose.

Nick said, 'Could you give us some background, starting from just before Rebecca went missing?'

'It was years ago.'

'Just try,' said Mia.

Baxter licked his lips, gazed narrow-eyed into a corner of the room as he mentally revisited the past. 'Becky went missing on a Friday. We were going out for a meal that evening to celebrate the fact she'd got a buyer for the gymnasium she'd been setting up. I was going to propose over dessert—'

He stopped abruptly, seemingly overcome with emotion. The detectives shared a telling glance.

'She was selling the gym?' said Mia. 'There was no mention in the notes.'

'Perhaps the police thought it had no bearing on the case.'

Nick was watching the man closely. 'We thought you were in Switzerland when Rebecca went missing.'

'I was. I mean, I was due to make my flight after the meal. When Becky stood me up I went anyway.' He made a choking sound, put the handkerchief to his eyes. 'I kept calling her but she never picked up. I called our friends but nobody had seen her....'

'How long were you away?'

'I came back the following weekend, after our main business was completed. I'd started to panic by then.'

'You said Rebecca stood you up on the Friday,' said Mia. 'Why would you think that?'

'What do you mean?'

'Your relationship had reached the point where you were planning to propose. You'd actually bought a ring. You were going to give it to her over dinner. Why think she'd just stood you up? Why didn't you start to panic then instead of a week later?'

'We were busy people,' he said, spreading his hands. 'We had a lot going on. It didn't cross my mind that anything might be wrong.'

'You were living separately at the time?' Nick asked.

'Yes, we'd always planned to move in together but it never happened. We were in a bit of a rut, to be honest.'

'How long had you been together?'

'About two years.'

'Were you excited about the baby?' Mia asked.

Baxter shot her a puzzled look. 'What baby?'

'The baby Rebecca was expecting.'

'There wasn't a baby,' said Baxter. 'Becky miscarried at eight weeks.'

Mia stared at him, taken aback. 'I'm so sorry – those misleading notes again. When did she lose it?'

Baxter puffed out his cheeks. 'It happened just before Christmas so … about five months before she disappeared.'

'She must have been very upset.'

'She was philosophical about it. The pregnancy was a shock more than anything. A baby would've interfered with her plans for the gym.'

'And yet a few months later she put the gym up for sale.'

'Things happen, plans change,' Baxter said, shrugging. 'I think she was more relieved than upset when she lost it. There was plenty of time for us to start a family … or so we thought.'

'We know you had to travel a lot with your job,' said Nick, 'but did Rebecca ever leave Nuneaton?'

'Yes, quite often in fact. She still had clients in London—'

'In her capacity as a personal trainer?'

'That's right. Becky had many high-profile clients. It's a very lucrative business.'

'How would she get to London?' asked Nick. 'By car? Train?'

'She used to drive. Why?'

'I was just thinking – the M1 would take her past Larchborough. The junction's not far from town, so that's one way to place her in the vicinity.'

'You're right,' said Baxter, almost clapping his hands in glee. 'She *was* due to travel down.'

'There you go,' said Nick, keeping his tone light and his dislike for Baxter concealed. He didn't believe a word. The man was thinking on his feet.

'So Rebecca was quite stable financially,' said Mia.

'Yes, things were good. Couldn't have been better, until …'

'You're staying in Milton Keynes at the moment,' said Nick.

'Yes. My sister's in the middle of a crisis. I'm helping her sort it out.'

'How long will you be staying?'

'Till it's sorted. I'm officially on two weeks' leave, but if I need longer there won't be a problem. My bosses are very flexible.'

'Will you be visiting Nuneaton?'

'Why should I?'

'It's where you come from. I just thought …'

'I was born in Milton Keynes. My relatives – what's left of them – are still there. I only moved to Nuneaton because of work.'

'Is that where you met Rebecca?' asked Mia.

'Yes.'

'And you were together for two years,' she said, consulting her notes.

'About that, yes.'

She gave him a puzzled glance. 'The case notes state that you were the sole recipient in Rebecca's will. Why was that?'

Baxter shrugged. 'Why not? We were totally committed to each other. She was to have everything of mine if I went first.'

'What about her family?'

'There was no family. I was all she had.'

'What happened to the gym?' asked Nick.

'I told you. We'd found a buyer.'

'But a missing person's assets are frozen for a good seven years.'

'True, but my name was on the deeds so the sale went through.'

Nick's eyes widened. '*Your* name was on the deeds?'

'Yes, didn't I say?'

'How come?'

'It was a joint venture. I put up the money and Becky was going to run it. I can show you the paperwork, if you like.'

'What about the equipment?'

'It was sold as a going concern. Everything was in the price.'

'Did you make a profit?'

'A small one. Nothing to write home about.'

There was silence for a few moments while they got those points down on paper, Baxter squinting to read the upside-down writing.

Mia turned to Nick. 'D'you reckon we've got enough?'

'I should think so ... for now.' He gave Baxter a broad smile. 'Thanks for coming in, sir. We appreciate it.'

'I can go?' Relief passed briefly across Baxter's eyes, but then his face showed irritation. 'Why couldn't we have done this over the phone? It was hardly worth coming in.'

Nick said, 'We did offer to come to you but you didn't want your sister upset. Remember?'

'True,' said Baxter, pushing back his chair.

Nick passed across a page from his note pad. 'Could you give us your mobile number, please? We'll need to keep you informed.'

Out in the car park Baxter approached his sister's blue Nissan with sluggish steps, sat in the driver's seat for many moments, quietly contemplating. And behind reception's double doors the detectives watched him avidly.

'Who was it said good liars need good memories?' Mia asked Nick.

'Dunno, but one thing's for sure … they didn't tell that bastard out there.'

'He was in Nuneaton when she disappeared?' Wells said into his mobile.

'So he's saying now,' Nick replied.

Wells let out a brittle laugh. 'What a twat.'

'That's what we thought, sir.'

'OK, mate, this is good. Get it all on the whiteboard. We'll start on Mr Baxter as soon as I get back.'

'Give Jack our best, sir.'

Wells pocketed his phone. 'It was Nick,' he said, in answer to Jack's querying glance. 'We've got some movement on the murder case. We're gonna need you sooner rather than later.'

Jack straightened his tie for the umpteenth time. 'What if the charge goes ahead?'

'It won't, mate.'

'But—'

'It won't,' Wells insisted. 'Christ, Jack, ever heard of positive thinking?'

'Sorry, sir.'

The waiting-room at Discipline and Complaints was sparse but sleek, its decor a calming mix of cream and green. They sat in tubular steel framed chairs upholstered in green leather. A water cooler stood in one corner, and potted plants sat on most of the beech wood surfaces.

'Posh here,' said Jack.

Wells bristled beside him. He was thinking of Silver Street's broken lift, the antiquated heating system, their toilet block that had been state-of-the-art in the dark ages. 'Don't get me started, mate.'

The words had hardly left his lips when a door was pulled open to their right and Inspector May ushered Jack into an adjacent office.

As Wells followed, May said to Jack, 'You've brought your solicitor. Very wise.'

Wells introduced himself, his face puce with the effort of holding his temper. 'No need for a solicitor,' he said.

The office held six desks, at which officers worked in silence. The atmosphere was hostile, claustrophobic, and Jack's already taut nerves jangled. They were led to a corner desk and told to sit.

Inspector May fixed Jack with a steely glance. 'You're here, as you're aware, DC Turnbull, because Jason Perry has alleged that on Monday the twenty-second of June you assaulted him in such a way as to occasion actual bodily harm. You do not have to say anything, but it may harm your defence if you do not mention when questioned something that you later rely on in court. Anything you do say may be given in evidence.'

Wells reared up in his seat. 'What the…?'

May ignored him, turned instead to Jack. '*Do* you have anything to say?'

Jack nodded, but was unable to speak immediately. He'd been cautioned. Bloody hell. The noose was tightening around his neck, and it took all of his inner strength to resist turning to Wells and pleading with him to do something. Those officers supposedly working so hard at their desks would love that.

'Perry's lying, sir. I didn't touch him. He was the one using his fists. I was trying to cuff him, that's all.'

'Our witness says otherwise,' May countered.

'*Our* witness?' said Wells. 'What do you mean our witness? We're supposed to be on the same bloody side.'

Inspector May gave Wells a fleeting glance. 'The witness states that DC Turnbull started the fight,' he said, sorting through papers on his desk. 'It's our job to weed out trouble-makers, those officers who give the force a bad name.'

Jack's stomach gave a sickening roll. 'But I'm not a troublemaker, sir. Perry's lying.'

'And the witness is lying too?'

'She must be.'

'Jack was beaten unconscious,' said Wells. 'Look at his face. He's not long left the hospital.'

Inspector May studied Wells. 'And Mr Perry is *still* in hospital. In a very bad way, we've been told.'

'So you'd rather believe a lying scumbag with a list of offences as long as your arm. So much for solidarity in the ranks.'

'It's not my job to believe anybody, Chief Inspector. I leave that to the courts.'

Wells let out a staccato laugh. 'You're not letting this go any further, surely.'

'We'll be sending all paperwork to the Crown Prosecution Service, yes.'

Wells was speechless; incredulity lengthened his jowls as he stared at the inspector. He rose from the chair, looked down on May from his imposing height. 'You're a tosser – do you know that? You're all tossers.'

'Sit down, Chief Inspector.'

'Perry's solicitor's going for compensation,' he said. 'That lying toe rag's gonna be quids in.'

'Sit down, Chief Inspector.'

'Not Jack though. No, Jack'll be forced to claim benefits … benefits that arseholes like Jason fucking Perry haven't contributed one penny towards.'

'Sit down,' May bawled. 'This is my jurisdiction and I will have you forcibly removed if you do not sit down right now.'

They locked eyes, their battle of wills enduring until Jack gave his boss a solicitous look. 'Do it, sir … please.'

Wells sat down. 'You haven't heard the last of me,' he told May. 'I'll be fighting this.'

'I dare say you will.' The Inspector had been holding a sheet of paper. He passed it now to Jack, along with a silver Parker pen. 'Read that carefully, please. Sign at the bottom.'

It was a Regulation 7 notice; it told police and court officials that the defendant had been made aware of the alleged crime brought against him. Jack scanned the brief details and signed on the dotted line, his hand shaking terribly.

'That's perfect,' said May, retrieving the form. 'Now, DC Turnbull, you need to contact the Federation. They'll see you're allocated a good solicitor.'

Parliament Street was busy with traffic and exhaust fumes hung in the air while passers-by babbled loudly. DCI Wells, however, was uncharacteristically quiet. He felt impotent; worried, too, that he might have been more of a hindrance than a help.

'Thanks for trying, sir,' said Jack, as though reading his thoughts.

'I haven't even started yet.'

'What do we do now?'

Wells sighed heavily. 'We get you that solicitor.'

By midday Mia was desperate to leave the office. Wells had phoned in with the news about Jack. They were taking a long lunch, he'd said; the entire force could go fuck itself. There was no mention of his earlier threat to pack it all in whilst hoping fervently that the big bosses might choke on his pension. It had been an idle threat, of course. No one in CID had for one moment imagined that Jack would actually be charged. But now the case was being handed to the Crown Prosecution Service, with no guarantees that they'd see sense and throw it out.

Everything was changing too quickly. Mia's cosy routine was being blasted to hell in a handcart. No more weekly trips to see her mother (who'd have thought she'd miss those so much?). No more happy bantering with Jack. Even Nick was changing. It was as though he'd been taken over by an entity from Planet Nice. Mia wanted the old version back. She knew where she stood with that one.

So at one o'clock, when Nick had asked yet again if she was OK – that weirdly concerned look on his face – Mia had grabbed her bag, muttered something about going to Boots, and then lurched out of the office.

She was standing outside Boots now, but she didn't go inside. Instead she crossed the road to Pencil Case, the discount stationery shop where Perry's witness, Valerie Clarke, worked as a customer service assistant.

She was perusing the correction fluids – not that she ever used them – whilst surreptitiously studying the staff. There were three women on duty – lunchtime being their busiest period – and none of them wore a name badge. Mia was wondering how she could identify Mrs Clarke when another of the assistants did it for her.

'Here, Val,' the girl called from the back of the shop, 'do you reckon I've got enough meerkats on this display?'

'More than enough,' said the woman behind the till.

So that was Valerie Clarke. She was plump; late thirties, perhaps; with blonde hair that showed dark at the roots.

As Mia stood in the cramped aisle, being jostled by other customers, she wondered what to do next. Why had she come here? She couldn't interrogate the woman, couldn't beg her to withdraw her statement. She'd just have to improvise.

Remembering that Mrs Clarke reared Yorkshire terriers, she picked up an address book with two cute examples of the breed on its hard-backed cover – really cheap at one pound fifty – and approached the till. The woman in front was purchasing three paperback novels for a fiver, and chatting with Valerie about last night's episode of *EastEnders*. Apparently Phil Mitchell was about to get his comeuppance. And not before time too.

When it was Mia's turn to be served, Valerie Clarke oohed and aahed over the two puppies as she rang up the one fifty.

'They're gorgeous, aren't they?' said Mia, handing over the cash. 'I've always had Yorkies.'

'Oh right,' said Valerie. 'You got one now?'

Mia assumed a pained expression. 'My little Pixie passed away in January. I've been looking for her replacement ever since, but I can't find a reputable breeder.'

Valerie's face broke into a smile. 'I breed Yorkies. I'll have a litter ready in a couple of weeks. You can see the mum and dad and everything.'

'No,' said Mia, in wide-eyed wonder. 'Isn't that a coincidence?'

'I can give you my number, if you like. Come along one evening. Give 'em the once over. I've got two girls and a boy. Sweet as sugar, they are.'

While Mrs Clarke searched for a pen and jotted her name and number on the bag holding the address book, Mia said, 'I wish I'd come in earlier now. Actually, I was going to on Monday only I was watching a fight outside HMV and by the time it was over I had to get back to work.'

Valerie leant across the counter, sucked air through her teeth. 'I saw that. Nasty, wasn't it?'

'Any idea what it was about?' asked Mia, lowering her voice to match Valerie's.

'The usual … shoplifting. We get a lot of that in here as well. Only we let them get on with it. Stupid risking a battering for the stuff we sell.'

Mia shuddered. 'Did you see all the blood on the pavement?'

'Yeah, I couldn't take my eyes off it.'

'Somebody told me it was a policeman who got beaten up.'

Valerie nodded. 'He ended up in hospital. Bloody shame, if you ask me. Things carry on like this there'll be nobody joining up, and *then* we'll be in a mess.'

'The other bloke should be a boxer,' said Mia, nodding approval. 'He was amazing.'

Valerie gave her a stern frown. 'Don't go idolizing buggers like him, love. It's the drugs that make 'em hard. Nothing else. Anybody with teenagers nowadays has a lot of sleepless nights. I should know. I've got one. He'll be the death of me.'

Mia felt a tap on her shoulder and turned to face an indignant old lady with a blue rinse. 'Have you finished?' she asked. 'Only some of us have got things to do.'

Mia gave the woman a lavish apology and picked up her purchase from the counter. Nodding towards Valerie's details on the bag, she said, 'I'd like to see those puppies, Mrs Clarke. Think you'll be in this weekend?'

'You just give me a call, love. I'll make sure I'm in.'

Mia was gazing at the window display of Help the Aged, next door to Pencil Case, pretending interest in the trinkets on view. She felt excited, optimistic; on top of things for the first time in days as she relived her conversation with Valerie Clarke.

The woman had sided with Jack. She'd admonished Mia for admiring the fighting skills of that no-good Jason Perry. She'd actually shown sympathy for the police. Why?

Mia decided she'd ring Mrs Clarke and call round at the weekend. If they could bond over the Yorkies the woman might open up, might confide the reason for her hostile statement in Perry's favour.

Mia stared at her reflection in the glass. *You must not buy a puppy.*

She was about to move off, grinning to herself, when the shop door tinkled and a hunched elderly woman accosted her on the pavement.

'Thought it was you,' she said, her tone accusing. 'Did you tell him?'

Mia thought the woman was familiar, but she couldn't put a name to the face. 'Do I know you?'

'I'm from the church.'

'Oh yes, we spoke in the car park. Sorry, I didn't catch your name.'

'Edna Templeton. Did you tell Charlie?'

'Tell him what?'

Mrs Templeton must have been all of four-foot-ten, and yet she had an extremely powerful presence. She fixed Mia was a wintry look, waggled an arthritic finger. '*He that covers his sins shall not prosper; but whoso confesses and forsakes them shall have mercy.* Proverbs, chapter twenty-eight, verse thirteen.'

Mia was expecting more, but the old woman had finished. She stood on the pavement in a rigid pose, her hooded blue eyes burning with a reproachful light.

'That's what you want me to tell him?'

The old woman put her hands together, steepled them as in prayer. 'Be his shepherd,' she said. 'Bring him back before it's too late.'

'I will,' said Mia, backing away. 'I'll go and do it now.'

Nick had typed up an abridged version of his notes from the Bryan Baxter interview. And it was those notes that were dominating the conversation when Mia returned to CID to find a calmer Wells at his desk.

'I want a full examination of Baxter's business dealings around the time of Rebecca's disappearance,' he was telling Nick. 'And I want to know everything about that gym – when it was bought; when it was sold; for how much, and so on.'

'I could do that,' said Mia, dumping her bag beside her desk. 'I don't mind working late.'

'No rehearsals tonight?' asked Nick.

'Not till Monday.'

'You'll get withdrawal symptoms.'

Mia gave him a tetchy glance. 'Actually, I'm going to the Sunday morning service.'

'And I thought you were just joking about that nunnery.'

Mia – refusing to be riled – told Wells about Kate Fisher's bruises. '*That's* why I'm going to the service,' she said, glaring directly at Nick. 'So I can keep an eye on them.'

Wells seemed genuinely staggered by Mia's revelations. Hardly a church-goer himself, and realizing that vicars and the like faced the same struggles as the rest of society, Wells did, however, believe that they should set an example and should at least keep their fists to themselves.

'Sir, we met an old lady at the church,' Mia said. 'She seems to think Reverend Fisher needs saving. She caught me in town just now and was spouting from the Bible. I reckon she knows what he's up to.'

'Keep me informed,' said Wells.

'OK. So do you want me to start on the Baxter stuff?'

'No, I've got Jack coming in for a few hours tomorrow. He can do it.'

Mia stared at him. 'What if the super finds out?'

'When was the last time Shakespeare graced us with his presence on a Saturday?' Wells huffed.

'Will you want me tomorrow?' asked Nick.

'I can't guarantee overtime.'

'Doesn't matter. I'm not doing anything.'

On the walk back from town Mia had pondered whether she should tell the DCI about her meeting with Valerie Clarke. Now she decided that disclosure was the best policy and went on to tell them everything Mrs Clarke had said. 'So I was planning to go and look at the puppies, see if she lets anything slip. Do you think it's a good idea?'

Wells didn't reply immediately. He sat fingering the stubble on his upper lip, his gaze fluttering over the chaos on his desk. 'You'll need to be careful,' he said. 'If she works out you're a copper we'll all be in the shit.'

'Don't worry, I'm with a theatre group now,' she said, grinning. 'I'll use my newfound acting skills.'

CHAPTER 9

BLOODY SOLICITORS. YOU pay them an arm and a leg and they're beyond your reach for almost a third of the week. They should at least employ a skeleton staff to man the phones at weekends. Did they think people only had problems between Monday and Friday? It wasn't good enough. Self-serving parasites, the lot of them.

Those thoughts and many others like them filled Bryan Baxter's consciousness from the moment he pulled back the curtains on that Saturday morning to reveal a stifling and wholly unsophisticated view of the estate on which his sister's house stood. The outlook from his bedroom at home encompassed a gigantic lake; romantic chalets nestling in the crooks of green hills; endless blue skies unsullied by even the tiniest cloud. There was no comparison. And the provincial nature of his surroundings did little to lift Baxter's mood.

He was irritable. He hadn't slept well. He'd spent most of the night staring into the darkness and reliving, word for word, his interview with the police. They'd seemed satisfied with his answers, had been politeness itself, but you couldn't trust that lot. Not fully.

He shouldn't have come back.

But Claire had been in pieces on the phone, had said she needed him. What she'd really needed – what she'd begged for the moment he arrived – was his money. Why hadn't she said? He could have transferred the cash within the hour. He could be sipping his coffee, nibbling his croissant, whilst taking in the view through the glass wall of his kitchen.

He could be helping the police with thousands of miles between them. A faceless voice on the end of a phone.

Here they were practically on his doorstep.

Here he was having to endure the constant bickering of his out-of-control nephews. *Boyish exuberance,* Claire called it. They were *testing the boundaries. Growing into their personalities. Working out the pecking order.* Bloody rubbish. They were five-and-six-year-old thugs, pure and simple.

And what of his brother-in-law, Nigel – Neanderthal Nige – the entrepreneur who wouldn't spot a good opportunity if it pulled down his trousers and gave him a blow job.

Jesus. He couldn't stand two weeks of this.

So what was he to do? Catch the first flight back or stay and brazen it out?

If he legged it the police might become suspicious. He'd already told them he was there for at least two weeks. And why had he said that? To make them believe he was a loyal caring brother and therefore an upstanding citizen, that's why. It had seemed the right thing to do at the time. And he did care about his sister; it was the rest of it he couldn't stand.

Christ, why did they have to find her? Why couldn't she have stayed hidden? The bitch had always been a liability. Why couldn't she have done this one thing for him?

Not a mention for two years. Not even a hint. He thought he was in the clear, had even started spending the money. He'd worked hard for what he had. If she ruined it all now …

He really needed his solicitor.

An unholy din started downstairs. The kids were at it again. Baxter rose from the bed, a determined line to his mouth. OK, he'd go down and give everyone a smile. He'd drink the instant muck that Claire called coffee. He'd make an effort to join in.

And he'd ring his solicitor first thing on Monday.

'Here he is,' said Mia, rushing to give Jack a hug. 'How are you, sweetie?'

'Glad to be back.'

'Did anybody see you come up?' asked Nick.

'No. Why?'

'No reason.'

He couldn't disclose the fact that Jack was to be there undercover, so to speak, like a clandestine member of the resistance movement behind enemy lines (Superintendent Shakespeare being the enemy in this particular scenario) because Jack still believed Shakespeare had sanctioned his return to work.

'Coffee's nearly ready,' said Mia, hovering by the percolator.

'What's this?' said Jack. He was holding up a yoghurt pot in which three straggly dandelions fought for survival.

'They were growing through the concrete in the car park,' said Mia. 'Nature's wonderful, isn't it? I thought they'd look nice on your desk – a sort of welcome back gift. I did wash the pot first.'

'You're mental.'

The coffee machine uttered its final loud gurgle, giving Mia a much-needed reason to turn away. Jack wasn't a wimp – far from it – but he still seemed so fragile that she could hardly bear to look at him. She'd spent much of the night sweating over her proposed meeting with Valerie Clarke. So much rested on her getting a good result. She couldn't balls it up.

'Can you see any better?' Nick asked Jack, as Mia handed out the coffee.

'A bit. I'll be able to see the screen OK.'

'How did you get on at the dentist?'

Jack grimaced. 'I'm having caps.'

'Tom Cruise, eat your heart out,' Mia laughed.

'I'm just glad I'm not paying.'

DCI Wells came in then, blustering towards his desk, all gangly limbs and nervous energy.

'Good, you're in,' he said to Jack. 'All right?'

'Fine, sir.'

'You've got a lot to do, mate.'

'Can't wait to get started.'

Wells was settling into his chair when his gaze fell on a pile of papers placed neatly in the centre of his desk. 'What's all this?' he said, holding them up.

'Ah,' said Mia, hurrying to give him his drink. 'It's a bit of info about the gym, just pages from the website. It doesn't tell us much, but there's a head office address. I was trying to find out when it was actually sold, sir. Give us some ammo against Baxter.'

'You did it this morning?'

'No, sir, last night. I wasn't here long.'

Wells sighed as he tossed the pages back on to the desk. 'You ain't doing yourself any favours, darling. You can't keep going twenty-four-seven. Sooner or later you'll have to stop and face up to things.'

'I know, sir, but I need to do it my own way.'

'If you say so.' Wells sipped his coffee then motioned towards the whiteboard. 'Had a chance to read any of it, Jack?'

'I've got the gist, sir.'

'It's Baxter we're focusing on. Bryan Baxter. Find out everything you can about him. The Nuneaton case notes are on your desk. They tell you something about the bloke, but not much.'

Jack found the file. 'So you want all of Baxter's business dealings for, what, the last two to three years?'

Wells nodded as he handed Jack the pages Mia had printed off. 'The case notes state that Rebecca owned the gym. Baxter's now saying it was his. Find out which version's right.'

Mia was rummaging in her bag for her note pad. She looked up. 'I've an idea Baxter wasn't the father of Rebecca's baby.'

'You might be right,' said Wells. 'We'll need his DNA sample at some point.'

'Good job I've got this then,' said Nick. He was holding up a clear plastic evidence bag containing the handkerchief that Baxter had used so lavishly during yesterday's interview. 'He left it behind. It'd be a shame to waste it.'

Wells raised a brow. 'We couldn't use that. Not without him knowing. It wouldn't be right.'

'I could always send it in under a different name.'

'Better not let me find out, mate. I'd go up the wall.'

'I won't tell you then,' said Nick, grinning.

Mia frowned. 'Baxter was good at acting upset, I'll give him that. They could use him in the theatre group.'

'I reckon he *was* upset,' said Nick, 'because we'd found the body.'

Wells drained his mug, held it out to Mia for a refill. 'As soon as we get all these strands together we can start building a case. But we've got to be quick. I don't want Baxter flying back to Switzerland.'

Jack was booting up his computer. 'I'll work all day, sir. Tomorrow, as well, if you like.'

'I don't want you overdoing it an' all,' said Wells. 'I've got enough with Tallulah Bankhead here.'

'Who?' said Mia.

'Never you mind.'

'I'll phone the hospital,' said Nick. 'See if they've found out what's wrong with Perry.'

'And I might as well call Valerie Clarke,' said Mia, handing Wells his mug. 'I'll do it in the corridor where it's quiet.'

'Valerie Clarke?' said Jack. 'Isn't she the witness?'

As Mia grabbed her bag and left the office, Wells filled him in. 'There's a reason she gave that statement, Jack. Mia's gonna find out what it is.'

Wells was going through his in-tray, separating everything to do with their murder case. When he'd finished there was a pile of papers half an inch thick. Most were copies of information already gleaned from phone calls and face-to-face discussions, but they would still need to be held. He left those at the side of his desk and returned to the pages still valid.

The top sheet was from John Lloyd. It told Wells that the pathologist was still to identify the source of those gilt and resin fragments found embedded in Rebecca's head wound. He would forward his results as soon as blah, blah, blah …

Wells tutted. He really needed an idea of the murder weapon, and he'd expected Lloyd to have come up with something by now. How hard could it be? It was some kind of tacky ornament. Wells didn't expect the exact date of manufacture, or a picture of the artefact, or even a map showing its location. Just a nudge in the right direction would do.

Mia bustled in, all smiles. 'I'm seeing Mrs Clarke tonight, sir. Six o'clock.'

'Can't be much wrong with Jason Perry,' said Nick, almost throwing the telephone receiver at its cradle. 'The bastard discharged himself last night.'

Wells sneered. 'Perhaps they weren't giving him the right sort of drugs on the ward.'

'So what's wrong with him?' asked Jack, not really wanting to know.

'They wouldn't say. Not without a warrant. They suggested we talk to his GP. He's in charge now Perry's refused hospital treatment.'

'Who's he under?' asked Wells.

'Staples Brook Medical Centre. Don't know which doctor.'

'Valerie Clarke lives in Staples Brook,' said Mia.

'There's a coincidence,' said Wells. 'Have a discreet look at Perry's address when you go to see her.'

'Right, sir.' Mia's mobile rang in the depths of her shoulder bag. Fishing it out she saw an unfamiliar number in the display window. 'Mia Harvey …'

It was Grace Chamberlain. 'Mia, sorry to bother you …'

'That's OK. What can I do for you?' *Meet for lunch hopefully. Or a drink would be nice. A girly chat perhaps….*

'It's probably nothing. Dad thinks it's nothing …' The girl sounded almost wild with worry.

'What's happened, Grace?'

A sharp intake of breath. 'There's a man. He's by my baby's grave, drinking himself into a stupor. Dad asked him to move on, but he wouldn't.'

'Is he causing a disturbance?'

'No, he's just sitting there.'

'Trouble is, Grace, we can't do much till he starts making trouble.' Mia felt her cheeks redden; those words always sounded so lame.

'But he's threatened Dad. He said he's already done a tart, and a vicar would finish the set. I think we've found your murderer, Mia.'

If only it were that simple. Crime scenes always attracted weirdos. Still, Grace had every right to expect protection for her daughter's plot – without having to exaggerate a potential problem to get it.

'I'll come along now,' said Mia. *We could always go for a drink afterwards. Or a nice lasagne. Or both.*

His name was Trevor Arnold. He was a rambler testing out a new route for Larchborough Wanderers Club. And his tipple of choice was peach-flavoured water from Tesco. He was a good metre and a half away from the grave and he'd paused at the cemetery to write up his observations whilst partaking of the coconut ice cake (a sugar fix was vital mid-trek) that had been lovingly concocted by the elderly mother with whom he still lived.

Wells had sent Nick along with Mia. Just in case the alcohol-swigging murder-proclaiming arsehole proved hard to shift. Now, as they watched Mr Arnold slither away, still apologizing, a ridiculously huge haversack hitched to his scrawny back, Nick said, 'He could have shared out the ice cake, miserable sod. I haven't had any since school.'

Mia stared at the thing pretending to be Nick. It had his shape to perfection; his good looks too. But a wire in the brain must be short-circuiting because the real Nick would *never* be that composed after his time had been wasted so blatantly. He'd be railing against the injustice of it all and treating everyone to his huge vocabulary of expletives.

'I *will* find out what you've done with him,' she warned the baffled DI. 'If it's the last thing I do.'

The detectives had almost reached the car park when they were waylaid by a nervous Charlie Fisher. 'I'm so terribly sorry,' he said. 'I didn't know Grace had phoned you.'

Mia gave him a smile. 'No problem, vicar. Better to be safe than sorry.' She motioned towards a large SUMMER FAYRE banner above the church doors. 'Another fund-raising event?'

'Yes, but it doesn't start till two. Come in. Both of you. Have a glass of wine. It's the least we can offer.'

'Lovely, thanks,' she said.

Fisher's face blanched beneath the beard – didn't television detectives always say they mustn't drink whilst on duty? – but Mia was unaware because Nick was prodding her shoulder blade quite viciously. Clearly, wine at the church fête was a step too far, even for the newly-sociable version of himself.

Inside the doors small cloth-covered tables filled every available space. These held cakes; jars of jam, marmalade and chutney; homemade wines; items both knitted and embroidered; flower arrangements and jumble.

Mia saw Frank Lessing moving between the tables, leaving small bags of change at each. She noticed Kate amongst the pews, a cardigan covering her flesh even though the muggy air threatened a storm. And she was surprised to find Tom Chamberlain there too. He was fiddling with a sound system, a pile of vinyl records at his side.

'Will parsnip do you?' Fisher asked, holding up a bottle from the wine stall.

God, no.

'Actually, I'd rather have a word with Grace,' said Mia. She wanted to know why the girl had phoned with such a barefaced lie.

'Oh,' said Fisher, not knowing whether to be pleased or concerned. 'She's in my office.'

'Stay here,' she whispered to Nick.

Mia found her sitting at the desk, a large glass of white wine clutched in both hands.

'What's going on, Grace?'

The girl held up her glass. 'Want some? It's Chilean … very fruity.'

And extremely moreish, Mia deduced, if that nearly empty bottle at her elbow was anything to go by.

'No, thanks.' She took the seat opposite, fixed the girl with an expectant stare. 'Well?'

'Well what?'

'You know what – you had me believe that man was a threat.'

Grace took a long swig of the wine, topped up her glass. 'He was in my daughter's space. He had to go.'

'He wasn't doing any harm.'

'I wanted him gone.' The words were spat out, along with a shower of saliva. 'Tom wouldn't do it. He wouldn't do even that small thing for me.'

No surprise there.

'Look, Grace, if you ever need to talk …'

'Oh God, not you as well.' She took another drink, gave Mia a chastising glance over the rim of the glass. 'I thought you were different, but you're just like *them*.'

Grace was reaching for the bottle again, but Mia got to it first. Placing it on the floor at her feet, she said, 'I need help too, Grace – I'm not ashamed to admit that. I need someone to listen to *me*. When you phoned I was hoping you might want to meet for lunch. *I* need to talk, if you don't.'

'You do?' Grace swallowed hard and tears brimmed. She looked like a small child drowning in a sea of loss.

Mia's heart went out to her. 'We could help each other. That's what friends are for.'

'Friends? We're friends?'

'I hope so.'

'So do I.' The girl seemed to take hold of herself. 'I shouldn't drink, Mia. It always makes me maudlin.'

'You're only human. You're allowed to let go once in a while.'

'Huh, tell that to those patients I keep lecturing about the evils of alcohol.'

'Everything in moderation,' Mia said, grinning. 'That was my Mum's motto.'

'Your poor mother. I'm so sorry.'

'Don't be. It was her time. Nobody goes until it's their time.'

Grace's face crumpled. 'No, some people go early … much too early. God, I'm so *wicked*.'

'No, you're not. Why would you think that?'

'Because it's my fault she's dead.'

Mia skirted around the desk and sank to her knees. 'Stop it, Grace. I can't begin to imagine what you're going through, but you've got to stop this. Your daughter was destined to go. I know that sounds harsh, but it was nothing to do with you.'

'Christ, what's wrong now?'

Mia turned to find Tom's bulky presence in the doorway. 'Your wife needs you,' she said, getting to her feet.

Grace, fully at the mercy of her demons now, was oblivious to her husband's arrival, was oblivious to everything, but the pain that had her in its grip.

Mia took a step towards Tom. 'Look at her. Go on … *look at her*. That woman needs you.'

He sneered. 'She's drunk.'

'Maybe. But come morning she'll be sober … and you'll still be an obnoxious piece of shit.'

'I beg your pardon?'

'You heard.' He was still blocking the doorway. 'Shift,' she said, digging him hard in the ribs.

Mia found Nick outside. He was lounging on the stone bench opposite the church doors, a half-smoked cigarette between his fingers.

He glowered at her. 'For your information parsnip wine tastes like Dettol with just a hint of sugar, and it has a really earthy aftertaste. Oh, and it smells like vomit.'

'You liked it then?'

'Fucking waste of a morning,' he muttered, flicking his cigarette into the shrubs.

'It wasn't a laugh a minute for me either,' she said. 'Anyway, you can stop at a cake shop on the way back. I need something sweet.'

'Your massive belly doesn't.'

'He's back … praise the Lord,' she said, arms lifted to the Heavens. 'You ought to come to church more often, Nick. It's done you good.'

Frank was cursing the weather. No rain for over a week and yet it was forecast for today. Sod's law. The fête would have been so much better outdoors. St Matthew's was usually cold as the grave, but already the atmosphere within its hallowed walls was close. Close and oppressive, as though something was about to break.

Something other than the storm.

At least the police had gone at last. Mia Harvey seemed to be there most days now, and that was unfortunate. For all of them. But how could they keep her away without looking suspicious?

Pausing to mop his brow Frank searched around for Charlie, spotted him sitting on a pew in front of the pulpit, his head bowed in prayer. Poor man. His anguish was almost a living thing now, and Frank had still not managed to wheedle out of him the reason why he should feel so wretched.

Frank had his own ideas though. And if he was right … well, hadn't he already taken measures to cover the crime?

And crime it was. There was no disputing *that* fact. The Bishop would never allow Charlie to continue his ministry after such a flagrant disregard of the rules.

But why should he be plagued with remorse now, when the misdemeanour was committed years ago? Had his conscience finally made itself heard? Charlie had always been so joyous, his love of God and community contagious.

Not anymore.

He'd changed the day that body was found. But then again they'd all been affected to differing degrees. Who wouldn't be disturbed by such a sickening discovery?

And if that wasn't enough the unfortunate chap had Kate to contend with. Yes, she'd helped to lessen his burden over the years. And, yes, she'd proved to be an asset during official functions. She could twist their bishop around her little finger, and that was some feat. But she wasn't making Charlie happy. Frank could see that; he wasn't blind. She'd tried to cosy up to him all morning, but Charlie wouldn't have it. Something was definitely amiss.

Kate wasn't scared of hard work though. She'd been a veritable whirlwind all morning. She was setting up the refreshments counter now. All competent and efficient. Earlier, Frank had asked her where she got her energy from; he'd like to pay a visit himself. She'd laughed, but it was a superficial sound with no real substance. Still, she wasn't his concern. And what a blessing that was.

Charlie was still in the same spot, still praying, and Frank was wondering whether he should go across and offer some comfort when Tom's voice cut through the silence. He was calling to Frank from the threshold of Charlie's office.

'Bring a bucket,' he was saying. 'Grace has just spewed everywhere.'

The storm, when it came, was spectacular, with lightning that blinded and thunderbolts so loud all those in CID had to shout to be heard. The rain was 'good rain' according to Wells; the sort that would perk up his garden no end. As Mia lived in a flat and had no garden to worry about, all rain to her was simply annoying.

By six o'clock, however, as she pulled up in front of Mrs Clarke's home, the storm had ceased, leaving the air fresh and roads and pavements glistening in the fast-returning sunshine.

Right, you're a dog-lover. Let's do it.

She'd never owned a dog. She'd had a cat, a gerbil, a few goldfish. But never a dog. Her mother had always been afraid of dogs.

Mia was approaching the front door when Valerie Clarke opened it, a tiny bundle of dark brown fluff held to her chest.

'You found us then,' she said, smiling. 'Come in, love.'

The puppies were in a back room. To reach it they had to tramp through the lounge where Mr Clarke was sprawled on the settee, watching *You've Been Framed* on a giant television set. He was pulling on a cigarette – not his first either, going by the thick fog of smoke in the room – and eating crisps from an oversized bag. When Valerie introduced their visitor he waved a hand, his eyes still on the screen.

Valerie giggled and said, 'He's hardly Brad Pitt, but he's got his uses.'

The back room was tiny; the bulk of it was taken up by a toddler's multi-coloured plastic playpen – home to the puppies and their mother. A battered Queen Anne chair covered in green chenille fabric and a portable television on a small table filled the remaining space. Yet again, the dusty air stank of cigarettes and Mia was overtaken by an urge to buy all the puppies, and the mother, if only to save their lungs.

'Sit down, love,' said Valerie, indicating the green chair, as though there were other seats to choose.

Mia had to remove a piece of knitting and its pattern before she could oblige. *This'll need to be washed. It'll reek of fags.*

'Which one's that?' asked Mia, pointing to the puppy still held tight against Valerie's breasts.

'One of the girls … Angelina,' she said, handing her across.

126

Mia held the puppy at eye level and stared into its little face. It weighed hardly anything, was covered in soft curls the colour of horse chestnuts, and was as warm as a comfortable bed in the depths of winter. Angelina was adorable, and Mia felt herself falling hopelessly in love as she stared into the puppy's huge brown eyes.

'And these two are Jennifer and Brad,' said Valerie, lifting them out of the playpen and placing them on Mia's lap. 'I've got a thing about Mr Pitt, if you hadn't guessed.'

With a strength that belied their size, Jennifer and Brad scrambled up to Mia's face – tails wagging furiously – and proceeded to lick off her makeup with tiny tongues that were surprisingly rough.

'Of course,' said Valerie, 'you can think up another name. You don't have to keep mine.'

'I quite like the name Brad, actually,' she said, treating him to a tickle under the chin. 'It's short and snappy.'

'You're after a boy then. Don't blame you really. It's cheaper to get a boy done than a girl.'

'Is it? That's good.'

What am I saying? I can't have a dog. I'm out all day.

Striving to focus once more on the real purpose of her visit, Mia said, 'I bet your son loves these, doesn't he?'

'Dylan? No, he's used to having puppies in the house. I started breeding them when he was hardly out of nappies.'

'He's very quiet. Is he about?'

'You must be joking. He's always off somewhere with his mates. Never tells us what he's doing.'

Mia pulled a face. 'That must be a worry.'

'He's sixteen next week. Thinks he's grown up. Gets on his high horse if me or his dad asks him where he's going.'

Angelina had one of the buttons on Mia's jacket between her teeth and was tugging hard. Worried that she might hurt herself Mia freed the button and held the puppy out of harm's way.

'Here, let me have the girls,' said Valerie. 'You keep Brad. Get to know the little hunk.'

Handing the puppies across, Mia said, 'I keep hoping I'll have kids one day, but really I think I'd be too scared. You know, with the way society's going. I reckon that's why I keep a dog.'

'I know what you mean.'

'That fight last Monday,' said Mia, her tone deliberately detached as she played with the film star's namesake. 'It frightened me. It's happening too often now. You're not even safe in the middle of town at lunchtime.'

'And it's not just the bad 'uns you have to watch any more, love. Good kids like my Dylan get sucked up in it.'

Something in the woman's voice made Mia forget the puppy momentarily and she looked up to find that Valerie was fighting tears.

'What's wrong, Mrs Clarke? Is it something I've said.'

'No, you're all right. We're just going through a bad patch with him.' She attempted a smile. 'Teenagers, eh?'

'Has he got in with the wrong crowd?'

'Something like that.'

'But this is a lovely area. I'd have thought kids would be safe here.'

'Drugs are everywhere, love. On every street corner. Wherever you live.'

'Don't the police do anything?'

'What *can* they do? They can't be everywhere. And if they do clear an area the pushers just move on, set up somewhere else.'

Valerie Clarke was so clearly a decent person. Mia was desperate to offer professional guidance. But, of course, she couldn't.

'At least that boy who beat up the policeman, the one in town … at least he'll go to prison. That'll be one less on the streets.'

Valerie seemed on the verge of replying, but instead she bent to put the puppies into the playpen. And when she straightened up Mia could see that weariness had taken hold, her stance was less erect. It could be the result of standing throughout their entire conversation – Mia having use of the only chair – but more likely it was worry that had drained her; worry that was even now subduing the woman's cheerful nature.

'Don't you? Think he'll go to prison, I mean?' Mia hated to push, but what other option did she have?

Valerie shook her head. 'He won't go to prison, love.'

'But he was caught. He put that policeman in hospital. They'll have to send him inside.'

The woman didn't answer immediately. She stood fiddling with her wedding ring, those intense blue eyes showing the hopeless tangle of her thoughts. Mia held her breath. *This is it.*

But, no. Valerie pointed a finger. 'I like your trouser suit,' she said. 'Where do you work – in a building society?'

'No, I'm a hairstylist.' *A hairstylist?*

'Mine doesn't dress that nice.'

'I don't, normally. I'm going to a wedding.'

Valerie's eyebrows rose. 'Bit late, isn't it?'

Mia was panicking now. Talk about digging yourself into a hole. 'I'm going to the reception. I wasn't invited to the church. Family disputes….'

'We've all got them,' said Valerie, laughing. 'I'll have to be moving soon myself. I pull pints at the Crown and Cushion Saturday and Sunday nights and I've still got to get my Jerry his tea.'

'You work hard,' said Mia, genuinely impressed.

'I clean at the remand centre two mornings a week an' all.'

'That can't be very pleasant.'

'It's vile,' said Valerie, grimacing. 'I'll do anything to keep our Dylan out of that place.'

Even perjure yourself in court?

It was hopeless. Valerie wasn't going to give. And who could blame her, really? Mia wouldn't discuss her family's business with a stranger, so why should she?

Brad had fallen asleep on her lap. Lifting him ever so gently Mia brushed her lips against the top of his little head and wished with all her heart that she could have him.

'I'm asking four hundred,' said Valerie. 'It's not cheap, but bear in mind he'll be wormed and he'll have had his injections by the time you get him. Plus, there's his Kennel Club certificate – that's worth a lot.'

Wormed? Injections?

Mia was beginning to realize just how little she knew about caring for a dog. And she was no nearer to wriggling out of their unspoken agreement. She badly needed inspiration. And then it came.

'His father,' she blurted. 'You said I could see his father.'

''Course you can. He's my mate's dog. She shows him at Crufts. Montpelier Fearless Montgomery the third ... how's that for a name? Let me know when you're coming and I'll have him over.'

Mia got to her feet and handed the sleeping puppy to Valerie. 'You've been really kind, Mrs Clarke. I wish I could do something to help.'

'You can tell me how much you charge for a colour and cut,' she said, a hand going to her dark roots. 'It's about time I spent something on myself.'

CHAPTER 10

IT WAS SUNDAY morning, nine o'clock, and Charlie Fisher was in the vestry, preparing for his first service. Or trying to. Weariness was making his limbs leaden, his fingers clumsy, and getting into his cassock and surplus was tantamount to grappling with a pair of wind-ravaged tents.

God help me.

This hell on earth couldn't continue. Something would have to change. But how could he come clean now? His actions – his diabolical deeds – flew in the face of all that his Holy Father held dear. He was a hypocrite, sermonizing weekly to the devout, when he himself had fallen.

How had he got himself into this situation? With little effort – that was the short answer. Entry on to the wrong path took but one small step. And his feet had moved almost without his consent.

He'd succumbed to her needs, had given her what she wanted. He'd sold his soul. And why? Because she'd threatened to go public – oh the shame! – and he'd jumped like a puppet to appease her. Then, once on that ungainly road, it was all too easy to compound the sin. In for a penny, and all that.

No more. The guilt was weighing too heavily. He wanted a way out. He prayed constantly for a way out. But God was ignoring his prayers.

Or was He?

Had God sent the police to end his interminable suffering? Would they soon put two and two together and come up with his name?

Fisher took up his stole, kissed its sacred fabric as he always did, and placed it around his shoulders with a heavy heart. There was a time when this small ritual – the putting on of his vestments – had made him almost burst with love for the blessed Father and the joy he derived from doing His work. Now he felt tainted. He might as well have been dressing for a television role, preparing to act a part, which, unfortunately, was too near the truth.

Checking his watch, Fisher saw that he had time to spare. Time enough to offer up a prayer. If God *had* sent the police then Fisher would tell Him he was ready to face retribution, was ready for this nightmare to end. But he had hardly started when Alison Parker breezed in, filling the vestry with Angel perfume.

'There you are, darling,' she said, closing the door carefully.

'What are you doing here? Seen the light at last?' Fisher smiled as he spoke, but there was little warmth in the words.

'Very funny.'

'Ali,' he said, his eyes burning with an almost maniacal brilliance, 'I *have* seen the light.'

'What do you mean?'

'It's all become clear to me. *God* had the body found. *He* sent the police … to end my suffering.'

She shook her head, frowned at him. 'Charlie, you're not making sense.'

He was smiling now, laughing almost. 'Don't you see? I've been praying for an end to this, and my prayers have been answered.'

'You're actually going to give yourself up?' she said, the whispered words loaded with anger.

'Not quite.' He hadn't the guts for that. 'But they'll find out soon enough. They're bound to.'

'And what about me? Eh? It won't take them long to get to me, will it? Then they'll look into my affairs, into … everything. Charlie, I love my life, my career … I love you too, but you're not going to ruin me just because you're feeling guilty.'

'I hadn't thought….'

'Then you'd better start thinking. I'm in this as deep as you are, so you'll say nothing, you'll *do* nothing to make the police suspicious. Do you hear me?'

He nodded, gave her a contrite glance. 'Why have you come?'

Alison snorted. 'To offer my help – *again*. I haven't heard from you since Thursday. I was worried. Stupid me.' She made for the door.

'Ali,' said Fisher, causing her to turn. 'I'm sorry. I …'

'Where's Kate?'

'She'll be along presently.'

'I'll make out I've a problem with the script. And you … you'll do nothing. OK? Forget all this God stuff. Be a man, Charlie.'

Once an actor, always an actor.

Reverend Fisher was the epitome of divine rectitude as he welcomed the faithful at St Matthew's main doors. How they loved him. He was God's Word made manifest. He shook their hands; hugged them if they insisted. He asked about Mrs Priestley's poorly cat, Mr Hobson's gout, Mrs Henderson's forthcoming operation … Fisher had a kind word for everyone; he'd always been good at improvisation.

And then he spied Mia.

'DS Harvey,' he said, holding out a hand, his smile fixed. 'Nice of you to join us.'

'Thought I'd give it a go, vicar. You never know, some of it might rub off.'

'Indeed,' he said, trying to ignore his rolling gut.

She sat at the back, attempted to blend in, but in all honesty Mia felt like a fish out of water. Still, it was all in a good cause. She glanced around for Kate, saw her in the right-hand aisle, chatting with her sister. Alison Parker, wasn't it? She wondered if Alison had any idea of the violence taking place in the Fisher household. Probably not.

There it was again, that 'keeping up appearances' thing. Kate all smiling and bouncy so Alison wouldn't know the vicar was beating her to a pulp every night. While Alison played the loving sister so Kate wouldn't guess he was dicking her to death. There was a lot to be said for being an only child.

Frank Lessing gave her a wave from the front pew. He was a nice bloke. She'd try and have a word with him later. He hadn't tested her extensive film knowledge in a while.

Mia was rummaging in her bag for a boiled sweet – it was like being at the pictures – when Edna Templeton shuffled along the pew and sat beside her.

'Did you tell Charlie?' she asked, her voice low. 'Did you save him?'

Mia nodded. She didn't dare speak for fear of her cheek bulging with the sweet. The old woman was bound to disapprove of her eating in church.

Luckily, Reverend Fisher chose that moment to close the outer doors and a hush descended on the congregation. Edna Templeton reached forward and retrieved a hymn book from a ledge on the pew in front. Mia copied her then sat back and relaxed, happy in the knowledge that she could suck her sweet in perfect peace.

OK, vicar, show me what you've got.

'Mia, come with me, I've got something for you,' Kate whispered, as the service drew to a close.

She followed Kate into Fisher's office and raised her brows enquiringly as the woman passed her a small piece of paper.

'It's Charlie's autograph. You said you wanted it.'

'Oh yes. Thanks.'

She'd throw it away at the first opportunity. Now she knew that Steve Webber – *Temple's Crest's* resident heartthrob – was a wifebeater, his scrawled signature had somehow lost its attraction.

'Are you all right, Kate? You're not coming down with something?'

'No. Why do you ask?'

'You're dressed for autumn. I thought you might have a chill.'

The woman's outfit was elegance personified. As per usual. She wore a violet-coloured ankle-length dress, made from the sort of material that never creased. It hung from her slight curves beautifully and was matched with black Gladiator sandals. Very chic. Her black military-style jacket was too bulky, however; it didn't go with the dress at all. Had he tried to throttle her this time? Was that why she'd covered her neck?

'I couldn't be better,' she trilled, a hand going to her throat. 'Still, bless you for being concerned.'

Mia didn't believe a word, but she let it go. 'I was hoping to see Grace here. Doesn't she come to church?'

'As a rule, yes, but she is unwell. She has a migraine.'

A bloody great hangover, more like. The office still smelt of wine; it was almost as if the old carpet had been doused in the stuff.

Mia was about to ask after Frank when she was dismissed with a curt, 'Anyway, don't let me keep you, darling. You must have lots to do.'

'Yes, lots,' said Mia. 'Is the rehearsal still on for tomorrow?'

'It is indeed. Seven o'clock.'

Outside, people loitered in small groups, exchanging gossip and generally catching up on the week's events. Mia couldn't see Frank anywhere, which was a shame; the old man really gave her spirits a lift. Edna Templeton was absent too, thank God. But Alison Parker was there, whispering intently with the vicar. How could they be so blatant? Had they no shame?

'Great sermon, vicar,' Mia said, stepping too near so that they had to break apart.

Fisher looked petrified, as though the Angel of Death had rested a bony hand on his shoulder. Alison was appalled at his reaction – if guilt had a face then they were looking at it – and in order to draw Mia's attention away, she said, 'Yes, our Charlie's still got it. He can still hold an audience.'

'Not interrupting anything, am I?'

'Absolutely not,' said Alison.

Fisher was fingering his beard whilst attempting a smile. 'Did you want me?' he asked.

'No, vicar, I want a word with Mrs Parker.' She fixed Alison with an enquiring look. 'If that's OK.'

Apprehension clouded the woman's eyes. 'With me? Why?'

Mia took her arm, led her to a quiet spot. 'I've been told you're a psychologist, Mrs Parker. Is that right?'

'Yes, I have an office at the hospital. And call me Alison, will you? I can't stand all that formal stuff.'

'Look … Alison … tell me to mind my own business if you like, but …' Mia took a deep breath and quickly related the conversation she'd had with Grace the previous day. 'I'm worried about her. I think she needs counselling.'

'Oh, I see.' Alison slid her hands into the pockets of her slacks as her narrowed gaze scanned the graveyard. 'I've tried to help Grace. We all have. And she does listen, up to a point. But there's a block – it's as though she doesn't want to get better, as though she feels she *should* suffer.'

'Is there nothing you can do?'

'Not without her consent.'

'So what's the answer?'

Alison shrugged. 'Another baby?'

'But that's impossible, isn't it? Grace told me.'

Suddenly Alison scowled, took a hand from her pocket and ran it through those glossy curls. 'I could *kill* Tom,' she said.

Mia smiled. 'I don't think much of him either, to be honest.'

'But to steamroll Grace into being sterilized – that was such an evil thing to do. Her baby had just died; her emotions were all over the place … He should at least have waited till she could think straight.'

Mia was gobsmacked. 'Grace was sterilized?'

'Yes.' Alison frowned. 'You said you knew.'

'If ever there was a reason to bring back hanging it's Tom bloody Chamberlain,' said Mia, flinging her shoulder bag under her desk.

'Good morning to you an' all,' said Wells.

'Sorry, sir, but I am so angry.'

'We guessed that.'

Mia had arrived at the office to find Wells and Jack hard at it. Nick was having a day off. She poured three coffees, all the while recounting Grace's sorry tale.

'It's a shame,' said Wells, 'but she signed the consent form so it was all above board.'

'That man's a control freak, sir. He *made* her sign it. The family weren't told until after the operation was finished. Tom doesn't want kids. I bet he was glad when his daughter died.'

Over at his computer Jack was remembering the moment Michelle had presented him with the positive line on her pregnancy test. They hadn't been trying for a baby. *He* hadn't, anyway, and his feelings of shock and panic had been overwhelming. A baby wasn't like a faulty toaster; you couldn't just take it back. Life had a way of changing you, though, over time.

'Jamie's the best thing that's happened to us,' he said. 'We were thinking about giving him a little brother or sister … but I doubt that'll be happening now.'

Wells let out a loud sigh. 'What do I keep telling you, mate?'

'To think positive, sir.'

'So when are you gonna start?'

Mia's miserable mood suddenly deepened. 'I didn't get anything out of Valerie Clarke, Jack. Sorry.'

'S'all right. Thanks for trying.'

Wells glared at her; he wasn't good at defeat. 'You got sod all?'

She outlined the bare bones of their conversation. 'She gave that statement to protect Dylan. I'm sure of it. I just don't know how he's involved.'

All of a sudden Wells was fired with enthusiasm. He kept repeating the boy's name whilst staring at his computer keyboard as though he knew how to use it.

'See if he's in the system, darling. There's more than one way to skin a cat.'

'Talking of cats,' said Jack. 'Did you end up buying a puppy?'

Mia snorted. 'As if.'

'How did you get out of it?'

'Sorry?'

'How did you manage to get away without buying one?'

Mia was staring hard at her computer screen so she wouldn't have to look at him. 'I just told her that … that I'd like to go back for a second look.'

Jack laughed. 'God, I wish Nick was here. He'd love this.'

She gave him a hurt look. 'I'm going back for you, Jack. To help you. I can be firm. I can say no.'

'OK, kiddies, that's enough,' said Wells. 'I don't want to be here all day.'

He was imagining his kitchen, swathed in the scents of roasting lamb and potatoes sizzling in goose fat. His favourite meal. It never tasted as good after a few minutes in the microwave. Pity.

'Did you have a look at Perry's house?' he asked Mia.

'I did, sir. It's a ground-floor maisonette, about three streets away from Mrs Clarke. It's a tip – Housing Association, I'd imagine – overgrown garden, dirty nets at the windows

… His neighbours all keep their properties really nice. I feel sorry for them.'

Wells sat back, hands behind his head. 'So this Dylan Clarke could easily be associating with Perry. Perhaps he buys drugs from him, or supplies drugs *to* him….'

'It's possible, but I can't find him in the system.' Mia motioned towards her computer screen. 'What if he's got nothing to do with the drugs scene? What if Perry's just threatening to implicate him in something to make Mrs Clarke play ball?'

Wells straightened up. 'You're going back to look at the puppies?'

Mia nodded, giving Jack a surreptitious glance. 'She might be more forthcoming next time.'

'When are you going?'

'We didn't arrange a date. I said I'd phone.'

'Leave it a few days, will you? Let me have a think. Perry's not going anywhere. His bail conditions are pretty stringent.' Wells retrieved a large round biscuit tin from beneath his desk and removed the lid. 'The missus made these scones last night. They'll go down a treat with another coffee,' he said, looking pointedly at Mia.

She collected the mugs and said to Jack, 'Found much out about Baxter, sweetie?'

'A fair bit.' Jack swivelled his chair away from the computer and found his note pad. 'The bloke must be rolling in dosh,' he said. 'Apart from his silly-money salary, he owns some houses that he rents out. He's got shares in two racehorses. He's joint-owner of a pub in Nuneaton. *And* he's got an alternative therapy clinic in London.'

Over by the coffee percolator, Mia said, 'I'm surprised, to be honest. He looked a bit down-at-heel when he came in.'

She handed out the coffees and took the biscuit tin from Wells' desk, giving two jam-laden scones to Jack and taking a couple for herself. She gave the remaining five back to Wells. He'd already polished off three and she was interested to see how many more he could manage.

Settling in her chair, she said, 'What about the gym?'

'He sold it in September 2007 to a German consortium called Hoffman Beck Incorporated,' said Jack, licking jam from his fingers. 'It's a chain, they've got branches all over Europe.'

'You'd have thought he'd be too upset to think about business. Rebecca had been missing for months by then.'

Jack shrugged. 'Anyway, I emailed the owners yesterday, asked them to get in touch. We might hear something in the morning. Well, *you* might. I won't be here.' They'd finally had to tell him he was working without Shakespeare's knowledge. He'd taken it well, all things considered.

'Sweetie, stop worrying,' said Mia, with a brightness she didn't feel. 'I know Valerie Clarke was a wash-out, but we've still got Perry's GP to go at.'

'That's right,' said Wells. 'You and Nick can make that your first job in the morning, darling. And get a warrant first, just in case.'

'OK, sir.'

Mia was watching the DCI finish off another scone. His fifth? Sixth? How did he stay so thin? She sighed. God, she was bored. So bored, in fact, that she'd even started eyeing the stuff filling up her intray.

'You know, sir, that *Cold Case* series on telly always looks so interesting, but this is really doing my head in.'

Wells shot her a piercing look. 'Shall I go out and knife somebody, give you something to do?'

Mia tutted. 'I was only saying …'

Jack chuckled. He'd really missed the banter. He loved his job, *really* loved it, and if that Jason Perry thing went to court … But, no, the boss had said to think positive and he would. What was the alternative anyway – lie down and let Perry pummel him half to death all over again?

'You do have a point though,' said Wells. 'We've nothing to build on. No lines of inquiry to follow.'

'Baxter's looking good to me,' said Jack.

'To me an' all, but we can't charge him on a hunch.'

'We need more publicity,' said Mia. 'Here, in Nuneaton *and* London.'

Wells snorted. 'Good idea, but where's the money coming from? Shakespeare's as tight as my arse.'

'What about her neighbours in Nuneaton?'

'Uniformed are on to them. They're going over everybody in the original case notes.'

'OK, what about her clients in London? Baxter said she'd still got some when she went missing.'

Jack said, 'I've been on to every gym and fitness company in London that's got a website and I've found nothing. Either she worked for herself and her own website's gone to cyberspace heaven, or she's been deliberately deleted.'

'We'll get Baxter in again,' said Wells. 'We'll have a proper go at him this time.' He picked up a wad of papers from his desk – that pile containing everything to do with the murder so far – and handed it to Mia. 'Take these, darling, if you want something to do. Make a file and put 'em in some sort of order.'

Bloody great. 'Thanks, sir.'

Jack's computer pinged. 'We have mail,' he said, in a bad American accent. 'It's the Germans. Never thought they'd be in today.'

He clicked his computer mouse and they watched as a grin spread across his bruised face.

'Sir, come and have a look at this.'

The email read:

HEALTHWISE GYMNASIUM,
NUNEATON, ENGLAND
Purchase date: 24 September 2007
Real estate agents: Benjamin Cooke
(Commercial) Ltd of Nuneaton.
Vendor: Ms Rebecca Crawford, 212 Wallace
Court, Nuneaton.
All documents relating to transaction are lodged
with our lawyers:

Hans Kruger Associates of Hamburg.
Please contact should you need more. We shall
be pleased to help.
Regards, Wilhelm Honnefelder (Executive
Director)

'Baxter's been telling porkies,' said Jack, in a sing-song
voice.

'Email the bloke back,' said Wells. 'Tell him we might
need copies of those documents.'

Mia was reading over Jack's shoulder. 'How did he manage to sell something in Rebecca's name?'

Wells grinned. 'Let's ask him.'

Nick hated Sundays. What could a single person do on a
Sunday? Flick through all the bad news in the papers and end
up suicidal? Go to a pub where everybody could see you were
Billy-No-Mates? Watch crap on the telly? No fucking way....

He'd stripped his bedroom walls weeks ago and had
planned to repaper today, had threatened to damage himself
if he didn't. Waking up to bare plaster every morning was the
pits. Christ, just waking up was bad enough.

Nick got as far as measuring the first strip. He even put the
dry paste in a bucket. Then he grabbed his car keys and drove
over to Jason Perry's street, parking a discreet distance from
the maisonette. It was only eight o'clock, and the lazy bastard
probably wouldn't surface till midday. But this was better than
climbing the walls he was supposed to be decorating.

Nick had smoked six cigarettes and finished off two
small bottles of Evian water when Perry showed himself a
little after ten o'clock. Couldn't the fucker sleep? He was with
his 'partner' – a mousy blonde who looked about twelve. She
was manoeuvring a brand new burgundy pram through the
doorway, all smiles and make-up. Perry had a pink holdall
over his shoulder – very New Man.

Nick left the car and locked it, praying it would still
have wheels when he got back. Then, keeping his distance,

he followed them to Stratton Common, a tiny handkerchief of a park on the edge of Staples Brook.

The park – funded by lottery money – had been designed in the hope that a bit of open greenery might help to reduce crime in the area: give the lawbreakers somewhere decent to congregate and they *might* stay out of trouble. No such luck. Within weeks of its opening the kiddies' primary-coloured climbing frames had been vandalized, the toilet block wrecked, and the small pavilion defaced with explicit graffiti. Local councillors never bothered to rectify the damage; they knew it would be a waste of money. So anybody decent still patronized Heaven's Gate or Larchwood Valley – even though those places were a car ride away – and Stratton Common was left for the scum.

The couple stopped in front of the pavilion. Perry took a small multi-coloured blanket from the holdall and spread it out so that their baby could lay there and learn how to kick while its subconscious soaked up the graffiti: words that would form the bulk of its future vocabulary, no doubt.

Nick had bought a newspaper from the kiosk and he sat on a nearby bench, pretending to read while he watched and waited. For what, he had no idea. But they needed to catch Perry red-handed, selling his stuff. They needed to show him up for the low-life he really was if those no-sense twats at the CPS were to drop the case against Jack.

Nick's horoscope read: *Your loneliness will evaporate this week. Love walks into your life wearing the colour blue. Get up close and personal. Drop your defences. Let yourself go.*

Perry's shell suit was pale blue. And Nick was dying to get up close and personal with *him*. Preferably somewhere dark so he could land a few punches. Or stick in a knife. Or blow his fucking brains out.

Jack might actually have to appear in court. It was unbelievable. Total bollocks. You do your best, only to find that life's led you to a great big vat of steaming shit. And you don't see any of it coming. Nick's mind wondered back to the day he and Jack first encountered Perry….

A teacher thinks with his balls instead of his fucking head. They choose curry for lunch. Why didn't they have a MacDonald's? They wouldn't have been anywhere near Argyle Street. Perry could've stripped HMV. He could have opened up with a machine gun. He could've run naked from one end of the street to the other. He could've done anything and it wouldn't have mattered because *Jack wouldn't have been there.*

He wondered how Mia had got on with the witness. Hopefully she'd got *something* they could use. Hopefully he was wasting his morning, watching two losers cooing over a kid. Just like normal people.

Something had been niggling at the periphery of Nick's mind. Something wasn't right. And now he realized what it was: Jason Perry was sober. Why wasn't he drugged up and pissed out of his skull?

Nick was pondering that thought when the ringtone on Perry's mobile blasted out, so loud a few passers-by turned to stare. *God Save the Queen* by the *Sex Pistols*. Nice.

Nick spotted a group of four yobs – one of them talking into a phone – disappear around the back of the pavilion. Jason Perry finished the short call and followed them, the pink holdall on his shoulder. After a few minutes the group dispersed in all directions. But Perry remained hidden: now was the time to strike. Nick folded the newspaper and left it on the bench. He had to be quick. He wanted the bastard on his own.

As it turned out there was no need to rush. He found Perry on his knees, the holdall in a pile of dog muck. He was clutching his right side, just below the ribs.

Nick helped him to his feet. 'You OK, mate?' The words were heavy with concern, but inside Nick was gloating.

'Yeah, bruv. Just a pain. Don't want the missus to know. She'll only start.' A sheen of sweat glistened on Perry's face, which was a deathly white.

Nick made a show of glancing around. 'I was looking to buy,' he said, 'but if it ain't a good time….'

Perry regarded him warily. 'I know you … yeah?'

144

Nick snorted. 'You fuckin' should, mate. I've had your stuff enough fuckin' times.'

'Yeah?' said Perry, frowning.

'Yeah. 'Course, you're usually wasted when I see you.' It was Nick's turn to frown. 'What's the story, mate? You stopped using?'

'Had to, bruv. Got a court case coming up. Compensation. Big numbers. S'licitor says I gotta lay off for the duration.' He groaned and clutched his stomach. 'It's fuckin' killing me.'

'Too bad.' Nick was looking around, hands on his hips. 'So you ain't sellin' no more.'

'Yeah, I'm sellin'. Just can't dip me hand in.' He reached for the holdall, clutched his side again. 'Ain't got much on me. Just some weed and a few rocks....'

Nick gave a low chuckle. 'No good to me, mate. I got a party comin' up. A *big* party. I want *everythin'*. Coke, the big H, Crank, some Es, Barbs, LSD, PCP, GHB ... Like I said, mate, I want the lot.' He'd worked the Drugs Squad in Manchester before joining Larchborough CID. Just as well.

Perry's mouth was hanging open. 'I'd better make a list.'

'If you can't do it, just say an' I'll take me business elsewhere.'

'I can do it.' He was sweating heavily now; great swathes of sweat were discolouring the blue top. Jason Perry didn't look at all well. 'When do you want it?'

'Soon as, mate.'

Perry was nodding. 'Give us a couple o' days, yeah? Gotta make a few calls.'

'OK, we'll meet here Wednesday night. Seven o'clock. How's that sound?'

'Cool.' Perry sucked in a breath, shook his head. 'It ain't gonna be cheap though.'

Nick swaggered, playing the big I Am. 'I'll have the readies. You just get as much as you can.'

Perry held out his hand. 'Deal.'

'Good. See you Wednesday.'

Well, uniformed will, at any rate.

CHAPTER 11

'SORRY TO MESS up your Sunday, Mr Baxter.'

The man gave Wells a cautious look. 'Why have you brought me in, Chief Inspector?'

'We just need to ask you a few questions, sir. Some new information has come to light.'

They were seated in interview room number one. Baxter was watching Mia as she slotted a new tape into the machine, giving details of date, time, and all persons present.

He swallowed hard. 'Hold on a minute, why are you doing that?'

'It's just procedure,' she said, with a friendly smile. 'Nothing to worry about, sir.'

'But you didn't record me last time.'

Wells grinned. 'This has got nothing to do with Rebecca Crawford's disappearance, sir. This is something altogether separate.'

'Oh?'

Baxter felt wretched. His mouth was dry and his bowels were as loose as a gangster's morals. Indeed, as he stared into their expectant faces, he was fearful he might shit his pants there and then.

Two uniformed officers had turned up in the middle of lunch, had practically *hauled* him into their car. In front of Claire and the family. In front of her *neighbours,* for Christ's sake. Oh yes, they'd all stopped cleaning their cars and mowing their bloody lawns to watch. Nosy bastards. He'd never live it down. And what if Gerhard got to find out? He'd tried his solicitor in the car. *Again.* Was put through to the answerphone message. *Again.*

Baxter squared his shoulders, fixed them with a defiant glare. 'I'm saying nothing till I get my solicitor here.'

'Any idea when he's likely to arrive?' asked Wells.

'Tomorrow at the earliest. He's not picking up his phone.'

'Oh dear.'

Baxter lurched forward. 'That's not a problem, surely. I can come back in the morning and you people can enjoy your day of rest. What do you say?'

'That does make sense,' said Wells, seeming to ponder.

'Good.' Baxter got to his feet.

'Did I say you could go?'

'But, I thought …'

'Sit down, please, sir.'

Baxter resumed his seat with all the grace of a petulant child. 'You're wasting your time, you know. I'm saying nothing till I get my solicitor. I've already told you.'

Wells leant back and regarded him coolly. He loved making wrongdoers squirm. Especially those who murdered heavily pregnant women.

He said, 'We've been on the old Internet, sir, looking into your many business interests….'

Baxter paled considerably. 'Are you allowed? There is such a thing as data protection, you know.'

As Wells knew very little about the Web and all it entailed, he said, 'DS Harvey, put the man's mind at rest, will you?'

Mia made a meal of looking through her note pad. Stopping at a supposedly relevant page she held it up, saying, 'We came upon the information quite legally, sir. You must know yourself that even one small tweet can lead to all sorts of interesting facts about a user.'

'No, I don't know,' said Baxter, craning his neck to glimpse her jottings. His heart was racing wildly as he mentally listed the many *interesting facts* they could have discovered about *him*. 'All right, you'd better tell me what you've found out.'

Wells raised his brows. 'Is there any point, sir?'

'What do you mean?'

'I'll only be wasting my breath if you're gonna stay shtum without your brief.'

'Stop playing with me, Chief Inspector.' He pointed to the recording machine. 'That can go against *you* as well as me.'

Wells seemed to consider those words for a long moment. Then he straightened up as though he'd come to a decision. 'Tell you what, sir, we'll forget our questions for now. We'll wait till your brief arrives.'

Baxter breathed a sigh of relief. 'Thank you.'

'But, as we're here …' Wells gave the man an amiable glance. 'That flamin' Internet's OK, sir, but it couldn't tell us anything about Miss Crawford so we're still in the dark about her disappearance. Truth is, the investigation's going nowhere. Are you up to helping us?'

'I've already told your colleague everything I know,' he said, nodding towards Mia.

'And very helpful you were too.' Wells fell silent, seemed to be wrestling with an idea. Finally, he sat back and gave Baxter a hopeful look. 'Listen, sir, if you could help us, if you could give us *anything* new, then we might be able to forget the little … *contretemps* … that brought you here today.'

Surprise was clear on Baxter's face. 'What about…?' He pointed to the recording machine.

'Oh, we can chuck that, don't worry. What do you say, DS Harvey?'

'It's a good idea, sir. Think of all the paperwork we'll be avoiding.'

'All right,' said Baxter, actually grinning now. 'What can I tell you?'

'Let's go back to when Rebecca disappeared,' said Wells. 'Everything in your garden was rosy, so to speak. You were planning to propose to the love of your life. You had a great job in Switzerland—'

'Still have,' Baxter interjected.

Wells nodded. 'In fact, everything was tickety-boo until Rebecca failed to keep your dinner date—'

Baxter held up a hand to stop him. 'Don't you remember?' he said to Mia. 'We established that Becky was on her way to London to see a client. That's how she came to be here in Larchborough.'

'He's right, sir, we did,' Mia was quick to reply.

'OK. So when was the last time you saw Rebecca, Mr Baxter?'

'The previous day.'

'You saw Rebecca Crawford the day before she disappeared. Is that what you're saying, sir?'

'Yes.'

'And how did she seem? Happy? Sad? Preoccupied? None of the above?'

Baxter shrugged. 'She was ... normal. The same old Becky.'

'She didn't give you any inkling that she might have to dash off to London at a moment's notice?'

'No, but she'd done it before. Some of her clients were very self-obsessed, thought she should be at their beck and call. Celebrities are like that.'

'And she didn't think to phone?'

'Perhaps ...' Baxter began, putting on a tragic look. 'Perhaps she was planning to, only she was ... *taken* before she could.'

'You think she was taken?'

'What else could have happened to her?'

'I wish I knew, sir.'

Mia cut in then. 'Mr Baxter, did Rebecca actually train with her clients?'

'Yes, indeed, she was very hands-on.'

'So, not only was she beautiful, she must have had the perfect body as well.'

'Absolutely,' Baxter agreed.

At eight months pregnant? Mia glanced down at her own stomach. 'There but for years of Indian takeaways go I,' she said, grinning.

Baxter's laugh was half-hearted. 'I was a very lucky man.'

'You must have been a very *worried* man at the time,' Wells commented.

'I was frantic,' said Baxter, eyes closed.

'And yet you went ahead with the sale of your gym.'

'I had to, Chief Inspector. Buyers don't grow on trees.'

Wells nodded and sat back. He was doodling a tiny headstone in the margin of his note pad while he considered his next question. Bryan Baxter had to be their killer. The man could only have risked selling the gym if he knew for certain that Rebecca Crawford was never coming back. And to be *that* certain then Baxter must have known she was safely buried miles away in St Matthew's cemetery. The big question now was: How the bloody hell did he manage the sale?

Wells regarded Baxter for a moment, was tapping his pen on the table top, and then he said, 'Who bought the gym, sir?'

Baxter puffed out his cheeks. 'Now, let me think.'

'You can't remember?' said Wells. 'I'm surprised.'

'I own lots of properties. I buy and sell all the time.' The man skimmed them a chiding glance. 'But you already know that, don't you? You've done all that sneaking about on the Internet.'

Wells shrugged off the remark. 'Why do you feel the need to buy and sell anyway? You've got that high-powered job abroad. You can't be hard-up.'

'I like to keep busy. I'm easily bored.'

'Oh right.'

Baxter watched worriedly as the DCI scribbled a few words. The atmosphere in that squalid room had changed; the pauses between their questions were suddenly loaded with foreboding. He felt hounded again, and in order to appear cooperative, Baxter said, 'Why don't I get my solicitor to bring the paperwork in the morning....'

Wells' jowls stretched into a grin. 'That'd be very good of you, sir. Thank you.'

In your dreams, old man.

He'd decided days ago that the minute he got that waste-of-space solicitor on the phone he would instruct him to destroy everything to do with the sale – they'd had a fire at the office, or a burglary perhaps – in return for a sizeable financial gift. They'd done much the same thing before. Some people would consider anything for money. And, luckily, his solicitor was one of those people.

'Is that it for today then?' Baxter asked brightly.

Wells turned to Mia. 'Anything you want to ask?'

'Actually, I was wondering if Rebecca trained any really famous people, anybody I might have heard of.'

Typical airhead female. Still, at least they were on a less touchy subject. Baxter smiled and said, 'Yes, there were a few Hollywood leading men. Some footballers. A young man from one of the soaps ... I couldn't possibly give their names though; client confidentiality is very important in that business.'

'Like data protection is on the Web?' said Wells.

'Exactly, Chief Inspector.'

'So Rebecca only trained men,' Mia said.

Baxter looked into the middle distance, as though contemplating her words. 'Do you know, I hadn't realized till now ... Yes, Rebecca did only train men.'

'I suppose,' said Mia, 'that the likes of Madonna and Gwyneth Paltrow wouldn't want to be trained by somebody better looking than they are.'

'Probably not,' Baxter muttered. He'd had enough now. He wanted to get away from that stifling room, from those dim people and their inane comments.

But Mia wasn't finished yet. 'Did Rebecca work for herself, Mr Baxter?'

'Yes, she did.'

'So she had it all – her own successful business; a man who adored her; fantastic looks …' She sighed loudly. 'I reckon we'd have had much more interest from the public if we'd put Rebecca's picture in the paper. People have more sympathy if the victim's beautiful. Still, we didn't have the case notes when the story went to press, so—'

'Is this going anywhere?' Baxter asked, arrogance loud in his tone.

'I told DCI Wells that we should have waited till we had a picture.' Mia gave a shrug. 'Anyway, is that why you wanted Rebecca to run your gym, sir? Because she was so beautiful and she'd be a good advert for the place?'

'I suppose so, yes.'

'I thought as much.'

Baxter's impatience was rapidly reaching crisis point. Why was he having to listen to that woman's ridiculously absurd *drivel*? He shot Wells a beseeching look. 'Chief Inspector, could I please go now?'

Wells was sucking on his biro and watching the man through narrowed lids. Slowly placing the pen on the table, he said, 'No, Mr Baxter, we can't let you go.'

'But, why?' the man almost wailed. 'I'll be back first thing in the morning with my solicitor. I promise.'

'*And* all the paperwork for the gym?'

'Yes, of course.'

Wells snorted. 'Pull the other one, mate.'

'What?' Baxter's horrified glance bounced between the detectives. 'But I've got to go. My family will be worried.'

'Tough,' Wells spat.

'How much longer?' he said, fumbling for his watch. 'An hour? Two?'

Wells frowned. 'Remind me, DS Harvey … what's the maximum sentence Mr Baxter could get under the Proceeds of Crime Act 2002?'

'Fourteen years, sir.'

'As much as that?'

'Of course, he'll get a lot more if we can prove he murdered Rebecca.'

'I didn't kill her,' he said, colour seeping from his face.

'No?' Wells growled. 'You sold her bloody gym though, didn't you?'

One small sentence dominated Baxter's thoughts as he struggled once more to control those incredibly irritable bowels.

They've got me.

'But the gym was mine to sell.'

'Not according to the current owners. Give me a minute and I'll tell you who they are.' Wells reached for the briefcase at his feet. He extracted a paper copy of that all-important email on which Rebecca's details were highlighted in pink, all the while outlining his actions for the benefit of the recorder. 'Here it is … Hoffman Beck Incorporated,' he said, placing the copy in front of the man.

A defeated Baxter fell back in the chair and gave a humourless laugh. 'Not as stupid as you look, are you, Chief Inspector?'

'No, mate, I'm not.'

'All right, what happens now?'

'*This* happens now.'

Wells leant forward and with immense pleasure he read the man his rights.

'How'd it go, sir?'

'Like a dream, Jack. George Slater's finding him a nice cosy cell.'

Mia perched on the edge of her desk and squirmed with delight. 'His stuck-up face was a picture when we showed him your email, sweetie.'

'Glad I've been some help,' said Jack, his own face glum.

'What's up?' said Wells.

The young detective lifted a disgruntled shoulder. 'Nothing, sir, I've just enjoyed the weekend, that's all.'

Wells was packing his briefcase. He paused momentarily, a smile on his lips. 'Let's hope you enjoy tomorrow an' all then. Eight o'clock start. Both of you.'

'But I can't….'

'I'm saying you can,' said Wells, settling into his chair. 'We've got our killer downstairs and just twenty-four short hours to find enough to charge him. We need you, mate.'

'What about the super?'

'Leave him to me.'

'Have we got time for a celebratory coffee?' asked Mia.

'No, I want my dinner. You can come an' all, if you like. The missus won't mind.'

'That's really kind of you, sir, but I've got things to do.' It was a lie, of course. But she had visions of Wells and his wife standing either side of her, shovelling wholesome food into her mouth as though she were a ten-stone toddler. Even mind-numbing loneliness was preferable to that.

'If you say so.' Wells gave her the email. 'Put that with the rest of the papers, will you?'

As she started searching her desk and began to panic, Jack said, 'I've got them, Mia. I've been having a quick look. And guess what I found. Turns out my sexy psychologist has had her teeth done.'

'You haven't got a psychologist.'

'I know, but she did try to chat me up in the hospital.'

'With you looking like that? The woman needs glasses, not fake teeth.' She took the papers from him, followed his pointing finger. 'Bloody hell … Doctor Alison Parker?'

'Do you know her?'

'She's our leading lady.'

Jack snorted. 'Your what?'

'Our leading lady at St Matthew's.'

'You've lost me.'

'God, Jack, we really need to bring you back in the loop.' Mia made a face. 'She lives in Stratton Heights … very nice too.'

'You didn't find Rebecca Crawford's name, I suppose,' said Wells.

'No, sir.'

Mia transferred the pile of papers to her desk. 'I'll take everything home with me, sir. I can make the file up there.'

While Jack switched off his computer equipment, his back towards Wells, he said, 'I had a bloke on the phone while you were downstairs, sir, with information about Jason Perry. He wouldn't leave his name.'

'Oh yes? What did he have to say?'

'Apparently, Perry's going to be supplying a large amount of drugs to persons unknown on Wednesday night in Stratton Common.'

Wells' grin was tentative. 'And did this bloke sound kosher?'

Jack was still busying himself at his desk, unwilling to meet his boss's gaze. He couldn't let on that Nick had made the call. Nick's tactics were dubious, to say the least, and any court proceedings resulting from them would be quashed immediately if they came to light, leaving Nick in big trouble. Jack would just have to stay as near to the facts as was possible; he hated lying to Wells. And anyway Nick had sounded positively euphoric during the call – made from a public payphone so that it couldn't be traced back to him – therefore, in a *way* Jack was talking to a stranger. The acerbic Nick never sounded euphoric.

'I'd say so,' said Jack, well aware that he was blushing as he straightened up. 'The bloke said Perry had done the dirty on his mate and now it was *his* turn to suffer.'

'Thank God for gang rivalries,' said Wells. 'Did you tell uniformed?'

'Yes, sir, and they're taking it seriously. There'll be officers in place at the given time.'

Wells grinned. 'This is really good news. For you an' all,' he said, turning to Mia. 'You might not have to buy one of Valerie Clarke's puppies.'

Or give her that colour and cut.

Thirty minutes later Mia entered her flat and was met by a yawning silence. She'd been almost drunk with joy when, two years previously, her offer for the property had been accepted. One of fifteen flats in a converted shoe factory, it boasted a sitting-room, separate kitchen, two bedrooms and a bathroom. The rooms weren't huge, but she had the use of two parking spaces and the neighbours were quiet so, all in all, it was perfect.

And, yet, it wasn't. She felt isolated. Her neighbours were *too* quiet; all of them guarding their privacy with an almost hostile determination. There was no communal garden. No communal *anything*. The only time she saw another face was in the lift or on the stairs where a quick hello was exchanged – if she was lucky.

Mia tossed her keys on to the hall table, shrugged off her shoulder bag and jacket, and went into the kitchen to fill the kettle. It was a little after seven o'clock and an evening of enforced solitude lay ahead.

How had she come to this? And how could she change things?

Mia loved her job, but the long hours put paid to any social life she might have had years ago. She'd made friends in the force, obviously, but they were either married or courting strongly, and Mia only met up with them socially at someone's leaving do or the Christmas party.

As the kettle boiled Mia decided to change into her pyjamas; she might as well be comfortable. On the way to her bedroom she paused at the open door to the spare room where the boxes of her mother's things were still waiting to be emptied. She couldn't face them. Not tonight. Closing the door firmly, Mia crossed to the living room where she put on the television set, selecting the Film Four channel. *The Day after Tomorrow* was on. That would do. She quite fancied Dennis Quaid. He could keep her company while she sorted out the murder file for Wells.

With pyjamas on and a mug of coffee at her side Mia sat cross-legged on the floor in front of the TV where she proceeded to sort the papers into various piles.

She looked again at Alison Parker's details on the list of cosmetic dentists. Was that just an innocent coincidence or a clue to something more? Lots of people had their teeth done nowadays. And not just singers or actors either. Professional people like Alison needed to look good for their clients. Why shouldn't she get herself a Hollywood smile if she could afford one? It had to be a coincidence. And anyway they'd got Baxter in the frame.

But DCI Wells didn't believe in coincidences. He always said that they were put there to focus the mind and encourage a more creative approach to tracking down the criminal scumbags of this world. Maybe he was right.

That particular dental practice had a Warwick address. And Warwick was midway between Larchborough and Nuneaton. More or less. Did that mean anything? Could Alison and Rebecca Crawford have become friends whilst comparing their treatment in the dentist's reception? Once again Mia scanned the list of names. Rebecca's definitely wasn't there. She looked for any Nuneaton addresses but, again, drew a blank.

There was one other patient from Larchborough however. The details read: A Molina, Hawk's Nest, Stratton Lea, Larchborough. Mia grinned. She was imagining Alfred Molina, the film star, living amongst them incognito. Stratton Lea was a small housing estate close to Stratton Manor, its semi-detached houses with their quarter-acre gardens quite sought after due to the spectacular views on offer in that part of town. It wasn't the first place one might look for a Hollywood A-lister, but perhaps Mr Molina was down to earth and hadn't let fame change him.

Mia was debating whether to drive up there with a pair of binoculars in the hope of catching a glimpse of Alfred when the doorbell rang. She froze, a hand holding the pyjamas together at her neck.

She glanced at her watch. It was almost nine o'clock. Hugging the wall for some obscure reason Mia made her way to the front door and peered through the peephole. Nick's distorted features peered back.

She opened the door a notch. 'What do you want?'

'Gonna let me in?'

'I'm undressed.'

'I'll try and control myself.'

Mia pulled the door wide and stepped back, cringing as he gazed longer than was necessary at her pyjamas.

'What do you want, Nick?'

He tutted. 'Your hospitality's rubbish, if you don't mind my saying.'

Mia threw him a contemptuous look and flounced off into the living room, leaving him to follow. 'OK, now you're in, what do you want?'

'Have you got any wallpaper paste?' he asked, reclining on her sofa.

'You've come all this way, at this time of night, to ask for wallpaper paste?'

'B and Q was shut,' he said, shrugging. 'And it's only nine o'clock.' He looked at the papers littering the carpet. 'What you doing?'

'Sorting out the case notes.'

'Want any help?'

'No.'

Nick motioned towards her empty mug. 'Making any more coffee?'

'The kettle's in the kitchen,' she said, strutting towards the hall. 'Help yourself while I get dressed.'

When Mia got back Nick was kneeling on the floor, sorting through the murder stuff. 'You haven't got very far,' he said, accusingly.

'Where's the coffee?'

'I couldn't be bothered. Got any wine?'

Mia glared at his back, was on the verge of throwing him out. Then she realized just how much she craved a bit of company.

'OK, one drink. But the minute you start all that "why are we here?" crap, you're out.' She went to fetch the wine.

'It's only cheap white,' she said, setting the glasses on her coffee table and filling them.

He looked up then, gazed at her clothes. She'd slipped into navy jogging bottoms and a pale-blue T-shirt; nothing special, but they were new and therefore hadn't yet stretched from too many washes. Mia thought they made her look slimmer.

'You're wearing blue,' he said.

'So?'

'I was reading about blue this morning.'

Mia handed him the wine. 'And what did you find out, that it's the colour fat losers wear?'

'Stop being so fucking aggressive – you look nice.'

'Has the boss put you up to this? Does he think I fall to pieces every time I cross the threshold?'

Nick gave her a frown. 'Do you treat all your guests like this?'

'You're not a guest,' Mia replied as she settled into an armchair well away from him. 'You're a what-do-you-call-it … an *interloper*.'

'And you're paranoid.'

'I've good reason to be,' she said, sipping her wine. 'You don't do *friendly*, Nick. You're better at *cruel* and *nasty*.'

Mia curled her legs up on the chair, made herself more comfortable. She was enjoying their verbal jousting.

'So, if you have come to check up on me, it's been a wasted journey. I'm fine, as you can see.'

'I came for some wallpaper paste, I told you.' He saluted her with his glass and then took a long sip, grimacing at the taste. 'Christ, this is sweet.'

'I like it sweet. And, anyway, I don't believe you've been decorating. You look too tidy.'

'Call me a liar then.'

She was right, though. The dry paste was still in the bucket; that single strip was still rolled up on his bedroom floor. Since his successful encounter with Jason Perry, Nick had been too wired up to settle at anything. So, after wasting the rest of his day he'd found himself driving towards Mia's flat. And, in a way, he'd been more surprised than she was to find himself at her door.

'Got anything to eat?' he asked.

She heaved a sigh, made it plain that he was pushing her 'rubbish hospitality' to its limits. In truth though Mia was only too happy to feed him; it beat watching old films on the telly. She disappeared into the kitchen, returning moments later with crisps, wholegrain biscuits, a tub of pâté … and a bowl of raisins to show Nick that she was a healthy eater.

'How was Jack?' he asked, spreading pâté on a few biscuits.

'Brilliant. He really saved the day.' She told him about the email from Germany and Bryan Baxter's subsequent interrogation – facts that Nick already knew because Jack had filled him in on the phone.

'Sounds like Baxter killed her, then.'

Mia nodded. 'We've got him in the cells. Jack's coming in tomorrow to help us nail him.'

'Shakespeare won't like that.'

'You haven't heard the best,' said Mia, forgetting to be aloof as she reached for a couple of crisps. 'Somebody snitched on Perry. Uniformed are going to catch him with a load of drugs on Wednesday.'

'That should help Jack's case.'

''Course it will. After Wednesday's collar the CPS'll have to take all of Perry's previous into account and they'll see he's not the innocent victim they think he is.'

'You don't say.'

Nick was giving her one of his amused glances that made him look exceptionally dishy and made Mia feel decidedly hot. 'Anyway,' she said, trying to remain poised, 'you might as well help with the file while you're stuffing your face.'

They halved the papers and worked in silence, Nick now and then sipping his wine and picking at the food.

'Christ, look at this,' he said, handing her a white form.

It was from the Crime Laboratory, and it told Mia that the DNA retrieved from Bryan Baxter's handkerchief – and sent in under the name of Billy Briers by Nick – didn't match the sample taken from the skeleton of their foetus.

'So Baxter *wasn't* the father of Rebecca's baby,' said Mia. 'I bloody knew it.'

'And the boss is just as fallible as the rest of us,' said Nick, smirking. 'That could have been on his desk for days.'

Mia was staring into the middle distance, pondering. 'Baxter reckons he saw Rebecca the day before she disappeared. But he couldn't have done. She was as big as a house and he was going on to me about her perfect figure.'

'He's been lying through his teeth all along, if you ask me.'

She rapped the form with her knuckles. 'This changes everything, Nick. With another man involved, it could mean Baxter isn't our killer.'

'Not necessarily. Rebecca was two-timing him, so Baxter could have killed her out of jealousy.'

Mia acknowledged the point with a nod. 'We'd better be vigilant. There might be something else we've missed.' She topped up their glasses. 'Oh, by the way, I haven't got any wallpaper paste.'

He gave her a quick glance. 'No problem. I'll get some tomorrow.'

CHAPTER 12

'THINGS ARE COMING together nicely, kiddies,' said a cheerful DCI Wells. 'Uniformed have finished with everybody in the original case notes and – guess what – nobody can remember seeing Rebecca Crawford for most of 2007.'

'And that's good how, sir?' asked Mia.

'Because it means that Rebecca must have been elsewhere for most of her pregnancy. So, where was she? And why did Baxter want us to think they were still in touch? And why – if it was so near to completion – did she abandon the gym? Now, I know we've still got to find answers to these bloody infuriating questions, but at least we've got questions to find answers for.'

'Baxter isn't the baby's father, sir,' said Nick, passing him the Crime Lab form. 'We found that among the papers last night.'

Wells' eyes narrowed. 'We?'

'Me and Mia. I called round to her flat.'

Nick spoke the words without the slightest hesitation. What he did in his own time had nothing to do with Wells. Mia, however, felt differently. As she saw the intrigue in his scrawny features, she couldn't help but feel awkward.

'There was nothing else of interest … in the papers,' she said.

Wells studied the DNA results, a smile hovering on his lips. 'And did you two form any opinions about the father last night?'

'No,' said Nick. 'But Mia now thinks Baxter might not be our killer. Whereas I still reckon he is, with jealousy as the motive.'

'Hmm, one of those theories is right.' Wells opened up his notebook. 'Uniformed also checked up on Rebecca's Nuneaton address. 212 Wallace Court. Turns out she was last seen there sometime in January 2007.'

'Is she still the owner?' asked Mia.

'She never owned it. She rented it.'

Nick shrugged. 'Why can't we just ask the landlord if she left a forwarding address?'

'Oh, we're going to, don't worry. But something tells me he won't be very forthcoming.'

'Why, sir?'

'Because Bryan Baxter's the landlord.' Wells grinned at them. 'See what I mean? All the pieces are coming together. Now we've got to make them fit. We'll have another go at him this afternoon. Let's make him sweat a bit first.'

Jack came in then, looking harassed. 'Sorry I'm late, sir.'

'S'all right, mate. How you feeling?'

'Confused, sir.' He stood before Wells, hands on his immaculately-dressed hips. 'I had a call from Inspector May this morning. That's why I'm late.'

Wells scowled. 'What did that tosser want?'

'He'd heard the CPS was scheduling my first hearing for the end of July, and he wanted me to know so I can prepare my case.'

Mia gasped. 'They're actually going ahead with it? But, sweetie, you could get five years.'

'I know.' Jack handed Wells an envelope. 'I had this in the post, sir.'

With all eyes upon him Wells pulled out a Barclays cheque. It was from the Criminal Injuries Compensation Authority. 'I can see why you're bloody confused, mate.' He held up the cheque. 'Jack's been awarded one thousand pounds compensation.'

'It doesn't make sense,' said Mia. 'What's he going to do, sir?'

'He's not going to panic, that's what.' Wells returned the cheque to the envelope and passed it to Jack. 'The end of July's still a month away, plenty of time for us to shaft that bastard Perry. And there's still Wednesday night to look forward to.'

'That's the tip-off Mia told me about – yeah?' said Nick, with award-winning nonchalance.

Wells nodded. 'And if it goes to plan Perry *will* be shafted – good and proper.'

'What about his GP?' asked Mia. 'D'you still want us to see him, sir?'

Wells glanced at his watch. 'Yes, go now, kiddies. And don't forget the warrant.'

Plans and strategies almost always work out smoothly in novels and televised dramas. Real life, however, has a tendency to erect a few hurdles along the road; it creates barriers that prevent people from reaching their all-important goals. And the particular barrier preventing Mia and Nick from obtaining a warrant to search Jason Perry's medical records came in the shape of magistrate Marjory Hickson.

Mrs Hickson had argued that, as the Crown Prosecution Service was now involved with Jack's alleged assault case, it was down to his legal team to secure evidence in his favour and his 'mates in CID' should leave well alone. Therefore, they were now entering Staples Brook Medical Centre unarmed and dispirited.

The waiting-room was empty. As they approached the desk Mia was jostling to get in front. But when she saw that the receptionist was young and pretty; saw too that the girl was almost licking her lips at the sight of Nick, she said, 'You'd better speak to her. Try to be nice.'

'Hi,' he said, flashing his best smile. 'I wonder if you can help me.'

'I'll do anything,' the girl breathed.

Nick displayed his warrant card; a move which had the receptionist almost panting. 'You're a policeman? How exciting.'

'I try to be – exciting, I mean – especially with someone as lovely as you.' He leant across the desk, lowered his voice. 'Did you know you've got the most beautiful smile?'

'Have I?'

'I go for smiles.'

'And you really like mine?'

'It's driving me crazy. I can hardly concentrate.' He leant even closer. 'First things first though. I'm here on a case. A very *important* case.'

Her dark brown eyes grew large. 'What can I do?'

'I need some information about Jason Perry of forty-five Wilford Road, Staples Brook. Can you give it to me, angel? Please? *Pretty* please?'

Mia, hovering a few feet away, didn't know whether to throw up or be impressed.

The receptionist's pretty forehead crinkled. 'I'd love to help, but I can't. I *can* tell you which doctor he's with.'

Nick placed a finger under her chin, narrowed his eyes. 'No need to bother the doctor, is there? That'd take too long. You tell me what I want to know and I'll show you how happy you've made me.'

The girl bit down on her bottom lip, wishing fervently that she could comply. 'I can't, honestly, I haven't got access to the notes. You'll have to speak to the doctor.'

Nick swallowed a curse. 'OK, who's his doctor?'

The girl, finally managing to drag her gaze away from his extremely pleasing features, was typing Perry's name and waiting for information to flood her screen.

'He's on Doctor Fisher's books,' she said, once more feasting her eyes. 'Do you want me to ring through?'

How else will he know we're here, you dozy cow? 'I'd be grateful if you could.'

The girl giggled. 'How grateful?'

Nick held his hand in front of her face, the thumb and forefinger almost touching. 'About this much.'

'Oh,' she said, pouting.

'I'll go and sit down while you make the call.'

Nick chose a seat nearest to the desk while Mia wandered across to a display of pamphlets. The receptionist's eyes stayed glued to him as she spoke into the receiver, her tone stilted and business-like. Why had he turned so cold?

Attempting indifference, she got to her feet. 'Go through that door there and you'll find Doctor Fisher in the third room on the right.'

Nick rapped on the door and, without waiting for a response, barged in. 'Doctor Fisher?'

'That's right.'

Mia was brought up short. 'I wasn't expecting *you*.'

Acute horror flashed momentarily in the doctor's eyes. 'I'm extremely busy,' she said, recovering quickly. 'What do you want?'

Grace Chamberlain uttered those words harshly, without a smile, without even a trace of recognition and Mia was seriously wrong-footed. Still, she bore in mind the woman's tragic history and the problems that were even now blighting her life – that excuse of a husband for one – and she made allowances.

'How are you?' she asked kindly.

'Extremely busy, as I've already said.'

'I was hoping to see you at yesterday's service. Your mum said you weren't well.'

'I had a migraine.'

'Are you OK now?'

Grace gave her a frosty look, skimmed her eyes over Nick. 'I will be when I can get back to my work. I'll ask again – what do you want?'

While Mia stood in shock at her friend's hostile attitude, Nick pulled up a chair and explained as succinctly as he could the reason for their visit. 'I appreciate that without a warrant we can't expect your cooperation, but our colleague's future's on the line here so we're appealing to your better nature.'

'Then you're wasting your time. I have a duty to Mr Perry and, although I sympathize with your colleague's predicament, I won't betray his trust.'

'Perry doesn't deserve your trust,' said Nick, barely holding his temper.

'That depends on your point of view. Now, I need to get on.' She nodded towards the door.

Mia stepped forward. 'Please, Grace …'

'I said go.'

The two women locked eyes. 'See you at tonight's rehearsal,' Mia said.

They left without another word, Nick slamming the door hard. Grace stared after them, breathing heavily as her thoughts returned to the previous night.

She'd had another row with Tom because he was insisting on going down to London again. To 'network', as he put it. He'd never get parts languishing in Larchborough. Didn't she want him to be a success? Didn't she want him to be creatively fulfilled? He wasn't her lackey, her pet poodle. He had a right to live his own life, realize his own dreams.

What dreams? It was sex he was after – lashings of it. Tom couldn't resist a pretty face. That 'networking' he spoke about most likely occurred in hotel rooms and a succession of marital beds.

Didn't she have rights too?

Throughout their marriage she'd carried Tom, had done everything in her power to keep him happy. She'd even agreed to no more babies when motherhood was *her* one and only dream. Wasn't that enough?

It was at that point in the quarrel when Grace finally acknowledged the truth. In her husband's eyes she was nothing more than a walking cash machine. She'd ruined her life, consigned herself to a future of unhappiness and regret for what? – a pretty boy whose ego and sexual appetites far outweighed his common sense and feelings of loyalty. So she'd told him to go to London. She'd *insisted*. And he could stay there for all she cared. Tom, of course, could see he'd gone too far and had spent the next hour placating her, fawning over her, until eventually she'd granted his wish for a few days away.

Later on – when she was sitting alone and fretting – her father had arrived with a story which made her already frazzled senses reel. He was in a terribly fragile state, desperate to unburden his soul, and he'd used his daughter as one would use a priest in the confessional, only becoming silent when every ghastly detail had been held up to the light. He'd sobbed, and Grace – although stunned – had held him tightly, telling him repeatedly that they'd pull together and get through this.

And they would. Her parents – her father especially – had always been there for her. Now she'd return the favour, even though he'd committed an offence which flew in the face of all her medical ethics.

First off, it was imperative that they get rid of Mia Harvey, which was a great shame in a way. Grace was beginning to enjoy their flourishing friendship. Having another female there to give advice was a huge comfort. But Mia *was* the police and therefore a threat to her family's future wellbeing. Holding firm to her decision Grace snatched up her mobile phone and tapped out a number.

'Dad? Dad, listen, I've just had DS Harvey here.'

Silence, and then a hesitant, 'Why?'

'Don't worry, it's nothing to do with you. But we've got to stop her sniffing around, Dad. If I were you I'd cancel the play.'

'I can't, I'd be letting too many people down. And what good would it do, darling? We'll still have police everywhere.'

'But Mia's getting too close. She's becoming a threat.'

'No, we carry on as normal. Ali said—'

'Why are you listening to her?'

'Ali said we mustn't raise suspicions and she's right.'

'She's just looking to cover her own back. I thought you wanted my help.'

'I shouldn't have burdened you. I shouldn't have—' Fisher broke off, his voice cracking.

Grace tutted impatiently. 'Keep it together, Dad. Just listen to me. Cancel the play.'

'I can't.'

'You can. Cancel the play. Get Mia Harvey off our backs.'

'Good news, Charlie, the police have finished with the crime scene.'

'What?'

'They've finished. We can lay Noah Bailey to rest at last.'

As Reverend Fisher looked up from his desk, mobile phone still in his hand, Frank Lessing stepped back in shock. The vicar's face was like marble, his beard almost black in comparison.

Frank's stomach did a sickening somersault. 'When're you going to the doctor's, Charlie?'

'I'm all right.'

'Let me get you a couple of tablets.' Frank made for the door.

'Stop fussing, I said I'm all right.'

Fisher's harsh tone halted the verger in his tracks. The old man sat in the visitor's chair before the desk and regarded the vicar's hunched figure. Poor Charlie was carrying such a heavy load. And there was no need. Should he tell him? Should he put the man out of his misery?

'Charlie, you don't have to worry any more. I've seen to it. I've burned the evidence.'

Fisher glanced up, managed a wry smile. 'What are you talking about, you old fool?'

'The burial records for 2006. They're a pile of ash.'

'You've burned the records? Why?'

'To stop the police finding out. They'd tell the bishop …'

Fisher shook his head. 'I'm lost, Frank.'

'I know. That's why I did it. I could see what it was doing to you, Charlie. The guilt was weighing you down. It still is.'

'What *guilt*?' The word was spat out, causing Frank to reel back. 'You can't just dispose of church records. What were you thinking?'

'I burned them for you, Charlie. You put little Anna – God rest her soul – in Rufus Medley's plot and you shouldn't have done it. Rufus bought that plot in the sixties. But it was the only one left at the time on account of the flood water and you wanted the dear mite nearby. Good job Rufus had no family when he died, nobody to oppose the cremation. Then when the police arrived I thought you were worried they'd find out so I burned the records.' He gave a hasty shrug. 'I'm saying, Charlie, I understand why you did it – I'd have done the same – and I don't want you losing the parish for love of little Anna.'

A low chuckle started in Fisher's throat and quickly built into a full-blown belly laugh. Frank looked on in wide-eyed horror.

'Charlie?'

'Bless you, Frank, you've cheered me up.' Fisher considered his verger through eyes moist with emotion. 'And thank you for looking out for me. It's good to know you're on my side.'

'You're not angry?'

'Why should I be? You had my best interests at heart.'

The verger raised his brows. 'No more worrying then? No more sleepless nights?'

'Things of the past,' said Fisher, smiling.

'Good.' Frank eased himself out of the chair. 'Better get back to them council workers. They'll be leaning on their spades, having a quick fag. They need me behind them.'

'Before you go …' Fisher tried to swallow, but his mouth was too dry. 'I've decided to cancel the play. It's too much with everything else we've got on.'

'True enough,' said Frank.

'Perhaps you could tell Kate when you've got a minute. It'll be better coming from you. She won't be able to browbeat you over the phone.'

'I wouldn't bet on it.' Frank got to the door and turned back. 'Nice to see you smiling again, Charlie … really nice.'

As soon as he was alone Fisher's smile became a tormented grimace. If only a pilfered burial plot was all he had to worry about. *Would* the bishop have banished him for it? That thought had never once crossed his mind. His family had been devastated by the baby's death, his daughter inconsolable, and he'd selfishly held their feelings uppermost in his mind. Fisher uttered a humourless grunt. Perhaps he'd been undeserving of his calling even then. If not, he certainly was now.

No matter, he'd cancelled the play and hopefully put paid to that detective sergeant's interest in his family. He'd set the ball rolling … and only his Lord and Saviour could know where it might finally judder to a halt.

'John Lloyd reckons the murder weapon was made of ground stone and resin, with the gilt as a possible decoration,' said Wells, holding up the pathologist's report. 'What does that bring to mind?'

Mia said nothing; she wasn't even listening. Grace's scathing tone in the surgery had really upset her. What could have happened since Saturday to justify such a nasty response?

Jack, too, was lost in his thoughts. With a court case in the offing and being no nearer to proving his innocence, the young detective was starting to doubt Wells' certainty that the case would be withdrawn. Things weren't looking good.

'A garden ornament?' Nick ventured into the silence.

Wells pulled a face. 'Not many garden ornaments by the river, are there? Does that mean Rebecca was killed elsewhere and transported to that spot?'

'There're plenty of angels and stuff on the graves, sir. Baxter could've used one of them. Say it was dark, nobody around, he picks up the first thing to hand….'

Wells was unconvinced. 'So he's by the river with a heavily pregnant woman in mid-summer when it gets dark at what … ten, ten-thirty? They argue, he gets angry and wants to kill her. He goes through the gate in the fence to the churchyard, chips away at an angel that's part of a gravestone, and she just hangs around while he does it. No, mate, it doesn't make sense. And what were they doing there in the first place?'

'He could have hit her first, searched for the ornament while she was unconscious.'

'No, don't like it.'

'So the murder *must* have been committed somewhere else,' said Nick.

'I reckon so. But how did he get the body there? Only two ways, as far as I can see. Across the churchyard and through the gate. Or he'd drive to where the anglers park and carry her along the bank, which is what … a couple of hundred yards? I agree with you in one respect, Nick, it must have been dark when he got her there.'

Mia had been listening to the latter part of their deliberations whilst looking at Rebecca's photograph from the case notes. She imagined the river at night – eerie sounds of water lapping against the bank, rats and God-knows-what-else scuttling around in the undergrowth, owls hooting. Her skin crawled. Whatever had gone on, whatever she'd done to incite murder in the man, Rebecca hadn't deserved to be dumped without ceremony in such an inhospitable place. Mia just hoped that the girl was dead long before she reached her grave.

She said, 'Sir, the killer must have known that particular spot would be a safe bet because of the flooding.'

'Yes?' said Wells, wanting more.

'Would Baxter have known though? He's not familiar with Larchborough. I'm just thinking … could the killer be somebody local, somebody who *did* know it'd be OK to bury her there?'

Nick jumped in. 'Don't forget, Baxter came from Milton Keynes originally. Almost on the doorstep. He could know Larchborough like the back of his hand.'

'Let's find out,' said Wells. He reached for his phone, called Jim Levers on the front desk. 'Jim, any sign of Bryan Baxter's solicitor yet?'

A wicked chuckle travelled along the line. 'The gentleman's been here a while now, Paul, and he's getting more than a bit uppity. These legal types, eh? No patience. Don't know the meaning of the word.'

A terse rumble sounded in the background: the solicitor's response to Levers's flippant way with words.

Wells grinned. 'Tell him his time's come, Jim. Me and Nick'll see Baxter in number one. Quick as you like.'

CHAPTER 13

BAXTER'S SOLICITOR, MATTHEW Pincer – senior partner of Pincer, Sharples and Marriot – was a brash, sharp-suited extrovert as a rule. However, when Wells entered the interview room with Nick, he noticed that Pincer looked strangely deflated, was sitting half-turned in the wooden chair, his back towards his client. Baxter, suit crumpled and stubble darkening his usually smooth complexion, was mirroring the man's body language. They looked like two book-ends, minus the books.

Wells was intrigued. Had the bolshie solicitor decided that he hadn't a hope in hell of winning this particular battle? While Nick fed new tapes into the recording equipment, Wells nodded a curt greeting to the solicitor.

Pincer simply scowled in return. 'It took you long enough. I'm a busy man, you know.'

Wells didn't reply immediately. He took the chair opposite Baxter, his leisurely movements angering the solicitor no end. When Nick was settled, their notebooks at the ready, Wells said, 'You conferred with your client, Mr Pincer?'

'Of course.'

Wells shrugged. 'I gave you extra time to concoct your web of lies. Why are you moaning?'

Pincer sat back, narrowed his eyes. 'Don't let your dislike for me colour your views on my client, Chief Inspector. It's unprofessional.'

'You're the expert on unprofessional conduct, Mr Pincer, not me,' said Wells, smiling. 'And it's true, I don't like you ... but I like Mr Baxter even less. Toe rags who kill pregnant women get right up my nose for some reason.'

Throughout their caustic banter Bryan Baxter sat quivering, eyes fixed to a spot on the opposite wall. He shot forward now, surprising them all. 'But Becky wasn't pregnant. I keep telling you. That's not Becky you found. I didn't kill anybody.'

'The post-mortem report and Miss Crawford's dental records tell us otherwise, Mr Baxter. Sorry, mate, the evidence doesn't lie even if you do.'

'But she lost the baby. How many times do I have to say it?'

'DI Ford,' said Wells, folding his arms, 'what exactly did Mr Baxter say about the miscarriage?'

Nick consulted his notes. 'It happened – allegedly – around the Christmas before she disappeared. Isn't that right, Mr Baxter?'

'Yes,' he said, nodding eagerly. 'She lost the baby at eight weeks.'

Wells looked towards the ceiling while he considered those words. 'Let's see, Miss Crawford was eight months gone at the time of death so ... yes, she'd have been about eight weeks that Christmas.' He fixed his gaze on Baxter. 'Which means she either lied to you about losing it. Or, more likely, *you're* lying to us. Which is it, sir?'

Baxter cast Wells a desperate glance. 'Why would I lie? What could I possibly gain?'

Wells changed tack. 'You told us you'd seen Miss Crawford the day before her disappearance. Why did you say that?'

'Because it's true.'

'Didn't you notice her belly? Christ, even personal trainers look like whales at eight months.'

Pincer held up a hand. 'Stop hounding my client, Chief Inspector.'

'OK, let's leave Miss Crawford for the moment,' said Wells. 'Let's focus on her gymnasium.'

Baxter shared a sly look with his solicitor then stared at the table top, his mouth a grim line. Pincer was brushing imaginary flecks from his jacket sleeve, refusing to meet the DCI's gaze.

'Nobody got anything to say?' said Wells.

Pincer jutted out his chin. 'I need to consult with my client on that particular point.'

Wells snorted. 'A while ago you were bollocking me for keeping you waiting. Now you're saying you didn't have enough time to consult properly.'

'That's right.'

'So you haven't brought the papers relating to the sale.'

'No, I haven't.'

'What a surprise,' said Wells, grinning.

'Don't blame me,' said Baxter. 'I tried his number enough times, only he was too busy sipping champagne on somebody's luxury bloody yacht.'

'I'm entitled to a weekend off,' said Pincer.

Baxter rounded on him. 'Not when I'm paying you a small fortune. I needed you there on the end of the phone, Matt, but you let me down.'

'How did you know you'd need your solicitor, Mr Baxter?' asked Wells, frowning. 'You a psychic?'

'What? No, I …'

'OK, I'm bored now, and my bum's starting to get numb,' said Wells, shifting his weight in the chair. 'I'll tell you what happened, based on the evidence we have so far. Contrary to your previous statement, Mr Baxter, you and Miss Crawford weren't heading for the aisle. I'd go so far as to say you weren't even a couple in 2007. I think she met somebody else and got pregnant by him—'

'Becky wouldn't do that,' Baxter cut in. 'She loved me.'

Wells couldn't admit to having DNA evidence denying Baxter's paternity on account of the fact that the sample was taken without the man's consent. Matthew Pincer would think all his birthdays had come at once if that juicy fact ever came to light.

Ignoring Baxter's interjection, Wells carried on. 'We know from our enquiries that Miss Crawford wasn't seen in Nuneaton for the majority of that year. She'd left her home – a property she rented from you, Mr Baxter – in the January. She must have moved away to be with her lover. After all, her work was centred mainly around London. There was no need for her to stay in Nuneaton.'

'What about her gym?' asked Pincer.

'Yes, what about her gym?' said Wells, eyeing Baxter. 'We'll come back to that.'

'Hold on,' said Pincer, on safer ground now, 'if your hypothesis is correct then my client was out of the victim's life many months before her death. Why aren't you hounding her lover?'

'Because your client's told one lie after another, Mr Pincer, and innocent people with nothing to hide tend to stick to the truth.'

Pincer grinned. 'Or could it be you're just too lazy to look further, and Mr Baxter's become a convenient scapegoat?'

Nick had been quietly taking notes, but he said now, 'I conducted our first interview with your client, sir. I made it clear that we just wanted any information he could give about Rebecca Crawford. He could have said he hadn't seen her since that January. Instead he gave us an elaborate story about planning to propose over dinner the following July, just prior to her murder.'

Pincer lifted a shoulder. 'So? What makes you think he was lying?'

'Bloody hell,' said Wells, laughing. 'He was either out of her life, or they were a couple till her death. You can't have it both ways.'

It was then that Baxter let out a strangled cry. 'All right,' he said. 'I'll tell you the truth.'

Disdain showed in Pincer's eyes. 'I need to consult with my client, Chief Inspector. I demand you give us a few minutes.'

'OK, but make it quick.' Wells started to leave his seat, motioned for Nick to stop the tape machine.

'No … stay,' said Baxter. He aimed a furious look at his solicitor. 'You'll get me a stretch for murder, Matt, and I didn't do it.'

'Five minutes,' Pincer said to Wells.

'No,' Baxter yelled. 'Get out, Matt. I'm dispensing with your services. I'll be better off without you.'

'You can't do that.'

'I already have. Get out.'

While Matthew Pincer gathered together his papers, thrust them hurriedly into his briefcase, Wells told the recorder, 'Mr Pincer is leaving the building … and good riddance.' He grinned at the outraged man. 'Cheerio, sir, nice of you to pop in.'

Pincer slammed the door with much force as Wells said, 'Sure you want to carry on, sir? We can wait while you find another brief.'

'No,' said Baxter, his chin set firm. 'I want to get this over with.'

Wells straightened up and folded his arms. 'OK … spill.'

Baxter glanced at Nick, at the pen poised ready to write, and just when it seemed he might have reconsidered his folly, he said, 'I know the sale of the gym was unlawful, but it *was* mine to sell. You've got to believe me. I'll hold my hands up to that, but I'm not going down for a murder I didn't commit.'

'Understandable,' said Wells.

'Fourteen years, you said. I'd get fourteen years.'

Wells considered Baxter's stricken features, noted his trembling hands as they rested on the table, and his attitude softened a little. The man looked petrified.

'Help us catch Miss Crawford's killer, Mr Baxter, and we'll help you. That's all I can say for the moment.'

Baxter gave a brief nod. 'Where do you want me to start?'

'Wherever you think's relevant.'

Baxter ran a hand over his forehead, took in a juddering breath. 'I met Becky at a dinner party in 2005 … April, it was. We had so much in common, both of us from working-class backgrounds, both of us desperate to make something of our lives. We became a couple almost immediately. She admired my entrepreneurial skills, said she was aiming for a portfolio like mine. Becky enjoyed her job, but found the celebrity lifestyle too shallow. She wanted a career with more substance, albeit in the same field. So, to start her off, I gave her money to buy the gym.'

'Have you got proof it was your money?' Wells asked.

'Yes, my accountant has all the details. I'll instruct him to make my accounts available.'

'Thank you, sir, carry on.'

Baxter pulled at his tie, unfastened the top button of his shirt. He was showing signs of acute stress but, even so, seemed desperate to tell them everything. 'The gym needed a lot of work, then there was the equipment to buy, and I paid for all of it. I didn't mind. I had the money. I just wanted to make her happy. And she was. But everything changed towards the Christmas of 2006. She became unwell, didn't want anything to do with me sexually. Then she told me she was pregnant.'

'Did she say the baby was yours?' Wells asked.

Baxter slouched in the chair, shook his head. 'She admitted to having an affair, said it'd been going on for months.'

'Did she give you the father's name?'

'No, she just said he was an actor she'd met.'

'Did she carry on seeing him?'

'No, he'd got cold feet over the baby, apparently. Becky was considering an abortion, said she wanted to stay with me.'

'But she didn't have the abortion,' said Wells.

'Obviously not.'

'She was still living in Nuneaton at this time?'

'I thought so. I'd let her have one of my properties – rent-free, of course. I was in Switzerland for most of January, and when I came back all of her things were gone. She'd left me a note saying it'd never work and I'd thank her in the end.'

'Did she leave an address?'

'No, but I managed to reach her mobile. One of the few times she actually switched it on.'

'Funny way to do business, leaving her mobile off,' said Wells.

'Becky had a separate phone for her clients. I didn't know the number, never thought I'd need it. Anyway, I told her I'd go along with anything she wanted, but what about the gym? I'd invested a small fortune. I couldn't afford to just let the place rot. She said I could find a buyer and she'd sign any papers etcetera …'

'So why did you sell it behind her back?'

Baxter fixed Wells with an impassioned look. 'I found a buyer, had everything in place for the sale to be agreed. I just needed Becky's signature. She was supposed to meet me for dinner—'

'Oh yes, you were gonna shove that bloody great diamond on her finger,' Wells interjected.

'Check with the restaurant. I'm sure they keep records. They'll tell you I booked a table for two. They'll tell you I left without ordering. Becky *did* stand me up. I called her number. Many times. I felt angry and let down. I'd bent over backwards to be reasonable, and she was messing me about.'

'So how did you manage the sale?'

'I'd acted as her representative throughout the process. The buyers had never met Becky, never even spoken to her …' He shrugged. 'I simply signed for her. It was easy. The money was going back into my account anyway. Where was the harm?'

Wells heaved a sigh, threw a fractious glance at Nick. 'What do you think, mate?'

Nick lifted a shoulder. 'We're no nearer to finding the killer, are we, sir?'

'Precisely. And you, Mr Baxter, are no nearer to getting off a murder charge. One minute you're feeling angry and let down, the next Miss Crawford's in a makeshift grave. You said yourself she was messing you about.'

'No,' said Baxter, panic sucking the blood from his face. 'Get me one of those sketch artists. I'll tell you what he looked like.'

'What who looked like?' said Wells, frowning.

'The man … Becky's lover.'

'You've seen him? Why didn't you bloody well say? Why waste all afternoon on portfolios and Love's Young bloody Dream?'

'Because I wanted you to understand my actions with regard to the gym. Becky's murder's got nothing to do with me.'

'It'll have everything to do with you, mate, when you're banged up twenty-four-seven. *When* did you see him?'

'When we decided to put the gym on the market Becky came to Nuneaton to visit the estate agents, sign forms and all that. The baby was showing by then and she looked fantastic. *Glowing* … you know? I realized I was still in love with her. I had this stupid idea of begging her to give us another chance. I'd be a good father to the baby. But the opportunity never came up. So when she left, I followed her. I thought if I showed her I was willing to follow her anywhere, she'd reconsider. Anyway, she drove straight to her man. I didn't get the chance to make my grand gesture.'

Wells got to his feet, his chair squealing on the dusty floor tiles. He paced, rubbed his buttocks, breathed deeply. 'Describe Mister Mystery for us.'

Baxter swallowed, his Adam's Apple jumping wildly. 'He was tall. Dark-haired. Attractive.'

Wells snorted. 'Tall, dark and handsome. Very Barbara Cartland.'

'He had a beard … a thick beard.'

'Was he old? Young?'

'Hard to say. I only saw him from a distance. The beard made him look old. He could have been anything between twenty and fifty.'

'And he's an actor,' said Wells, pacing again. 'One of her famous clients?'

'I don't know.'

'You didn't recognize him from the telly?'

'I don't watch TV. Or films.'

Wells felt a bead of perspiration travel between his shoulder blades. He was frustrated. All they needed was one small definite fact about the lover and the rest would fall into place. Wells considered Baxter. The man looked worn out, his eyelids bruised and heavy like a toddler's when sleep was too close to deny.

'Listen, mate,' said Wells, sitting down again, 'you're gonna have to give us more than that. Did Miss Crawford give you *any* clue to this man's identity? Where was he from? Was he filming at the time? Come on, mate, give us *something*.'

'I don't think he'd worked for a while.'

'How do you know?'

'When Becky told me about the affair I was hurt and upset. I accused her of being a money-grabber, said he must have more money than me or she wouldn't have looked at him twice. She said I was wrong, he hadn't got any money.'

Wells was puzzled. 'What are you saying? He couldn't find work?'

'She just said he'd had only limited success but she loved the man, not the image.' Baxter lifted a weary shoulder. 'I wish I could tell you more.'

Wells shook his head. 'You ain't helping, mate. Now we're looking for a tall, dark, handsome actor who hadn't worked for some time. London must be crawling with the bastards.' He shifted his position, curled an arm around the back of his chair. 'OK, let's narrow it down. Which part of the city did you follow her to?'

'I didn't follow her to London, Chief Inspector.'

'Where then?'

'I thought I'd told you. I followed Becky here. I followed her to Larchborough.'

A *frisson* of excitement charged the air in CID as Wells recounted Bryan Baxter's testimony. The detectives had something to focus on at last.

'… so we're after a good-looking bearded actor with links to Larchborough,' Wells concluded. 'Stratton End, to be precise. That's where Baxter said they ended up.'

'Is he telling the truth though?' Jack ventured tentatively.

Wells cast him an amiable glance. 'He was fighting for his freedom in there, mate. He knew he was in the frame. So, yes, I reckon he was.'

'Where is he now, sir?'

'I sent him home. The bloke needed a wash. He stank – or somebody did, and it wasn't me,' said Wells, sniffing his armpits. 'He'll be back later to do the Photofit.'

Jack frowned. 'But he's still guilty under the Proceeds of Crime Act, surely, sir.'

'Credit me with a bit of sense, Jack. I told him to stay put for the foreseeable. I said if he did a runner he'd be liable for all expenses incurred in bringing him back. He's not going anywhere, trust me. Money's really important to that bloke. Anyway, if his accountant backs up the story then I'm buggered if I want to waste time on the paperwork. Baxter was getting his own money back. And who can blame him?'

Throughout Wells' account one name loomed large in Mia's mind; a name that clearly hadn't occurred to the others.

'Reverend Fisher,' she blurted.

'What about him?' said Wells.

'He's the killer.'

'Yeah, right,' scoffed Nick.

Mia peered earnestly at Wells. 'Fisher used to be an actor, sir. He had a lead part in *Temple's Crest* back in the eighties. He's tall, dark and handsome. He's got a beard. He's the vicar at St Matthew's, so he'd know better than most that Rebecca's body wouldn't be disturbed. And where's the church? Stratton End. Plus, he's knocking his wife about – a woman who's smaller than Kylie Minogue, for pity's sake – so it's not beyond the realms of possibility that he'd resort to murder if pushed.'

Wells looked as though he'd just checked his lottery numbers and all six matched. 'Bloody hell,' he muttered. 'OK, how's the best way to play this?'

'I'm going to the rehearsal tonight. Hopefully, he'll be there.'

'No, you're not,' said Jack. 'Sorry, Mia, but a call came in while you were getting my lunch. I forgot to give you the message.' He held up a yellow Post-It note.

Jack didn't dare leave the office to buy his own lunch – he only risked the loo when his bladder was full – for fear of bumping into Superintendent Shakespeare.

'What was the message?' Mia asked.

'The play's been cancelled. They didn't give a reason.'

'Who called?'

'Dunno. An old bloke.'

'Strange.' She told Wells about Grace Chamberlain's aggressive behaviour at the surgery.

'Did you do anything to make them suspicious?' asked Wells, frowning.

'Suspicious of what? I only went along for something to do.'

'OK, we'll get something in tomorrow's paper. *Man helping police with their enquiries*. It's not a complete lie. And if the reverend is our man, it might put his mind at rest.'

'You're not bringing him in?' asked Nick.

'I want something on him first. I don't relish Shakespeare's reaction if we arrest a vicar and it turns out he's got nothing to do with the case.' Wells focused on Mia. 'Are you sure he's battering his missus?'

'Positive, sir.'

'Any chance she'd testify?'

'Not in a million years.'

'She might have to, if that's all we're left with.' Wells started packing his briefcase. 'Right, my belly wants its dinner so we'll call it a day. In the morning we try to get something on Fisher. Though where we'll start is beyond me.'

'I know just the woman,' said Mia. 'I know where I can find her as well. She'll be my first job.'

A notice on its window told Mia that the Help The Aged shop opened at nine o'clock. It was now nine-fifteen and still the door was locked. Of course, with volunteers involved rules were not always adhered to. It was really annoying.

Cupping her hands to the glass door Mia peered into the bowels of the shop and saw that a light was on out the back. And then an elderly man came into view carrying a pile of clothing. Mia waved her arms in an effort to attract his attention. The man, depositing his load on the counter, gave her a dirty look, but made for the door nonetheless, flicking on lights as he went.

Pulling the door open a crack, he said 'What do you want?' with the air of a householder disturbed by one of those annoying coldcallers.

'Is Mrs Templeton here?'

'Who wants to know?'

Mia found her warrant card and held it up to the man. Taking his time, he read the details, compared the photograph to Mia's face.

'Bit young for a detective sergeant, lass,' he said, letting her in.

'Am I?'

'I was in the force myself. Uniformed division. Retired in eighty-six. Thirty years in Silver Street, I was. Loved the job.'

'Then you'll remember my Dad,' she said, forgetting her quest momentarily. 'Robin Harvey. Superintendent.'

The man grinned. 'Served under him. Real pleasure. Your Dad was a gent.'

'That's so nice of you, Mr …'

'Call me Harry,' he said, holding out a hand. 'What's Edna been up to – drugs or thieving?'

'Oh, Harry,' said Mia, her laugh strained.

'She's out the back,' he said. 'Edna irons. I put out. Go through.'

The back room was small and chaotic. A forty watt bulb threw deep shadows across the jumble, in the centre of which stood Edna Templeton at the ironing board.

'Who let you through?' was her opening line.

'Harry,' said Mia. 'I need a word, Mrs Templeton.'

'What about?'

'Reverend Fisher.'

Edna put down the iron and faced Mia, hands in the pockets of her wraparound pinafore. 'You told me you'd sorted him out.'

Picking her way through the jungle of black bags – Health and Safety would have a field day – Mia approached the old lady. 'I have to ask what you know about Reverend Fisher and why you think he's in need of saving.'

'Who can say, I have kept my heart pure; I am clean and without sin? Proverbs, chapter twenty, verse nine.'

'What does that mean, Mrs Templeton?'

'Read your Bible, you'll soon find out.'

'You asked me to help the vicar. I need to know why.'

'Charlie's lost his way.'

'Why? What's he done?'

'Evil men do not understand justice, but those who seek the Lord understand it fully. Proverbs, chapter twenty-eight, verse five.'

For God's sake! 'What's he done wrong, Edna?'

The little woman reared up. 'Charlie's only human. Sometimes we humans can't help ourselves.'

'Edna, I can't help unless you tell me what he's done.' The woman remained silent. 'OK, if that's the way you want it.'

Mia turned to go, was almost at the door when she heard, 'He's mixing with the wrong lot.'

'I'll need more than that,' she said, taking out her notebook.

Edna's shoulders sagged. Would her words be cast in stone? Would they condemn Charlie for ever?

Mia noted the distress in the old woman's eyes and softened her approach. 'Can we go somewhere more comfortable? I'll treat you to a nice cup of tea.'

'No bribes,' said Edna, panicking. 'We'll talk here or not at all.'

'OK.' Mia's pen was at the ready. 'You said he's mixing with the wrong lot. Who are they?'

'How should I know? Do you think I hang around street corners?'

'Reverend Fisher does though, obviously.'

'He's a good man. He's being tested,' said the old woman, close to tears. She pulled at the front of her pinafore, fighting her conscience. There was no way out of this. 'Charlie meets … *people* … in the street.'

'He's a vicar,' said Mia, thoroughly disappointed. 'He might be trying to help them. It's his job.'

'No, he's too … *friendly*. He never wears his dog-collar. He's up to no good, I know he is.'

'How long has this been going on?'

'A couple of years. He meets them around Stratton End. Various places. I live in Parsonage Street. Used to be a good area. Not any more. I go to bingo, walk back past the Hippodrome and I've seen him … with *them*. The first time his little granddaughter had only been in the ground a couple of months.' She shook her head, her mouth set in a disgusted *moue*.

'Can you describe any of these people?'

'Women mostly. Cheap sorts. Too much make-up. High heels they can barely walk in. One was smoking, swigging from a can of beer … and her ready to drop.'

Mia's stomach gave a tiny lurch. 'She was pregnant?'

'Ready to drop, like I said. God help the poor baby.'

'When was this?'

'A while back. Haven't seen that one for a long time.'

Mia fished Rebecca's photograph from her shoulder bag. 'Could this be her?'

'I'll not look at pictures,' said Edna, pushing the photograph away. 'I've had one heart attack already.'

Mia stifled a sigh. 'OK, you said he's friendly with these people. What does that mean?'

'What do you think? Charlie gets on with them but he knows he's doing wrong. He meets them where it's dark. Doesn't want to be seen. Anybody walks by he hides his face.'

'Has he ever seen you watching him?'

'Dear Lord, no,' Edna gasped. 'He'd die of shame.'

'Does he go off with these people?'

'I don't stick around to find out.'

Mia glanced over her notes. 'What do you think of Mrs Fisher?'

Edna seemed thrown by Mia's change of direction. 'What's Kate got to do with anything?'

Mia shrugged. 'Their marriage can't be that good if the vicar's resorting to prostitutes.'

'Pro…?' Mrs Templeton railed against the word. 'Wash your mouth out, lady.'

'What else could these girls be?'

The old woman was shaking her head. 'You've got the wrong end of the stick. They're not all women. There's men as well.'

'Prostitutes have pimps, Edna, and pimps are always men.'

'You ought to be ashamed.' The woman's face crumpled, tears glistened on her lids.

Mia wanted to comfort her but a small mountain of jumble stood between them. 'Why now? Why start worrying about him now?'

After a fair amount of eye-dabbing, Edna said, 'There's a battle raging in Charlie – good against evil – and it looks

188

like his conscience is winning at last. He's not himself. Hasn't been for a couple of weeks. It's eating him up from the inside. He needs help.'

A flutter of tension started in Mia's stomach. 'When did you notice this change in him? Around the time the body was found?'

She gave a reluctant nod. 'The straw that broke the camel's back. All them policemen tramping around his granddaughter's final resting place – it'd tell on anybody, wouldn't it? A soul can only take so much. Will you help him? Will you keep him out of harm's way?'

Mia couldn't help but smile as she put away her notebook. 'Oh, I'll keep him out of harm's way, Edna, don't you worry.'

'A paltry community service order?' said Mia. 'After what he did to you?'

'And two months suspended for the DVDs,' said Jack.

Mia had rushed back to the station, eager to share her news about the vicar. But she'd opened the door of CID on to a shocked silence. Jack had just received a call from his solicitor, Craig Jordan, informing him of the sentence awarded to Jason Perry at the youth's court appearance that morning. The whole team was appalled.

Jack uttered a scornful sigh. 'Jordan said I'll be up before the magistrates myself soon so the case can be submitted to crown court. I've had it, Mia.'

She gave Wells one of those looks he dreaded. 'But Perry's pleaded guilty to the attack, sir. The CPS should be dropping Jack's case.'

'Don't think I've forgotten Joey and Syed,' he growled. 'Jim Levers said he'd keep an eye on their arrest list. The minute an unexplained injury comes to light I'll have their bloody balls.'

'Why bother?' said Mia, sinking into her chair. 'We're on the wrong side of the thin blue line. We're expendable.'

'Huh, cheer me up,' Jack muttered.

'Who's pulled your chain?' said Nick, frowning at her.

'Nobody,' she replied, glaring back.

'Come on, kiddies, no bickering in front of Daddy,' said Wells. 'What did you find out about Holy Joe?'

Mia related all details of Reverend Fisher's nocturnal habits.

'So he's picking up these prozzies in the Hippodrome area,' Wells pondered.

Nick thumbed through his notes. 'Baxter said he followed Rebecca to the Crown and Cushion. That's about a block away from the Hippodrome.'

'It's looking good to me,' said Mia.

The DCI wasn't quite so sure. 'How does it help us?'

'He's hardly your average vicar, sir – unless modern theological courses have modules on how to negotiate with pimps.'

Wells chortled. He liked that. 'But we've only got the old lady's word.'

'I could get on to my girls,' said Mia. 'It's not every day they service a vicar.'

'I doubt he'd be broadcasting his day job but, OK, ask around. And be discreet.'

'We need Fisher's DNA,' said Nick.

Wells said, 'I want something on him first, something to warrant the test. We'll focus on him, but until we've got something concrete we keep an open mind.'

'There must be websites,' said Jack. 'You know, where actors can put photos and details for casting directors. Shall I see what I can find, sir?'

'Good idea,' said Wells. 'In the meantime we get anything we can on Holy Joe.'

'I'm going to see him,' said Mia.

'On what pretext? I don't want you storming in there heavy-handed.'

Mia held up a white envelope. 'I got this in the post. Mum's headstone's ready. I need the vicar to do a bit of a ceremony when it's put on.'

CHAPTER 14

'YOU GONNA BE all right with this?' said Nick.

Mia turned in the passenger seat of his car. 'With what?'

'The headstone.'

'Why shouldn't I be? Just hope there're no spelling mistakes.'

Wells had instructed Nick to drive Mia to the church. He'd prattled on about 'two pairs of eyes being better than one', but she knew he just wanted Nick to hold her hand.

'Maybe you should give it the once over first.'

Mia didn't even want to see the headstone on the grave. She was still experiencing feelings of abandonment. Ridiculous, really, at her age. Perhaps she needed counselling. She came to a sudden decision: she'd go through her mother's things tonight. Those few boxes were the block. Once they were sorted she'd be able to move on.

'Let's just get it over with,' she said. 'And don't let Fisher know we're on to him.'

In the car park Mia stomped off, leaving Nick to lock up. And she was almost at the church entrance when she heard, 'Morning, stranger. Long time no see.' It was Frank Lessing.

'Not my fault,' she countered with a smile. 'Why was the play cancelled?'

'Charlie's heavy schedule. Something had to go.'

'Pity it was the play.'

Frank shrugged. 'He's been overdoing it lately.'

'Yes, I heard he's been a bit under the weather.'

Nick arrived then, held out a hand which Frank shook warmly. Since his heart-to-heart with Charlie, Frank could afford to be hospitable towards the police.

'My mum's headstone's ready, Frank. Is Reverend Fisher about?'

'In his office.'

The church's interior was cool, its atmosphere sublime. Or it would have been if an almighty row hadn't been going on in the vicar's office. Sounds of a scuffle reached the detectives. Raised voices overlapped in a tangle of hostility. Nick threw open the office door to be confronted with a scene so surreal they were dumbstruck.

Charlie Fisher was astride his wife on the floor. He had her wrists in a tight grip. He was pulling her about and yelling. Kate was whimpering and begging him to stop. Both were unaware of the detectives at the door. Nick acted swiftly. He grasped Fisher's upper arms and yanked him to a neutral corner.

'This isn't how it looks,' Fisher spluttered.

'Tell that to the fucking magistrates,' said Nick, feeling for his handcuffs.

Mia hurried to help Kate. Those old bruises she'd spotted days ago were now overshadowed by angry red marks from this new attack. Mia pleaded with her to sit up, but the woman refused to budge.

'I think she's in shock,' Mia told Nick.

'Call the paramedics,' he said, hauling Fisher to his feet.

The vicar became hysterical. 'No … no paramedics….'

'Kate, sit up,' Mia coaxed.

The woman was in the foetal position, clutching her stomach and groaning. Mia didn't know what to do.

'Kate, tell me where it hurts.' Mia threw an angry look at the vicar. 'Did you punch her stomach, Reverend?'

'No,' Fisher cried. 'I was trying to help her.'

'Yeah, right,' said Nick.

'Honestly, I'd never hurt my wife. I'm trying to *help* her.'

As Mia got through to the emergency services Fisher's shoulders slumped. He knew he was beaten.

'She wants her drugs,' he said, his voice surprisingly strong. 'They're in my pocket.'

'She's got a medical condition?' said Nick, searching the vicar's pockets.

Fisher stared down at his squirming wife and there was so much love, so much *benevolence*, in his eyes that Mia was momentarily taken aback.

'She's dependent on them,' he said, his voice cracking. 'Kate's an addict.'

'When did your missus start using?' asked Wells.

Reverend Fisher was affronted. 'I don't think *using* is—'

'Just answer the question.'

The vicar gave a nod of acquiescence. 'Soon after our granddaughter's death. Kate was suffering badly. Losing the baby and having to witness our daughter's tremendous pain, it was …' He shook his head. 'Kate couldn't handle it. She was depressed, found it hard to function. As the weeks progressed even getting out of bed was an effort. Her doctor prescribed antidepressants but they didn't work.'

Fisher was installed in one of the interview rooms with Wells and Nick. The tape machine was redundant. They wanted the full story before deciding which – if any – charges should be brought against him.

He'd taken off his dog-collar and was slumped in the chair, bathed in sweat, clothes askew, rubbing at his wrists occasionally. And although he'd protested all the way to the station Fisher was now calmly accepting of his fate. He was in their hands. He'd confess all. It was a huge relief.

'Then what?' said Wells. 'Did the GP change her to something stronger?'

Fisher shook his head. 'Kate didn't want anything stronger. She didn't want the antidepressants. It was our daughter who persuaded her to take them. Looking back now, I wish to God she hadn't.'

'Why?'

'They were highly addictive.' Fisher let out a scornful laugh. 'Doctor's don't tell you that, do they? They don't tell you people with certain personalities should steer clear. Well, Kate was one of those people. She quickly got used to the dosage; needed more and more to achieve the same effect. We didn't know, of course. She was good at hiding it.'

'Your daughter's a doctor – why didn't she cotton on?'

'Grace was hardly functioning herself. She'd just lost the baby, and she had … *issues* … with her husband.'

'Oh yes, he'd talked her into being sterilized.'

Fisher regarded Wells coolly. 'You seem to know an awful lot about my family.'

'It's my job to know, vicar. When did you suspect your missus was addicted?'

'I didn't. Not at first. She started to change. Slowly. Small changes. Hardly noticeable. She'd argue over the slightest thing when before we were always in accord. She became too rigid – you know, everything in its place, that sort of thing – when she'd always been so lackadaisical—'

'What did you do?'

'Told her to relax, not to sweat the small stuff. Only she wouldn't listen.'

Wells sat back, folded his arms. 'Is that when you started hitting her?'

'What?' said Fisher, clearly staggered. 'How could you think such a thing?'

'Don't bother denying it, mate. DS Harvey's seen the bruises.'

'I've never hit my wife. I've *restrained* her. I've had to. When I'm late with her pills she gets quite … *emotional*. She lashes out at me. I have to stop her from going too far. She could hurt herself.'

Wells took a small brown bottle from his briefcase and put it on the table. Fisher's eyes never left it.

'Amphetamines, Vicar. Found in your pocket by DI Ford. Where did they come from?'

Fisher's gaze remained on the bottle. 'I bought them.'

'Who from?'

'Some chap I met on the street.'

'Which street?'

'Vicarage Street.' He tried a smile. 'Ironic, don't you think?'

'That's in Stratton End? Near the Hippodrome Cinema? You've been trawling that area a lot, haven't you, vicar?'

Fisher's haggard features paled. 'How did you know?'

'You've been spotted, mate. We thought you were picking up prostitutes, but all the time you were buying drugs for your missus.'

'Prostitutes? I wouldn't—'

'When the doctor's tablets stopped working you thought you'd get stronger stuff, keep her more manageable.'

'No,' he yelled. 'Kate's doctor stopped the prescription. She was going back too often to have it filled. He said it was best if she found other ways of coping. He suggested bereavement counselling.'

'You must have agreed, surely,' Wells pressed. 'You could see the pills were doing more harm than good.'

'No, I couldn't. Not then. I knew Kate was suffering. We all did. But I'd no idea it was because of the medication. Then I found packets of over-the-counter stuff … strong stuff … hidden in all sorts of places. I confronted her and she broke down, told me everything. She begged me for help, said she couldn't cope on her own any more. I started buying pills off the street. I run a soup kitchen in the winter; I knew where to go. We thought we'd keep her stable … functioning … and then gradually wean her off.'

'We?' said Wells. 'Was your daughter in on this?'

Fisher looked horrified. 'Grace knew nothing about it. She wouldn't have agreed.'

'Who then?'

A haunted look came to Fisher's face. He started chewing on the hairs around his bottom lip. 'I'd rather not say.'

'You're gonna have to, mate.'

The vicar stared at Wells, saw that a stalemate had been reached. 'My sister-in-law. Alison Parker. She was helping me … helping Kate.'

'Alison Parker from the hospital? The psychologist?'

Fisher nodded. 'I had to confide in somebody. My wife has always been close to Ali, and with her clinical expertise … I thought she'd be the best person to approach. But Ali's completely innocent in all this. She was just advising me on the best way to handle things.'

'Just advising you?' Wells gave a harsh laugh. 'She didn't do a very good job.'

'She was trying her best.'

'Really? Anyway, not to worry, we'll see what she's got to say.'

Fisher's fear-filled eyes widened. 'Please don't talk to her.'

'Why? Frightened you'll never get your leg over again?'

The vicar stared at the DCI in disbelief. 'What are you suggesting?'

Wells had a vicious smile on his lips. 'You've been shagging your sister-in-law for a while now, haven't you, vicar? Don't bother denying it – you've been seen.'

'How dare you.'

Those words were uttered through Fisher's bared teeth; anger replaced the fear in his eyes. Adrenalin pumped through Wells' system. Was this the real Charlie Fisher, at last?

'Not nice to be found out, is it? Especially when you're a vicar and a load of decent people look up to you.'

'Ali was helping her sister,' said Fisher, fiercely annoyed. 'And if you dare to suggest anything else, I'll sue. I swear to God.'

In an effort to keep this new momentum going, Wells said, 'It'll make quite a story: local vicar keeps wife in drugged stupor, leaving him free to shag her sister. The reporters'll have a field day.'

Fisher struck the table with his fist; a move so unexpected both detectives jumped. 'We were helping my wife,' he yelled, those teeth on view once more.

'You were feeding her habit,' said Wells, his own voice rising. 'How was that helping her?'

Those words clearly hurt. Fisher's anger faded in a heartbeat and the mild-tempered man was back. He slumped in the chair, the shake of his head a helpless gesture. 'We thought we could cope, but the more drugs I bought, the more Kate wanted. And if she didn't get them all hell broke loose. It was easier to simply give her what she wanted.' He shot Wells a pleading look. 'I've been in mental torment for so long. Life's unbearable. I'm living on my nerves the whole time, frightened she'll make a scene in front of people, frightened I'll be caught buying the drugs …'

'You weren't helping your wife this morning,' said Nick. 'You wanted to hurt her. She was begging you to stop.'

Wells rested a hand on Nick's arm. 'Try to remember, mate, that when you're living on your nerves like the Reverend here, there's times when violence is the only answer.'

'No,' said Fisher, hotly.

'We've had plenty of bastards like you in that chair, mate. First one with a dog-collar though.'

'Makes it worse really,' said Nick.

'I know it looks bad,' said Fisher.

'Bloody right, mate.' Wells considered the man for a moment. 'Why didn't you get your missus some proper help? Why let it get to this?'

Fisher focused on Wells, all emotion spent. 'Pride, Chief Inspector. Pride and avarice. I love my job … my *calling*. I love my church. I love being the centre of people's devotion. I don't want to lose any of it.'

'How would doing the right thing jeopardize your job?'

'It'd been going on too long. I was in too deep. My bishop would never have condoned what I'd done.'

'Then why do it in the first place?'

Fisher gave Wells an earnest look. 'You had to be there at the beginning. Everything wasn't all black and white. I looked through the grey and thought I was doing the right thing. I really did think I could wean Kate off the drugs.'

'You're a fool then. Hardened professionals don't always succeed.'

Fisher nodded. 'It's been a hard lesson to learn.'

'Hard lesson to bloody learn.' Wells leant across the table, his face mere inches from Fisher's. 'You've got a temper – we've seen it here this afternoon. You're partial to a bit of nooky on the side – forbidden fruits. You come across all holier-than-thou, but you're nothing, vicar … worse than nothing.'

Nick's mobile vibrated in his pocket. He retrieved it and read the message, showed it to Wells who nodded. Fisher was staring down at his hands.

Wells reached for his briefcase, took out Rebecca's photograph and laid it on the table. 'Tell us how you knew her.'

Fisher looked at the photograph and gave a shrug. 'I've never seen her before in my life. Who is she?'

'Rebecca Crawford – that bag of bones we found in your church grounds. Rebecca was seeing an actor in Larchborough around the time of her death. Care to comment, vicar?'

Fisher shrugged. 'I'm not an actor.'

'You used to be.'

'Yes, years ago, in another life.'

'Very much in *this* life, I'd say. And this actor we're talking about had a beard just like yours. Sort of narrows it down, don't you think?'

Fisher managed a smile. 'This is absurd. I wasn't the only actor with a beard.'

'True. And they were all living here at the time. You could hardly walk down the high street without tripping over one.'

'You're clutching at straws,' said Fisher, trying to hold on to that smile.

'We're gonna need a DNA sample, vicar.'

'Why?'

'If you've read the papers you'll know that Miss Crawford was heavily pregnant when she died—'

'Dear God, it gets better – you think I fathered her child as well?'

'You can give us the sample today, or we can apply to the courts. It's up to you.'

Fisher threw up his hands. 'Why not? My career's finished. Take your sample. And I want a solicitor before I say another word.'

'Don't blame you, mate.'

'What happens now?'

'You'll be cautioned and taken to the cells.'

Fisher's jaw dropped. 'You're keeping me here?'

'What did you think we were gonna do … treat you to a few days in Spain?'

'You can't.'

'We can. We can keep you for twenty-four hours without charge. And while you're partaking of our hospitality, vicar, we'll get the DNA result back – although we might have to treat the technician to a holiday to achieve it – and then the excitement really starts.' Wells grinned. 'You're not the only one who loves his job.'

'You're making a big mistake,' said Fisher, his expression stony as the detectives made to leave.

Wells stared down at him. 'How come you haven't asked about your missus? Don't you care?'

'Of course. Why do you think I'm so eager to get home?'

'You won't find her there. She's still at the hospital.' Wells raised his brows, gave Fisher a withering look. 'That text we had just now … it was from DS Harvey. Your missus had to have her stomach pumped. Seems *somebody* gave her an overdose.' Wells tapped him on the shoulder. 'You've got a lot of explaining to do, vicar.'

'He didn't turn up?'

'No, sir,' said a dejected Jack. 'Uniformed kept a watch for over an hour.'

'Christ …' Wells threw his briefcase on to his desk, pulled off his jacket and hurled that alongside it. 'So much for our bloody informant.'

Nick sank into his chair. 'Perhaps Perry got the time wrong.'

'Uniformed couldn't hang around all day. They'll be in the shit for wasting resources as it is.'

'It was worth a try,' said Jack, the words meant for Nick. 'Anyway, how'd it go with the vicar?' Wells filled him in, making much of the man's moments of temper. 'Sounds like a result, sir. Shame about his wife though. Will she be OK?'

'We'll know more when Mia gets back,' said Wells, settling at his desk. 'What you been up to?'

Jack gathered together a pile of papers and held them up. 'These are off various actors' websites – *Cattlemarket.co.uk*, mostly.'

'Any luck with Rebecca's address?'

'No, I've tried all the usual – tax office, social services, electoral roll. I got nothing.'

'Maybe she hadn't got her own place,' said Nick. 'She could have been living with somebody.'

'I bloody hope not,' said Wells. 'If Fisher's our man she'd have needed a place of her own. I know his missus was out of it most of the time, but I reckon she'd have noticed another woman in the house.'

Mia burst in then. 'Sir, you'll never guess who I've just seen in Accident and Emergency.'

'Elvis?' he said, bringing a laugh from Jack.

'Jason Perry. They were sending in the crash team when I left.'

'No wonder he wasn't in the park,' said Nick.

Jack looked petrified. 'Is he all right?'

'I couldn't find out. Nobody would tell me anything.'

'Christ, Mia, he'd better be, I don't want to go down for murder.'

There were framed photographs taken in happier times. A few ornaments that Mia had bought during school trips. Hair brushes. A can of hairspray. A selection of toiletries. Those sparse items were arranged on the mattress in Mia's second bedroom.

She reached for one of the photographs. It had the three of them – Mia and her parents – outside the ruins of a Welsh castle. They were laughing, as though the person behind the camera had just told a really hilarious joke. Mia and her father were shown with their arms linked while Barbara stood a small distance apart; on the periphery – as always – but happy just to be there. How Mia now wished she'd grasped her mother's hand in the seconds before the shutter fell.

Barbara's outfit in the photograph – green sweater and navy blue slacks – was immaculate. She'd always dressed well, had always cared about her appearance; all of which made sorting through the tired and over-washed clothes brought from the nursing home in a black plastic sack all the more distressing.

Mia had initially thought of taking them to a charity shop, but the more she delved into that sack, the more shocked she was by their condition. Why had she not noticed how shabby everything was during her weekly visits? Mia tried to remember a time when she'd gone through Barbara's wardrobe and chest of drawers, and couldn't bring to mind one single occasion in the past couple of years. What must the carers have thought of a daughter happy to leave her mother in virtual rags?

Mia stuffed the clothes back into the sack, sniffing back tears as she did so. The ornaments could go to a charity shop. The photographs she'd keep. Everything else could be binned.

Guilt ate her up. She'd spent most of the day judging others: Reverend Fisher and Jason Perry, to name but two. How dare she do that when she was so far from perfect herself?

Mia was lugging the sack along the hallway – she'd dump it by the outside bins in the morning – when the doorbell rang. Thinking it might be Nick, and quite pleased if she was honest, Mia wiped her eyes and opened the door to find Grace Chamberlain staring back.

She gave Mia a weak smile. 'Can I come in?'

'How did you know where I live?'

'I phoned the police station, said I was a long-lost friend …' Grace averted her gaze. 'I'll understand if you want me to go.'

'Don't be silly.' Mia stood aside, allowed her to step into the narrow hallway. 'The living room's on the left. Mind that sack.'

Coronation Street was on the TV. Mia switched off the set and sat in an armchair while Grace perched on a corner of the sofa. The atmosphere was fraught, neither knowing what to say.

Mia jumped to her feet. 'Can I get you a coffee?'

'No thanks, I won't stay long.'

'Grace, I can't discuss your dad's case, if that's why you're here.'

'Actually, I came to give you this.' She retrieved a piece of paper from her handbag and offered it across.

It was a list of symptoms and a likely prognosis written in Grace's untidy hand. It told Mia that Jason Perry was in the latter stages of liver disease brought on by his excessive drug and alcohol abuse.

Mia sank into the armchair. 'So his bruises are a symptom.'

Grace nodded. 'And nothing at all to do with any fight he might have had.'

'He's going to die?'

'He's fighting for his life even as we speak.'

'Good.' Mia folded the paper. 'Can I keep this?'

'Of course. And I'll testify in court if I have to. I'll do anything you want.'

'Oh yes? And what do you want in return?'

Grace's colour deepened. 'Dad came to see me on Sunday. He told me everything … about Mum … about how he'd been buying drugs … When you came to the surgery I was looking on the Internet for rehab clinics. I wasn't thinking straight. I just wanted you gone. I'm sorry.'

'Have you spoken to your dad?'

'They let him phone me this afternoon.'

'Then you'll know he's in line for a murder charge.'

Grace sprang forward. 'But he couldn't hurt anybody. It goes against everything he believes in.'

'He's hurt your mother enough times.'

'No, he hasn't. You know how aggressive addicts can get when they're after a fix. Dad's had to restrain her at times to protect himself, but he's never willingly hurt her.'

'You're beginning to sound like him.'

'It's the truth.'

'The investigation won't stop just because you're protesting his innocence, Grace. The evidence is stacked against him.'

'What evidence? You can't have evidence because Dad didn't kill anybody.'

Mia couldn't help but feel for the girl. 'I'm really sorry. I worshipped my dad as well. It must be hard to suddenly realize he's only human.'

'This is going to kill him,' said Grace, giving her a pleading look.

'So? He killed Rebecca.'

'But he never even met the girl.'

'You can't know that.' Mia sat back, made herself comfortable. This was going to be a long evening. 'We've had more than one testimony – from people who've known your dad for years – that his behaviour changed when Rebecca's body was found.'

'I know, but think about it. He was breaking the law almost daily and suddenly he'd got police officers crawling all over the grounds. He was scared it'd all come out.'

There was one thing Mia couldn't fathom. 'Why are you defending him? You're a doctor. Aren't you really angry he turned Kate into an addict?'

'He's a good man. He did what he thought was best.'

Mia snorted. 'He fits the profile of our murderer, Grace, and there's nothing you can say to change that.'

'Some friend you've turned out to be,' said the girl, grabbing her bag.

'I'm not your friend,' Mia snapped back. 'You made that clear enough on Monday.'

'I shouldn't have come.'

Mia rushed to her feet as Grace headed for the door. 'Don't go. Please. Let's not part like this.'

The girl stopped on the threshold, her head bowed. She turned slowly, showed Mia the grief that was spoiling her lovely face. 'Will you help us?'

Mia led her back to the sofa. 'You need a drink. How about some wine?'

'No, thanks, I'm driving. Have you got any tea?'

'Wait there.'

Mia was filling the kettle when Grace came into the kitchen.

'How's Kate?' she asked, tossing teabags into the mugs.

Grace was studying a picture on Mia's wall calendar: Loch Ness in the sunshine. 'Stable, but she was still unconscious when I left so I don't know *why* she overdosed, or *how* …' She dashed across the tiny space, stared at Mia's profile. 'Dad *was* trying to help her.'

'That what he told you on Sunday?'

'Yes, and I believe him. He's the kindest man I know.'

'Pretty stupid as well.'

'Haven't you ever made a mistake?'

'Plenty,' was Mia's quick response. She was thinking of her mother, conveniently abandoned in the nursing home. 'We all make mistakes. We're all capable of being selfish too, hurting our loved ones without even realizing. Your dad's no different, Grace.'

Mia made the tea and carried the mugs through to the living room, leaving her to follow. Setting them on the coffee table, she said, 'Did you know about his affair with Alison Parker?'

Grace was reaching for her drink when those words stopped her. 'Don't be ridiculous. What gave you that idea?'

'Haven't you seen the way they act together?'

She gave a humourless laugh. 'You've known us for all of five minutes and think you've got everything sussed.'

Mia took her mug and calmly sat down. 'Sometimes it takes an outsider to see the true picture.'

She was expecting Grace to storm out again and was surprised when she stayed seated, hands shielding her face. A moment later those hands came down, revealing eyes made black by tear-ravaged mascara. 'If he hadn't been with me when my baby died…. Oh God, Dad's helped me so much. He's *saved* me. And now I must save him. I must do the right thing … however painful.'

Mia joined her on the sofa, offered a tissue to use on those eyes. 'Then leave us to do our job. If he's innocent, we'll know, I promise.'

'He *is* innocent.'

'Oh sweetie, you can't know that.'

'I'm certain of it … because I know who the real killer is.'

In the space of a second Grace had leapt to her feet and was pacing the small room – eyes wide, mouth stretched into a bewildered O – like a woman possessed. She was hyperventilating and Mia grabbed her arms, brought her to a standstill, shook her violently.

'What have I done?' she said, struggling to escape Mia's grip. 'Oh God, what have I done?'

'It's OK … you're OK.' Mia sat her down, dropped the tissue box on her lap. 'You're safe here. You can talk. You can tell me anything. There'll be no repercussions.'

The girl had started to tremble. Mia made her sip some tea and then returned to the armchair. Best to give her some space.

Grace fixed her with a determined look. 'My parents have always supported me, always *loved* me. I can't let them down now … not for a shallow self-absorbed man who doesn't even know the meaning of the word.'

This time it was Mia's eyes that widened. 'Are you talking about Tom?'

'He's never loved me. He only loves my money.'

'Grace, are you saying Tom killed Rebecca Crawford?'

'He bedded her for months. He was the father of her baby….'

'And he killed her? Is that what you're saying?'

Grace gave a slow nod. 'Yes, Mia, that's exactly what I'm saying.'

CHAPTER 15

'OK, KIDDIES, LISTEN up,' said Wells, replacing his telephone receiver. 'Tom Chamberlain's been apprehended and the Met have allocated two officers to drive him back here, pronto. Estimated time of arrival 10 a.m.'

'He was at the address Grace gave me then?' said Mia.

Wells nodded. 'Playing 'hide the sausage' with a tasty Page Three girl, by all accounts.'

Mia had phoned Wells with Grace's revelations a little after nine o'clock the previous evening. Wells immediately contacted the Metropolitan Police where plans were put in place to intercept Tom at a downmarket hotel in Soho – his usual hideaway when visiting the capital, according to Grace. The tasty 'model' had caused quite a rumpus, apparently, when uniformed officers burst into room number twenty-seven and hauled Tom from beneath her heavily tanned and unbelievably taut body.

Grace had spent the night at Mia's flat. Once she'd started to confide, her stream of words proved difficult to stem. Therefore Mia had had no choice but to act as confessor, nurse and big sister all rolled into one until the small hours. As soon as the surgery had opened Mia phoned to tell them Grace wouldn't be going in and then dropped her home on her way to the station.

This was good news for Reverend Fisher. He was released from police custody at first light; albeit with the caution still in place should he harbour any ideas of absconding. Not that that was likely. The vicar had rushed straight to the hospital where Kate, awake but still groggy, had been calling for him continually.

Jack was oblivious to all of this. He'd been summoned to Superintendent Shakespeare's office first thing. And he now entered CID to a smattering of applause. They knew he'd soon be off the hook.

'Well?' said Mia, all smiles.

He gave a despondent shrug and made for the coffee percolator.

'Come on, mate, tell us,' said Wells.

'Jason Perry died at two o'clock this morning,' he said.

'That'll please Valerie Clarke,' said Mia.

'Couldn't have happened to a nicer bloke,' said Nick.

'But what about his kid?' said Jack, taking the coffee to his desk with all the vitality of an anaemic sloth.

'Oh yeah, who's gonna teach him the drugs business now his old man's gone?' said Nick, frowning. 'I know … the next lowlife his skanky mother hitches up with.'

'What did Shakespeare say about your case?' said Wells, impatiently tapping his pen on the desk. 'When's it gonna be dropped?'

'Perry's medical notes are going over to CPS, sir. Craig Jordan should be giving me the all clear later today.'

'Good. So cheer up, you twat.'

'It's a shame for Perry's little boy,' said Mia, 'but at least your Jamie won't have to visit you in prison.'

'He was only nineteen,' said Jack, still in shock.

'And it's his own fault he's dead,' said Nick. 'Christ, Jack, don't waste your energy.'

Wells clapped his hands together smartly. 'OK, you can all say a prayer for Jason bleedin' Perry in the lunch break. Till then we get on with some work.'

He was bringing Jack up to date with unfolding events in the murder case when the detective suddenly let out a loud whoop. He was holding up a sheet of paper he'd printed off yesterday from the *Cattlemarket* website.

It showed a publicity shot of Tom Chamberlain.

With a very fetching beard.

It was a very nervous Tom Chamberlain who sat in interview room number one, listening intently to Scott Brooks, the duty solicitor brought in less than an hour before. As Wells breezed in, followed closely by Mia and a uniformed officer, the solicitor reared up, ready to start his patter. But Wells beat him to it.

'I'll come straight to the point,' he said. 'Tom Chamberlain, I'm arresting you for the murder of Rebecca Crawford on a date unknown in the summer of 2007.' He skirted the table, wielding a cotton bud at Tom's fraught features. 'Open your mouth, mate. I want a DNA sample.'

The solicitor put up a hand. 'I can't allow that. My client has rights.'

'So did Rebecca Crawford.'

Wells handed the sample to the uniformed officer for immediate delivery to the Crime Laboratory while Mia dealt with the tape machine. By the time all were seated Tom still hadn't uttered a word.

Wells put the publicity shot on the table for him to see. 'That you, sir?'

'Yes.'

'When was the photograph taken?'

'Not sure – about three years ago.'

'Good, so you had that beard in the summer of 2007.'

'I think so, yes.'

'Chief Inspector,' said Brooks, 'you've got to give me something to work with here. I've been offered hardly any details as to why Mr Chamberlain's been brought in.'

Wells sat back, regarded the man with irritation. 'I said when I came in. Weren't you listening?'

'But how do you know my client killed Miss Crawford? On whose evidence?'

'His missus,' said Wells.

'Grace?' said Tom, looking agog. 'She told you I've killed somebody?'

Wells nodded. 'She said you'd been having it off with Miss Crawford for a good many months. She said you got the girl up the duff.' He shot the solicitor a repugnant glance. 'I suppose that put a spoke in his wheel, Mr Brooks. He wouldn't want pregnant mistresses littering his road to success.'

Tom shot forward. 'I've never met anybody called Rebecca Crawford. Grace is trying to get back at me. I left under a bit of a cloud on Sunday and I should have been back yesterday. She's teaching me a lesson.'

Wells folded his arms, aimed his pointed stare at Tom. 'And why would she do that, sir?'

'She's possessive. I'm kept on a really tight leash.'

'Doesn't stop you sniffing around anything with a pulse,' said Mia. She couldn't help herself; he was everything she hated in a man.

'Could we stop the personal jibes and let my client have his say?' said Brooks.

'Good idea,' said Wells, giving Mia a warning look.

Tom pulled at the neck of his polo shirt, all the while meeting the DCI's expectant gaze. 'It isn't easy living with my wife. She's so incredibly needy. I have to go up to London regularly for auditions, screen tests … It's a relief to get away. I really earn those trips. I have to literally beg for permission to go. I'm more like a pet than a husband.'

'My heart bleeds for you, mate, but get to the bloody point.'

Tom lifted a shoulder. 'I'm trying to explain what my marriage is like and why I … sometimes look for a little fun elsewhere. We all need our egos bolstered. But I couldn't kill anybody. That's obscene.'

'So Grace is making it up?' said Mia. 'Like she made up the story of you forcing her into being sterilized?'

'I didn't *force* her,' said Tom, his laugh hollow. 'You can't force Grace to do anything. The sterilization was her idea.'

'As if I'd believe that. She spent hours last night telling me how much she wanted a baby.'

'That's right, she did,' said Tom, desperate to explain. 'Look, Charlie and Kate have always spoiled her. Everything Grace wanted Grace got. Well, she wanted a baby and then it was taken away. She was affronted. How dare God do that. For the first time in her life she was experiencing loss and it was bloody awful. So she made sure it'd never happen again.'

Mia was shaking her head. 'I don't believe you.'

'Check her medical records. Find the surgeon. He'll tell you. My wife's a control freak, Mia, but our baby's death was beyond her control. And I've been suffering for it ever since.'

Mia laughed. '*You're* the control-freak, Tom. You were scared to let her have another baby in case she decided to give up work and you'd have to get off your backside and actually start earning some money. You're a parasite.'

'Personal jibes,' said Brooks, pointing a finger.

'I'd love to earn some money,' said Tom, his colour rising. 'But Grace won't move back to London. How can I get work stuck here?'

Mia tutted. 'That old excuse again. Move there yourself if you're so desperate to get a job.'

'I'd love to. I haven't got a penny, but when I'm slumming it in London I'm far happier than I've ever been in that monstrosity we laughingly call a home.'

'Then do it.'

'I can't. Every time I threaten to go Grace loses it, says she'll kill herself, kill *me* … She's unhinged. She gets it from her mother. Kate's always tottering on the edge, if you ask me.'

Mia snorted. 'And yet you married Grace. Out of all the scores of women who throw themselves at you, you chose her. Why, Tom? What first attracted you to the very well-off and highly successful doctor?'

211

Tom fell back in his chair, seemed almost to have given up hope of ever winning over the pithy detective. 'Grace hadn't got anything when we first met at university. But she was beautiful and uncomplicated. It was love at first sight. Her parents lived in London then – Charlie had just finished his theological course – and I'd stay with them most weekends. We all got on so well that when Grace chose St Bart's for the surgical part of her training we moved in with them. I'd been studying history – I'd planned to lecture – but I changed course after I met Charlie. I'd always wanted to act and he inspired me to take it up as a profession.

'Everything was fine for ages. Grace got a practice, Charlie was given a curate's post, and I was getting small parts in obscure dramas on satellite channels. Life was exciting. We got married in Charlie's church, had our reception in a local pub. Not very romantic, but we didn't care. We were in love.'

'I hope there's a point to this story,' said Wells, looking at his watch.

'Things couldn't have been better,' Tom went on hurriedly. 'But then Charlie was offered St Matthew's. His own parish at last. He couldn't turn it down. So when he and Kate moved here we rented a flat. And that's when she changed, wanted everything her own way. I never had a say. When she got pregnant she decided we'd move here. Sod my career. So when she heard of the practice vacancy in Staples Brook it seemed like fate was calling and she went for it. It's been hell ever since.'

'You had to live in our grotty little town,' said Mia. 'Poor Tom.'

He gave her an admonishing look. 'I was brought up in similar surroundings. I'm not posh. I'd have been happy to live here with the Grace I married, but the pregnancy wasn't easy. She suffered a lot, wanted me with her all the time. I missed auditions, opportunities. Then when the baby died … I wanted to comfort my wife but she wouldn't let me anywhere near her. She wanted me where she could see me, but continually kept me at arm's length—'

'So you started sleeping around,' Mia cut in.

Tom seemed to shrink in the chair. 'I did meet a girl. Before we moved here. We'd hit that rough patch and this girl … she arrived at a time when I was vulnerable.'

'Rebecca Crawford,' said Mia.

'No,' said Tom, getting angry.

'And when *she* fell pregnant you tried to get rid of her. Only she wouldn't go, so you killed her.'

'That's not true.'

Wells grinned. 'You killed her, mate, and we're gonna prove it.'

'How?' asked the solicitor. 'My client's already said he's never met the deceased.'

'OK, Mr Brooks, let's jog his memory.' Wells retrieved Rebecca's photograph from his briefcase and held it up. 'Ring any bells, Mr Chamberlain?'

Tom's features lengthened as he stared at the photograph. 'What's going on?'

'You recognize her,' said Mia. 'Don't deny it.'

'I feel sick,' said Tom, a hand going to his mouth.

Wells grinned. 'She's come back to haunt you, mate.'

Tom was staring at the photograph, a hand still covering his face. 'That's Anna,' he said, before throwing up all over his publicity shot.

'This is definitely the woman you were seeing?' said Wells, holding up the photograph.

Tom nodded. 'But she wasn't calling herself Rebecca Crawford. Not when I knew her.'

They were in another of the interview rooms; number one was undergoing a clean. Tom's vomit had gone everywhere. His clothes too had been spattered so he now wore a white vest and black jogging bottoms borrowed from one of the uniformed officers.

Mia was inserting the interview tapes into the machine and explaining for its benefit the reason for their break in procedure. With that done she sat as far away from Tom as the small table would allow. He still looked unwell.

'So she was calling herself Anna,' said Wells.

'Anna Molina,' said Tom. He was still looking at the photograph, drinking in every detail. 'I met her at one of Alison's parties. Alison Parker … Grace's aunt. Anna was training her for the London marathon. They were good friends. Anyway, we hit it off straight away and pretty soon we were lovers.' He leant forward and touched the photograph. 'It was really Anna's body you found? There's no mistake?'

'Rebecca Crawford's body,' Wells corrected him. 'Her dental records confirm it. If this "Anna" story's true she was having you on, mate.'

Tom suddenly became agitated. 'I'm not lying. She had a house in Stratton Lea. Hawk's Nest.'

'Hold on,' said Mia. She extracted the cosmetic dentist's list of clients from the case file in front of her and offered it to Wells. 'That name and address are on here, sir.'

'Why was she using another name?' asked Wells, frowning.

Tom gave a helpless shrug. 'I don't know.'

'The baby was yours?'

His nod was half-hearted. 'I panicked when Anna told me she was pregnant. Our daughter had only been dead a few months and Grace was still in a very bad state. So I told her we couldn't go on; the pregnancy had changed everything.' Mia gave a disgusted huff, causing Tom to round on her. 'I'm not proud of myself. I didn't know what else to do.'

'Was she living in Larchborough by this time?' asked Wells.

'Not then, no. I realized I'd made a big mistake. I loved her. So I asked her to take me back. That's when she moved here. Grace wasn't letting me get to London very often, so we thought it'd make things easier.'

'No wonder Grace was suspicious,' Mia spat.

'As far as I was concerned my marriage was over. There was no love left, only cold looks and recriminations. Grace was an empty shell. She still is. She's incapable of loving anybody any more.'

Wells sat back, folded his arms. 'So Anna … Rebecca … who-bloody-ever … moved to Larchborough when? January 2007?'

'That sounds about right,' said Tom, nodding.

'Did she ever mention Nuneaton?'

'She used to live there. That's where Alison met her, actually.'

'When was the last time you saw her?'

Tom tried to think. He looked so bereft, so awfully pale. If Mia hadn't cultivated such a strong dislike for him she might have tried to work up a little pity. As it was she had him bang to rights: he was Rebecca's killer.

'Towards the end of June 2007,' he said, eventually. 'We were making plans at her house. I was going to tell Grace everything and then move back to London with Anna.'

'What stopped you?'

'I had a four-week shoot in Luxembourg. A straight-to-DVD film. Only a small part and the money was crap, but it'd look good on my CV. I was going to tell Grace after that. But when I got back Anna had gone. I tried to find her. I was praying she'd get in touch….'

Wells gave him a cynical glance. 'Why didn't you contact us when you couldn't find her?'

'How could I? Grace would've found out.'

'So what?' said Mia. 'You were planning to tell her anyway.'

'But Anna had gone. Everything had changed.'

Mia snorted. 'You'd lost one cash-cow so you were holding on to the other.'

'For God's sake, money isn't everything.'

'It is when you haven't got any.'

'This film,' said Wells. 'Can you prove you were in it?'

'Yes, I've got the DVD. And you can check with my agent. She'll confirm everything.'

'Quite a solid alibi,' said the solicitor.

'If he's telling the truth,' said Wells.

'I am. I might be a lot of things, but I'm not a killer.'

'Nobody ever is when they're sitting in that chair,' said Wells. 'How hard did you look for her? Did you go to her house?'

Tom had to stifle a sigh. He thought they were about to let him go. 'Of course I did. But I could only look through the windows. I hadn't got a key.' He shrugged. 'Everything looked the same. Hardly surprising though – Anna had rented it fully furnished.'

'Did she have a car?'

'Yes, but I couldn't check if it was there because the garage was locked.'

Scott Brooks snapped shut his notepad. 'Let my client go, Chief Inspector. You know you've nothing to hold him on.'

Wells, with uncharacteristic compliance, waved a hand for Tom to leave. 'But if he puts one foot outside Larchborough it won't be his wife after him, it'll be me. And out of the two of us I've got the biggest temper so he'd better think on.'

'I won't go anywhere,' said a grateful Tom. 'I'll do anything you say.'

Wells gave him a gruff nod. 'Leave your agent's details at the desk on the way out … and try not to spew over that vest.'

'You don't like him very much, do you?'

'No, sir, I think he's vile.'

'Is he vile enough to kill though?'

Mia lifted a shoulder. 'He got himself into a mess. Perhaps murder was the easiest way out.'

'Killing ain't easy, darling.'

'It is for some people.'

They were still in the interview room, waiting for Bryan Baxter to be brought up from the cells. Scott Brooks had been asked to sit in on the interview as the man's own solicitor had been given the elbow. The end of Baxter's twenty-four-hour detention was fast approaching and Wells wanted to make the most of what time was left.

He'd phoned through to Nick with instructions to get the agent's details from reception and check that Tom Chamberlain had indeed been involved in the Luxembourg film. Jack was to find the landlord of the rented house in Stratton Lea.

Baxter looked decidedly worse for wear as he entered the interview room, a uniformed officer clutching his left bicep.

'Anna Molina,' said Wells, without preamble. 'Ever heard the name, sir?'

'It was Becky's professional name.'

'Why couldn't she use her own name?'

Baxter looked towards the solicitor, who immediately offered his hand. 'I'm Scott Brooks, sir. I've been asked to sit in as your temporary legal representative.'

'When you've finished your social niceties,' said Wells, 'perhaps you'd be good enough to answer my question.'

He was in no mood to faff about. For some reason he was halfway to believing Tom's account. The man might be a philanderer, but Wells didn't think he had the guts to kill. Baxter, on the other hand, had money tied up with Rebecca. Also he was jealous of the man she'd chosen over him. And jealousy was an age-old motive for murder.

'Sorry,' said Baxter, flinching. 'Becky worked with a lot of high-profile celebrities which made her an easy target for the down-market rags always on the lookout for a seedy story. She took on a different name to protect her privacy.'

'Why didn't you tell us before?'

Baxter shrugged. 'I don't know.'

'Hawk's Nest, Stratton Lea. Does that address ring any bells?'

'No,' he said, with another shrug.

'You're lying. You've told us one lie after another. You've changed your tune so many times, mate, I don't know what to believe.'

'But I've helped you. I told you about Becky's lover.'

'Yes, but that was only half the story. Let me fill in the gaps.' Wells stretched out his legs, the pose relaxed, but his tone had a definite bite to it. 'I reckon you did get a look at Miss Crawford's lover – but a long time before you said. You were jealous. You couldn't stand seeing her with this other bloke. You came to Larchborough that night in July 2007. Not to beg her to take you back. You came to kill her.'

'That's rubbish,' Baxter spat. 'Prove it.'

'And you made up that story about the actor with the bloody great beard to put us off the scent.'

'But he exists,' Baxter cried.

'We know,' said Wells, straightening up and looking Baxter in the eye. 'We've spoken to him. And you know what? – he says he wasn't even in the country when the murder took place.'

'Oh I see, you'll take his word but not mine.'

'His story's checkable, mate.'

'Have you checked it?'

'Being done as we speak. He'd have to be a first-class prat to feed us a lie that'll be found out so quick. But your story – we can't check that so easy.'

'The restaurant …'

Wells snorted. 'Any twat could book a table and sit there looking miserable for a couple of hours. Don't mean a thing, mate.'

'Help me,' Baxter begged the solicitor.

Brooks made a face. 'Don't know the facts of the case. Sorry.'

'I'll tell you the facts,' said Wells. 'He bashed a young woman's brains in then put her six feet under. Eight months gone she was. And you know why he did it? Because she'd messed him about. She'd got him angry. Him an important entrepreneur an' all.'

'I want Matthew back,' said Baxter. 'Call him for me.'

'You'll have plenty of time to sort out your solicitor in the remand unit, mate.' Wells rose to his feet. 'Get him to the custody sergeant, DS Harvey. It's about time we got this show on the road.'

'Craig Jordan just phoned,' said Jack. 'I'm officially a free man.'

Wells grinned. 'About bloody time.'

Nick waited for the DCI to get settled at his desk and then handed him two sheets of paper. 'Faxes from Chamberlain's agent,' he said.

Wells scanned the sheets. One was the film contract with Tom's signature; the other an invoice showing payment for his services.

'Six thousand quid? He said the pay was crap.'

'I wouldn't mind that for a month's work,' said Jack.

'Me neither. Anyway, the dates tally so that's him off the hook.'

'You're charging Baxter?' said Nick.

Wells nodded and went over the relevant details of his interview. 'Mia's getting him sorted downstairs.'

'No, she's not. I'm here,' said Mia, charging through the door with her usual exuberance. 'Baxter's going ballistic, sir, talking about a stitch-up to anybody who'll listen.'

'He can do what he likes. Everything points to him.'

'Does it though?' she said, frowning.

'Oh Christ, don't start that. Baxter had motive *and* opportunity. Don't forget he started off saying he was abroad when it happened. Then we find he was in Nuneaton the whole bloody time. He's lied from the word go.'

'But we haven't got any proof.'

'You think we've got the wrong bloke?'

'I just think Tom's more likely.'

'You're like a little terrier, darling. When you get your teeth into somebody you never let go.' Wells held up the faxes. 'This is proof from his agent that Chamberlain was in Luxembourg when Rebecca was killed. Now, unless he flew back in the middle of the job there's no way he could have killed her.'

'It's possible,' said Mia.

'What's possible?'

'That he flew back.'

'OK, so now you want us to check all flights from every airline out of Luxembourg for the whole of that month. No, hang on, we'd better expand the search to all neighbouring countries, just in case he crossed the border to make it harder for us.' Wells let out a harsh laugh. 'Come on, darling, it ain't feasible.'

'But what if we don't find any evidence that Baxter did it, sir?'

'We make sure we do. We'll have plenty of time. He'll be on remand for months.'

It was the remand time that was concerning Mia. Baxter could be banged up for the better part of a year. Possibly longer. And if he *was* innocent; if Tom *did* kill Rebecca … It just seemed a shame that Baxter could have his liberty taken away for something he hadn't done. Wells called her a terrier, hanging on for dear life to a notion that might be incorrect. But he was just as bad. He'd convinced himself that Baxter was their man and nothing would shake that conviction. Still, it was pointless going on about it. She'd just have to keep Tom in her sights, keep those little terrier teeth sharp.

'You're right, sir, I suppose.'

'No *suppose* about it, darling.' Wells grabbed his briefcase. 'Right, let's all get home. Tomorrow we start looking for that proof.'

'Nick, could I ask a favour?' said Mia. 'I've still got Grace Chamberlain's car at home and I want to return it. Could you follow me in yours and then drop me back? It shouldn't take long.'

'OK. You can feed me afterwards. I was just thinking my cholesterol levels are a bit low.'

'Listen to that, Jack,' said Wells, grinning. 'And I didn't even know she was after a bloke.'

'Ha-bloody-ha,' said Mia.

God … men and their one-track minds.

Anyway, she *was* after a bloke.

She was after Tom Chamberlain.

Let's hope he's there when I drop off the car.

Tom was skulking by the recycling bins when Mia pulled Grace's black BMW into their wide gravelled driveway. And he bounded towards her as she parked outside the up-and-over garage doors, leaving plenty of room for Nick.

'What are you doing with Grace's car?' he asked, even before she'd killed the engine.

'Long story,' said Mia, getting out to face him. 'More to the point though, what are *you* doing out here?'

'She's bolted all the doors.'

Nick's car pulled in then. Mia studied the house while she waited for him. It was a large detached of Gothic design. Mia thought it was hideous.

'Grace won't let him in,' she said as Nick sidled up.

'Not your lucky day, is it, sir?'

'Will you do something?' said Tom, all the while scanning the street beyond his border hedge.

Mia handed him Grace's car keys. 'Like what?'

'Get her to open the door. I can't let people see me like this,' he said, indicating the jogging bottoms.

Nick was approaching the front door when Grace threw it open. She'd been drinking again. Nick could smell whisky on her breath.

'Why have you let him come back?' she slurred. 'He killed that girl. He should be in prison.'

'Darling, let's talk,' said Tom, rushing to her side.

Grace grabbed the door. 'Get away from me, Tom.'

'Let's go inside,' said Nick, taking her arm.

The living room resembled a *Dracula* film set: lashings of black wood and faux period furniture – none of it comfortable, as Mia discovered when she sat with Grace on the wood-framed sofa. A number of table lamps struggled to illuminate the gloom even though an early evening sun still shone outside.

Tom was hovering by the huge fireplace. 'Why did you say I killed her, darling? Can't we at least talk about it?'

Grace ignored him, turned to Mia instead. 'Why is he still walking free?'

'It was down to our boss. I didn't have any say.'

Tom's face brightened. 'He knows I'm innocent. That's why he let me go.'

Grace shot him a look of utter contempt. 'Innocent? You were seeing that woman behind my back. You gave her a baby.'

Tom started pulling at the waistband of his jogging bottoms. 'Could I go upstairs and change out of these? They're grotesque.'

'Pack a bag while you're up there,' said Grace. 'I want you out of my sight.'

'But I've got nowhere to stay.'

'Just do it,' said Nick. 'We'll sort everything out later.'

'Oh for God's sake.' Tom scuttled from the room, a hand brushing his hair.

'Grace could do with some coffee,' said Mia. 'Will you make some, Nick?'

'Me?' he said, astounded.

'Yes, please,' said Mia, glaring at him.

When he'd gone she said, 'My boss might think Tom's innocent, Grace, but I'm still on his case. You've got to help me though. You've got to stay sober.'

'Your boss … he doesn't still think Dad did it?'

'No, he's got somebody else in the frame.'

'But you can't let an innocent man go to prison. It wouldn't be right. Tom killed that girl.'

'And I believe you, but just saying the words doesn't make it true. We need proof and I can't find it on my own. Will you help me?'

A kaleidoscope of emotions passed across Grace's face as she rose to her feet. She gave a resolute nod.

'OK, what do you want me to do?'

CHAPTER 16

'MR THORPE?' SAID Nick. 'Mr Dean Thorpe?'

'Who wants to know?'

Nick held up his warrant card. The man visibly relaxed and pulled wide the door he'd been holding open a mere crack.

'Enter,' he said. 'Nobody can say old Thorpy ain't a pal of the police.'

Nick had come with Jack to an address in Argyle Street to talk about Rebecca Crawford's rented house in Stratton Lea. They followed Mr Thorpe along a covered entry and up a flight of rickety stairs to an office which was surprisingly plush.

'Take the weight off,' said Thorpe, offering them a couple of chairs. 'What can I do you for?'

Nick undid his jacket and made himself comfortable. 'I'm Detective Inspector Ford, sir, and my colleague's Detective Constable Turnbull.' He took Rebecca's photograph from his pocket and showed it to the man. 'We're investigating the murder of this woman. We believe she rented one of your properties in 2007. Hawk's Nest in Stratton Lea.'

Thorpe's smile faded rapidly. 'That's Anna. She's dead? When? How?'

'You remember her?'

'You bet. She's a real sweetheart. We'd meet for a drink now and again. No hanky-panky like. She's young enough to be my daughter. How can she be dead?'

Nick took out his notebook. 'Think back to the summer of 2007, Mr Thorpe. Did Anna terminate her lease? Did she just disappear? When did you last see her? Anything you remember could be very useful.'

The man rubbed at his jowls. 'Blimey, let's see … I knew something was up when she got late with the rent that July. Anna don't like direct debits so she'd bring me the cash. You telling me that's when she got done?'

'Yes, sir.'

'Blimey, and I thought she was just messing me about. A lot of them do, you know.'

'What happened when she didn't bring the rent?'

'I kept phoning her, but she never picked up so I went round. All her things were still there. I thought, well, she ain't done a runner. Maybe she'd been called away. A family emergency or something.'

'Did you find her handbag in the house?' asked Jack, writing it all down.

'No.'

'What about her car?'

'That was in the garage.'

'Didn't you think it was strange she'd gone off without it?'

'No.' He made a face. 'Maybe I should've.'

'What happened then?' asked Nick.

'By the October she still hadn't come back and I'd got a professional couple after a place so I put Anna's stuff in storage and leased the house to them.'

'Have you got a list of her things?'

Thorpe opened a drawer in his desk and pulled out a large ledger. Finding the relevant page he handed it across to Nick. 'It's all above board. I shove everything in my warehouse and tell your lot I'm doing it. I've had to do it loads of times – that's why I didn't think nothing about Anna going off. If the items haven't been claimed after the relevant period I sell them on. Your lot know I do it.'

'Can I photocopy this?' asked Nick.

'Give it here, I'll do it.' Thorpe took the ledger to the photocopier sitting on a smaller desk in a corner of the office. 'My Charlene normally helps out only she's off to a health spa with her mother. Birthday treat. I'm coping on my own till Monday.'

Nick accepted the photocopy from Mr Thorpe. 'Where's your warehouse, sir?'

'Back of Tesco's, just round the corner. I'll take you there now, if you like.'

The warehouse was a huge space with tall metal containers around its perimeter, leaving room in the centre for larger items such as beds, cookers, fridges and garden furniture. Three cars were covered in tarpaulin sheets.

Jack lifted one of the sheets. 'Bloody hell, Nick, there's a Jag under here. Who'd leave this behind?'

'You'd be surprised,' said Thorpe. 'I found a wad of fifty-pound notes once. Had to hand that in though. Your lot wouldn't let me keep it.'

He led the detectives to a container on the right-hand wall and opened it with his master key. 'This is Anna's stuff. Her car's the small Golf over by the door.'

There wasn't much to see: baby clothes, all neatly placed in zip-up polythene bags; a pink suitcase full of women's clothing; a large makeup bag; pairs of shoes in various styles, and a number of jackets and coats.

'This is all there was?' said Nick.

Thorpe nodded. 'Anna had the house on a short lease. She was planning a permanent move to London.'

'We'll need to have this stuff collected,' said Nick. 'You'll get a receipt.'

She was supposed to be at the dentist after telling Wells that a filling had come loose, but Mia had more pressing concerns and they couldn't wait.

She pulled into the car park at St Matthew's – glad to see Reverend Fisher's Renault in its usual spot – and grabbed her things in a rush. The last thing she wanted was a lengthy chat with Frank, should he be lurking amongst the gravestones.

Mia found Fisher stooped over the communion table, head bowed before the ornate thirty-foot Crucifix which dominated the chancel. Her hurried footsteps echoing beneath the vaulted ceiling caused him to turn sharply. Terror showed in his eyes.

'What do you want?' he asked, his voice quivering. 'Are you here to arrest me?'

'No, vicar.'

She came to a halt at the chancel steps, the breath catching in her throat. He seemed to have shrunk a couple of inches in the twenty-four hours since she saw him last; flecks of grey showed in his beard. How could a person age in so short a time?

'Will you sit with me?' she said, taking the front pew. 'We need to talk.'

He was slow to join her, his body language guarded. 'I've nothing more to say. I've told you everything.'

'How's Kate? Is she all right?'

Fisher turned his head away, let out a piteous groan. 'How can she be all right? She's possessed by the Devil's helper and I've been feeding its hunger.'

Mia pulled him round to face her. 'You've got to stop torturing yourself, vicar. She'll get proper help now. She'll get better.'

'Why are you being so kind? You hate me. You all do. You think I beat up my wife.'

Mia let out a sigh. 'I've spoken to Grace and I see things differently now. I've spoken to Alison as well. She told me everything … about how she helped you with Kate—'

'What?' Fisher looked petrified.

'Don't worry, I'm on your side. I'll do anything I can to help you, to help all of you.'

'She'd bought some pills,' he said suddenly. 'Kate. That's how she overdosed. She was taking her own along with mine. She'll go into a clinic. The doctors say it'll be hard, but if she's determined she'll get better.'

'That's good news ... isn't it?' said Mia, squeezing his arm.

Fisher swivelled round, looked her straight in the eye. 'I didn't kill that girl. I swear before God. I couldn't do such a thing.'

'I believe you. That's why I'm here. I need evidence to prove that Tom did it and I want you to help me.'

'Tom couldn't take a life,' he said, that look of anguish back again.

'Vicar, he was having an affair with the murdered girl. She was carrying his baby—'

'I know all that. Grace told me yesterday.' Fisher got to his feet and paced in a square before the pulpit. 'All the time I was ministering to my congregation my own daughter's marriage was falling apart and I didn't even notice. What sort of father am I?'

'You had a lot on your plate. And Grace is good at hiding her feelings.'

'But she shouldn't have to. Not with me.'

'OK, let's both of us start helping her now.'

'How? Tell me how.'

'Like I said I need evidence against Tom. He's staying at the Coach and Horses for the time being. I've asked Grace to go through his things, check his computer, credit card statements ... You see, we don't know exactly *when* the girl was killed. The timeframe's too hazy. Say he did do it and after he buried her Tom had his clothes dry cleaned and that showed up on his credit card statement ... I know I'm clutching at straws, but one small clue like that could change everything.'

'What can I do?'

'That stretch of land where the body was found – was it ever maintained after the fence was built?'

He nodded briskly; his enthusiasm roused. 'For quite a while, actually. We cultivated it with a view to creating a sort of meadow-land with wild flowers to attract insects and wildlife. A number of local schools were involved. It gave the kids a focus. But funds got too low so we had to abandon it.'

'*When* did you abandon it?'

'A couple of years ago. I'll have the exact date in my office.'

'Was it still going on in 2007?'

'Definitely. Until that summer anyway.'

Mia felt a sudden adrenalin rush; she might be on to something here. 'Vicar, was Tom involved with your project?'

Fisher laughed despite himself. 'Afraid not. It wasn't Tom's scene. Anyway, Grace was pregnant; she wanted him with her. No, it was just Kate, Frank and me to start with, plus the kids, their teachers and other volunteers.' His expression changed. 'Of course, after our granddaughter died Kate lost interest; she didn't help after that. Towards the end though, before the money ran out, Grace joined us. I was so proud of her. The baby had been dead for about a year and her emotions were still raw, but she got stuck in. She said it was good therapy.'

'But no Tom?' said Mia, sighing.

'He'd come with Grace now and again, but he'd just watch.'

Mia stood up and hitched her bag on her shoulder. It didn't take long to have a tooth filling replaced. Wells would be wondering where she was.

'Have you got any record of the work you did on that land?'

Fisher nodded, already heading for his office. 'We kept a weekly diary for the schools, and of course I had to log all our expenditure.'

'I'll need to take everything home,' said Mia, hurrying to keep up with him. 'I'm doing this without my boss's permission.'

'That's all right. Let's just pray that God leads you to the truth.'

'Amen to that, vicar.'

Mia wasn't a big drinker but she'd opened a bottle of wine – that white crap that Nick had pulled a face at while guzzling it like a man who'd been lost in the desert for a month – and she was on her second glass as Richard Gere tried in vain to hide that adorable puppy from Joan Allen. *Hachiko* was her favourite DVD. The story was cinema's equivalent to a nice warm hug; the handsome man/cute animal formula worked every time for her.

Mia's day had been fraught – hence the need for wine and a slice of Hollywood's finest cheese – with DCI Wells crowing continually that a conviction was in sight. And having to fake a frozen mouth till lunchtime didn't help either.

She'd bolted the door. Even if Nick turned up, quoting Elizabeth Barrett Browning and giving her tantalizing glimpses of a sapphire and diamond engagement ring through the letterbox, that door would remain shut.

Tom Chamberlain was their killer and tonight was the night she'd prove Wells wrong.

Reverend Fisher had given her a pile of lined exercise books in which he'd recorded every type of seed, shrub and riverside bulb his team had planted along that stretch of land. He'd logged every tool, from trowel to mechanical digger.

He'd also drawn an extremely detailed diagram of the area. And it was that diagram which captured Mia's attention.

The vicar had marked off the land into numbered sections. In another book, under those numbers, he'd recorded the dates work had started on each area, the tools used, processes undertaken, and the names of those involved.

A quick look told Mia the mummified body was found in section number fourteen and that their money ran out during work on number twelve. Undeterred, she found the page for number twelve in the hope of finding Tom's name there. Reverend Fisher had left nothing to memory, recording every minute detail, so even if Tom had merely handed out seeds to little Janet from class six, the anal-retentive vicar would have written it down.

But Tom's name wasn't there.

OK, she'd go at it from another angle.

She found the book listing all monies paid out. Pieces of machinery, garden centre purchases and bits and bobs from B and Q were entered on the left, while a column on the right showed the costs.

Mia smiled to herself as she took a sip of wine. Fisher's handwriting was immaculate, his columns spirit-level straight. But occasionally – towards the end of the project – Grace's spidery scrawl would spoil the look of the page. Why can't doctors ever write properly?

On the television Richard Gere had died and the dog's life was changed for ever. Of course, his family was distraught too, but they didn't matter; that dog was the star. Mia usually made a grab for the tissues at this point, but tonight Mr Gere's dramatic heart attack went unnoticed.

She'd found a discrepancy in the dates.

In the expenditure book Grace had recorded that on Monday 22nd July a heavy-duty Rotavator had been hired for one week from Birchwood Garden Centre at a cost of forty pounds. And yet, according to the project books, all work had been abandoned over a month before. Why? Because the money had run out.

Grace could have entered the wrong date, of course. She was still grieving over the death of her baby. It's quite possible she wasn't thinking straight.

Mia grabbed her mobile and scrolled down to Grace's number, watching Richard Gere's black-coated family approach the funeral cars as she waited for the girl to pick up.

'Grace? Hi, it's Mia.'

'Are you phoning with news? Have you arrested Tom?'

Give me a bloody chance. At least the girl sounded sober. She was thankful for that.

'Not yet. Listen, your dad gave me the diaries he kept while you were all doing that work on the flood area and the dates don't add up.'

'Why?'

'It says here the work was abandoned in the first weeks of June and—'

'No, I mean, why are you looking at the books?'

'Because I'm trying to get something on Tom, I told you.'

'Stop wasting time then. Drag him in and make him confess. That's what you police usually do, isn't it?'

Mia frowned. 'On TV perhaps, but real life's a bit different, Grace. I need evidence first.'

'Then get some and stop wasting my time. Tom wouldn't *dig*, for God's sake.'

'He must have done *some* digging, Grace, if he buried that poor girl.'

'That poor girl?' An almost hysterical laugh travelled along the airwaves. 'Are you actually feeling sorry for her? She stole my husband. She ruined my life. Tom didn't lift a finger to help with that project. He was too busy making love to his mistress in her tacky semi-detached.'

'How do you know she lived in a semi, Grace?'

'Her type always does.'

'Did you know her address?'

'Of course not.'

'Did you ever meet her?'

'No. Why are you badgering me? Just do what you're paid to do and leave me and my family in peace?'

The call was disconnected and Mia found herself listening to silence. She was trembling. Why had Grace gone at her like that? There was no need. She was doing her best.

Still more than a little disturbed, Mia phoned Reverend Fisher's mobile and heard lots of voices in the background when he picked up.

'Vicar, it's Mia Harvey. Sorry, are you at the hospital?'

'Just on my way out,' he said. 'Kate's a lot better tonight.'

'That's great. Listen, I'm going through your diaries and I'm hoping you can sort something out for me.'

'I'll try.'

'Did Grace carry on with the work after you'd abandoned the project?' Mia held her breath. A nagging doubt was striving to be acknowledged and she prayed the vicar would banish it from her mind.

'Not that I recall. Why do you ask?'

'Grace hired a Rotavator towards the end of July. I just wondered why she'd do that.'

'That's right, I remember now.' He was getting into his car. Mia heard the dull thud of his driver's door as he closed it. 'She *was* going to carry on, said the work took her mind off everything. She hired the machine – paid for it herself, God bless her – and did about two night's work then lost interest. That's typical of Grace.'

'Did Tom help her?'

'No, he was filming abroad. I think that's the reason she gave it a go, to get out of the empty house.'

'OK, vicar, that's great. Thanks a lot. Bye.'

Shit!

For the third time that evening Mia selected a number and pressed the call button.

'Paul Wells …'

'Sir, it's Mia. We need to get Grace Chamberlain in for interview.'

CHAPTER 17

'WHAT THE HELL'S going on?' said Grace.

Mia ignored her, focused instead on feeding tapes into the recording equipment. DCI Wells took his seat and positioned the vicar's exercise books into neat piles, trying in vain to keep his annoyance under wraps. That thorn in his side, Matthew Pincer, was seated to the left of Grace. Of all the solicitors for her to choose …

'Morning, Chief Inspector,' said Pincer with a grin. 'Long time no see.'

'Not long enough for me, mate.'

The solicitor clutched his chest. 'Ouch … that hurt,' he said, still grinning.

Grace grabbed Pincer's arm and gave it a jerk. 'You think this is a joke? Carry on with that cavalier attitude and you won't be laughing for long.'

Pincer was startled. He wasn't used to being admonished by his clients.

'Cat got your tongue?' Grace asked Mia as she sat beside the DCI.

'I'd rather you focused on me,' said Wells. 'DS Harvey's just here to take notes.'

'And why am I here?' asked Grace, giving him a frosty glance.

Wells patted the exercise books. 'We need to clarify a few things.'

'Have you charged my husband?'

'No.'

'Why not? What's going on?'

'I'll ask the questions,' said Wells.

'When are you going to start?'

'When you shut your trap,' he replied, a little too loudly.

Grace was on the verge of protesting, but she pulled back. Her brief nod invited Wells to continue.

'Mrs Chamberlain,' he said, unbuttoning his jacket, 'when did you find out your husband was seeing the dead girl?'

'I didn't know he was at first. I just knew he was seeing someone.'

'How did you know?'

'How do you think?' said Grace, skimming her eyes. 'Tom made it plain he'd rather be in London than with me. We'd grown apart. It didn't take a genius to figure out he'd found somebody else.'

'He reckons you were the one who didn't want to know.' Wells retrieved the transcript of Tom's interview from his briefcase and scanned it briefly. 'He said, and I quote: *As far as I was concerned our marriage was over. Grace was an empty shell. She's incapable of loving anybody any more.*'

'Tom would say that. He's like a child, blaming everybody but himself.' The words were uttered with defiance, but Mia watched as a modicum of hurt crept into the woman's eyes. 'Anyway, I'd lost my baby and I was facing a childless future thanks to him. How did he expect me to react?'

Wells raised an eyebrow. 'But you asked to be sterilized. It was nothing to do with your bloke.'

'Is that what he told you?'

'Yes, but we didn't take his word; we asked the hospital staff.' More papers were lifted from his briefcase. Wells held them up. 'These are copies of your medical records, Mrs Chamberlain, and they tell us that you asked about the procedure. *You* paid for the operation to be done privately at a time suitable to *you*. So you can throw that sympathy card out of the pack 'cause it ain't any good any more.'

Grace rounded on the solicitor. 'Are you going to let him speak to me like that?'

Pincer was still brooding over her previous attack. 'It's his prerogative,' he said, flatly.

Returning her caustic stare to Wells, Grace said, 'So? What of it? Tom would have made a lousy father anyway.'

'Really?' said Wells. 'He was looking forward to Miss Molina's baby.'

'I doubt that very much. He killed both of them, don't forget.'

'How did you feel about the baby?'

Grace surprised them all by laughing out loud. 'It served him right. There he was having the time of his life with *my* money and for once he had to face the consequences.'

Wells frowned. 'Call me thick, but I'm confused. You say you didn't know who your husband was seeing, and yet you knew about Miss Molina and her baby. The two facts don't add up.'

Grace was floundering, eyes darting all ways, mouth opening on to nothing. The detectives had seen that look many times on suspects struggling to come up with a feasible explanation.

'I … I didn't know who the woman was to start with so I did what you do – I investigated, I searched for evidence. Tom's transparent, incapable of hiding anything. I soon found out who she was.'

'What did you do then?'

'I stopped his trips to London. I was pregnant. I needed him here with me.'

Wells pulled a face. 'But that only made matters worse. When did you find out Miss Molina had moved to Larchborough?'

'Did she? I wasn't aware.'

'Why did you go to Miss Molina's house in Stratton Lea?'

'I've never been to that part of town.'

'What if I told you your car was seen outside the house?'

Grace tutted and waved a finger at Wells. 'Now you're trying to trick me. I didn't have my BMW back then.'

'I wasn't talking about your BMW,' said Wells, with a smile. 'It was your previous car that was seen there.'

Grace paled momentarily. 'It wasn't mine. It couldn't have been.'

That much was true. Wells had only asked the question to gauge her reaction. And she'd responded exactly as he'd hoped. When Mia phoned him the previous evening Wells had scoffed at her suspicions. But now he wasn't so sure. He opened up the expenditure book and offered it to Grace.

'Why did you hire that Rotavator?' he asked, his finger next to the entry.

Grace stared at the page and shrugged. 'I was helping my father to clear the site.'

'The work was abandoned weeks before, Mrs Chamberlain, so I'll put the question to you again.'

'And I'll repeat my answer … *again*,' said Grace, angry now. 'I was helping my father.'

'No you weren't,' said Wells, returning the book to its pile. 'You were preparing a grave for Miss Molina.'

Grace's mouth sagged open, its corners stretching into a rigid grin. 'I'm a doctor. I make people better. I don't *kill* them.'

Wells shifted his weight in the chair. 'How did your baby die, Mrs Chamberlain?'

'Her lungs weren't working properly,' said Grace, frowning. 'She died from lack of oxygen.'

'Sure you didn't smother her?'

'What?'

'You were alone with your baby when she died. Who's to say you didn't make it happen?'

'That's preposterous,' said Grace, rearing up.

Wells spread his arms. 'I can't prove it, but there was a lot of controversy at the time according to the consultant in charge. A baby's healthy one minute and then she's dead. It makes you think.'

'She had a birth defect,' said Grace, panicking. 'I'll show you her death certificate if you don't believe me.'

Wells snorted. 'That doesn't prove anything.'

Grace turned on the solicitor. 'Tell him to stop.'

Pincer conceded her yelled request with a nod. 'Unless this line of questioning is relevant, Chief Inspector, you'd better stick to the matter in hand.'

'OK,' said Wells, shrugging. He leant forward, elbows on the table. 'You were used to your bloke's floozies, weren't you? But Miss Molina was different. She was a threat. She might actually take him away. And then he made her pregnant.' Wells widened his eyes, sucked in a breath. 'Oh dear, another reason for him to choose her over you—'

'Tom doesn't want children,' Grace interjected.

'Doesn't he? Or is that a line you've been using to get sympathy all these years? Poor Grace loses her baby and nasty Tom makes sure she can't have any more.'

Grace averted her gaze. 'You don't know what you're talking about.'

'How did you kill Anna Molina?' asked Wells, sitting back. 'What did you use as a murder weapon?'

'I didn't kill her.'

Mia had heard enough. 'Then how did you know it was Anna in that grave? You came to my home on Wednesday night knowing that she was the girl we'd found. You could only have known if you'd put her there.'

'Rubbish,' said Grace, trying a laugh.

'Is it? We hadn't a clue ourselves until we spoke to Tom.'

'But I've already told you, I found out Tom was involved with her. When I read about her death in the newspapers it made sense that he was her killer.'

Mia shook her head. 'All the papers called her Rebecca Crawford. Even Tom didn't know Anna Molina wasn't her real name. When we showed him her photo he was so shocked he threw up all over the desk.'

'Because he knew he'd been found out. It's a textbook reaction.'

Mia pointed her pen at Grace. 'If you hadn't come to my flat you might have got away with murder.'

'Don't be silly.'

'But we had your dad in the frame and you panicked. You couldn't let him take the blame for something you'd done. Confess now, Grace, and it'll go in your favour. A guilty plea could take years off your sentence.'

'I'll not confess to something I didn't do.'

'OK, but it'll be a lengthy trial. Your mum won't be able to cope. She's got her own battles to face. And it'll pile even more stress on to your dad. Would you really put them through all that?'

Grace fell silent, stared down at her lap. Then, as if coming to a decision, she said, 'Could I have a moment alone with my solicitor?'

They were back in the interview room after a thirty minute break, during which time Reverend Fisher had been called to the station. He sat alongside his daughter, holding her hand, shock sucking all colour from his face. Mia sat motionless. Matthew Pincer was stony-faced; this case wouldn't be his usual walk in the park. Grace, however, seemed strangely elated, as though a huge burden had been lifted from her shoulders.

'Tom went off to Luxembourg without his mobile,' she said, with an almost joyous glint in her eye, 'and by the time I found it, his plane was already in the air. So I thought I'd see what was on it. He'd never know.'

'And you found Miss Molina's details?' said Wells.

She shook her head. 'I found loads of text messages – very *intimate* messages – from someone signing herself "A".'

'How did the messages make you feel?' asked Wells.

'Angry. Hurt. Frightened. I knew I was difficult to live with and that's why Tom played around, but those messages ... they were so tender, so loving. You're right, Chief Inspector, I did feel threatened. We had that once and I wanted it back.'

'What did you do?'

Grace gave her father a sideways glance. 'I sent "A" a message, pretending to be Tom. I said the flight had been delayed and the bitch was away – that's how they referred to me – and I needed to see her urgently.'

'So she came to your house,' said Wells, folding his arms.

Grace nodded. 'I was going to ask her to leave him alone – beg her if I had to. I realized I didn't want to lose him. But when she turned up – when I saw she was pregnant – I was so jealous. The pregnancy suited her. She looked beautiful. Whereas I was sick for the whole nine months. It didn't seem fair.'

She shuddered as though someone had walked over her grave. Reverend Fisher wrapped an arm around her shoulders and squeezed her gently. 'Just tell the truth, darling. You're doing so well.'

Grace gave him a smile. 'She was surprised to see me – obviously – and nearly didn't come into the house. But I said neither of us could go on like this and things needed to be sorted ... if only for the baby's sake. I found myself warming to her. Can you believe that? She had such a calming presence, rather like an aura.'

Wells frowned. 'So why did you kill her?'

'She told me her name was Anna.'

Those words were spoken with such simplicity, as though killing someone because of their name wasn't in the least insane. Mia struggled to get into the girl's mind-set, to imagine the scene. And that was when realization dawned.

'Oh God,' she said, a hand rushing to her mouth. 'That was your baby's name.'

Grace nodded. 'Tom chose it. He said it was the most beautiful name in the world. He said it reminded him of everything that was good and beautiful. He named our baby after his mistress.'

'I'm so sorry,' said Mia, bringing a quizzical look from Wells.

'Oh, don't worry, I'm over it now. But at the time I couldn't believe he'd do such a thing. And yet there she was, large as life, telling me their affair had started ages before I'd even conceived.' She paused to meet Wells' gaze. 'I didn't kill my baby, Chief Inspector; I wanted her to live so badly. God had different ideas, however, and all I had left was her grave. But even that was spoilt. How could I ever look at it again – with *her* name carved on it – without being reminded of Tom's betrayal?'

'How did you kill her?' Wells asked, striving to remain impassive.

Grace removed Fisher's arm from her shoulder. She couldn't admit to her horrendous deeds whilst feeling his touch. 'We were in my kitchen. I'd made us some coffee and was sitting opposite her at the table. She was telling me about their plans to move back to London, about how she knew I didn't want Tom any more. I wasn't really listening. I couldn't get the image of my daughter's headstone out of my mind.

'Anyway, I'd bought my parents a stone cherub for the garden – their wedding anniversary was coming up – and it was on the floor to my right. I grabbed it, walked around the table, and bashed it against her head as hard as I could. Don't ask me why. It felt like I was watching myself doing it.'

'Where did you hide the body?'

'We had a large freezer in our garage. I got everything out and put her in there. Afterwards, I returned her car – the keys and her address were in her bag. I got rid of the bag, of course. Can't remember where now. Sorry. Of course, after I'd buried her I sent the freezer to the tip. I didn't fancy using it after that.'

Wells watched Grace closely. She was too prosaic, too *normal*, for his liking. The girl's emotions were on a roller-coaster high, but they'd soon hit the ground again. And when that moment came she'd need help.

He said, 'How did you get her body to the grave?'

'In the boot of my car. At the churchyard I used a wheel-barrow to get her over to the spot I'd prepared.' She lifted a shoulder, gave him a smile. 'It was easy. God always gives us strength when we need it.'

Reverend Fisher let out a groan and buried his face in his hands. Now it was Grace's turn to comfort him. Hugging him tightly, she said, 'I'm sorry, Dad, but it had to be done. Haven't you always said I should use my initiative?'

CHAPTER 18

'GRACE CAN'T GO to the remand unit,' said Mia.

'Why not?' said Wells. 'She took a life.'

'But she's ill, and she'll only get worse banged up with a load of yobs.'

Nick let out a sarcastic snort. 'What about a health spa?'

'Or a nice family-run hotel somewhere hot,' said Jack.

The team was back in the office after formally charging Grace with first degree murder. She'd been released into her father's custody at the vicarage until Monday morning when she'd appear before magistrates so that legal proceedings could begin.

'What are we going to do about Baxter?' Jack asked Wells.

The DCI shrugged. 'We should have him for appropriating funds but it was his money – his accounts confirm it – so I'm all for letting him off.'

'And what about the vicar?'

Wells fell back in his chair and pushed out a long breath. 'God knows.'

Nick laughed. 'His Christmases'll be a bloody sight easier inside.'

'You're so funny,' said Mia, tutting. 'He wasn't buying those drugs to make a profit. He's not a criminal. He was trying to help his wife.'

'And a right mess he made an' all,' said Wells.

'Can't we cut him a bit of slack, sir? His daughter's going to be banged up for life, his wife'll be in rehab for ages … His life's already in pieces.'

'This ain't *Jim'll Fix It,* darling. We can't make everybody's dreams come true.'

'But nobody outside this office knows what he did. The super doesn't know. Can't we just lose the paperwork?'

'We'll see.'

Jack was packing away the case notes. He said, 'You know what – I bet Rebecca Crawford was a right skank.'

Mia gasped. 'That's a vile thing to say.'

'Why? She used different names with different men. We can't find any family. I reckon she was a con artist. She was just playing those suckers.'

'She's dead, Jack. Have a bit of respect.'

'Just offering my opinion,' he said, shrugging.

'Well, don't—'

'I want somebody to phone Tom,' said Wells, before the argument could gain momentum. 'Tell him he can get back home. Then you can all get off.'

'Have you got plans for today, sir?' asked Mia.

'Yes,' he said, pulling a face. 'Joey and Syed finish their shift at two o'clock. I've got a bit of grovelling to do.'

CHAPTER 19

THE HEADSTONE LOOKED lovely. Her father's details had been retouched with gold so that they matched Barbara's. Mia had been dreading this moment, but was strangely comforted by that extra attention to detail.

'No spelling mistakes,' said Nick as he stood beside her, hands in his trouser pockets.

'No,' she said.

'You OK?'

'Yes, I think it looks great.'

She turned away as tears threatened. She didn't want to break down in front of him.

'Come here,' he said, taking her in his arms.

They stood as one for many moments, Mia surrendering to him. Finally she pulled away.

'Why did you come, Nick?'

He shrugged. 'We're friends. That's what friends do.'

'Are we friends? You're not just taking the piss?'

'Christ, talk about being paranoid....'

'I'm sorry,' she said as he moved away. 'I'm glad you're here. You can't know how much.'

A twig snapped behind them and both turned to see Reverend Fisher, fully gowned, making his way towards the grave. He took Mia's hand and gave her a smile.

'How can I ever thank you?' he said, his eyes twinkling in a face still ravaged by grief.

'For what?' Mia asked.

'For giving me my freedom. For allowing me to continue with my ministry.'

'You've our boss to thank for that, vicar. He couldn't see any good reason to prosecute. He reckons you've suffered enough.'

'God bless him for that.'

'How's your wife?' asked Nick.

'Struggling,' he said, with a catch in his voice. 'So am I. They won't allow visits. Too distracting.'

'It won't be for ever,' said Mia. 'Does she know about Grace?'

Fisher shook his head. 'I can't tell her. I'll wait till she's better.'

'Grace might get the minimum sentence,' said Mia, trying to sound upbeat. 'She *was* provoked in a way.'

'It's all in His hands now,' said Fisher, pointing to the sky. 'Anyway, are you ready to start?'

'Not yet.' Mia had piled the dead funeral wreaths beside the grave. Reaching for them, she said, 'I'll just dump these in the skip. Mum always liked everything tidy.'

'Let me,' said Fisher, taking them from her.

As he walked away Mia studied the grave. In the autumn, when the soil had settled, she'd plant loads of bulbs: crocuses and daffodils and narcissus. She might even put a dwarf rose bush in the centre. She'd look after the plot. She'd give it the attention she should have lavished on her mother.

Mia allowed her tears to fall then. 'I've so much guilt, Nick. I don't know how I'll live with it.'

'You will,' he said, moving to her side. 'I'll help you.'

THE END

245

THE DS MIA HARVEY SERIES

Book 1: Desperate
Book 2: Obsessed
Book 3: Silent Grave

Please join our mailing list for updates on DS Mia Harvey, **free Kindle crime thriller, detective, mystery books and new releases.**

www.joffebooks.com

Printed in Great Britain
by Amazon